SETH KNYTE

The Years of our Lives

First edition

ISBN: 979-8-9902844-1-8

Editing by James Anders Banks
Cover art by Mark Baker

This book was professionally typeset on Reedsy.
Find out more at reedsy.com

To my beloved family, whose unwavering support and love have been my guiding light through every twist and turn of life's journey. And to Jessica, whose inspiration and encouragement breathed life into every word of this tale.

"You never know when a story will appear."

Prologue

So, it all started with me, Ryan Weaver, and my best friend Alexa Hawthorne. Alexa and I had been best friends for around twelve years now. We lived in a smallish town with around only twenty thousand people. Our town was called Lendinbrisk. Almost no one had ever heard of it. Anyways, our town of Lendinbrisk was located in the northern part of Maine. We lived in a heavily wooded area of the U.S., where the most development we had was at our Blockbuster. Yes, I know Blockbusters died a long time ago, I was just using it as a reference. So, now you know that our town hadn't developed since the early 2000s I can go into my story.

I'll start from the beginning. My friend Alexa and I had always been "golden children" in the sense we never did anything wrong. Alexa was around five foot tall with brownish-blonde hair and piercing blue eyes. She always carried a small grin making her seem like an angel, however, appearances are not always as they seem. Alexa and I didn't do things that are inherently bad out in the open, we were very secretive about the things we did. I was never big on doing dreadful things, but Alexa loved them. She would do things like, you know how public restrooms always have graffiti. Well, she was the one to carve those words. That's tame compared to the other things she got up to.

One day, while we were walking home from school, Alexa was talking about how much she hated her training. "God, Ryan, why are you always in your head, distracted? Earth to Ryan," she said, shaking me back to reality.

I responded to her, "I actually think... That's why, Alexa. Unlike you, I

1

have things on my mind."

She shook her head dismissively and replied, "Always so cocky, mister mysterious."

I flashed a smile back, saying, "Yep."

With that, our conversation ended as we split off when I reached my destination. My safety and warmth: my house. This winter had been horrible, even without all the drama at school.

I ran up our old Maine staircase. I made it into my room and slammed the door behind me. See, I wasn't like most kids my age, as you could guess. When I spaced out, I was thinking of ideas for the stories I would write. I always carried a pen or pencil on me. "You never know when a story will appear," that was my motto. Ideas are often forgotten, so I'd write them down to remember them.

But I'd been experiencing some writer's block recently. I needed a change of pace, something new and fun to bring me back to my former stature. I think we all need things like that to happen throughout our lives. Without these life-changing moments, it's easy to get stuck in a rut, so to speak. I was always a very cynical person, and not without reason. I enjoyed the company of myself more than others really.

My great friend since we were grade schoolers, Alexa, was all I had to talk to, besides my parents. Which was okay with me because she was good company. She was a real outdoorsy type of person, however, and that just wasn't my style. I enjoyed being inside a place like a library more so than outdoors. Alexa also loved to "prank" people, and she was good at it. At least in her own way. They were less like pranks and more like traps designed to scare people.

She would often fill up bags of old deer meat and wrap them up in tarps. Making them look like there'd been a murder with the body lying out in the woods. She'd cut a small hole into it, so the stench permeates the area. Then she would leave the "prank" there for days until some hunter found it and reported the "murder".

I always knew it was her when something crazy happened because, for the most part, everyone in my town was docile. Everyone saw me and Alexa as model students, always getting perfect grades. In many ways, we were. However, with the lack of excitement in our town, Alexa was getting restless. She started to pull those types of stunts often, almost getting caught on multiple occasions. Those times I would always step in and save her skin, giving her an alibi and a way to be safe.

I'd been thinking so much I forgot to look at the clock. I realized this and turned to the clock, seeing 8:23 P.M. flashing back at me. "God, how have I been up here for five hours?" I said to myself. I walked down the staircase again, surprised to see my parents cooking. It was Friday. They always went out on Friday. We never cooked on this day. I walked up to them and asked, "What's wrong? Why are you cooking today? You usually go out."

They turned back to me surprised, saying, "Well, we know winters here suck and just wanted to make you dinner before we left. It is the holiday season, time to give, and so on."

I smiled and hugged them each once, replying, "That's why you guys are the best." The smell of stir-fried chicken and fresh green beans, with the sound of sizzling bacon, completely clouded my judgement. The aroma was divine. They sure did know how to make my favorite food. I could already taste the fresh ramen with the delicious juices from the chicken and bacon and assorted vegetables mixed throughout.

I set the table for one person. Grabbed my favorite drink and poured it into a cup. Then I grabbed a napkin and chopsticks, knowing full well everything had been julienned. They brought me my serving right as I sat down, and bid me farewell, going out to their usual dinner date. I am an only child and had had an extremely fortunate life and would never complain, especially about the food in front of me. I hungrily started savoring every last bite of this heavenly meal.

I finished and got my brain back on track, remembering exactly what I had been thinking about. I was wondering how I could do something exciting in my small town in Maine. Away from all the big cities and huge amusement parks like Disneyland and Disney World. All of these things seemed so far out of my reach. I wondered if I would ever get out of this rut I was in. Like everyone else in the world does from time to time. But somehow it always managed to turn up fine and dandy. I'd always been confused about that because it was like life is a lot like the movies. Whereas no matter how dreadful things get, if you can look for the good in them then everything will be fine. For example, a lot of people have mixed feelings about the things they watch. However, we had this ability to pick things we like out of things, no matter how bad we see them as.

Humans truly are amazing, look around, every single one of us is similar but not one is an exact copy of the next. We're all unique, and I know that sounds so cliché but it's true. No one else can think as you do, act like you do, talk like you do, walk like you do, do anything you do. This is because you're the one doing it solitarily and it can't all be mimicked exactly. I think that we often let our egocentric mindset ruin so much of our perception. We're always focused on ourselves and would rather help ourselves than someone else. Another issue is that when we help others, we are always looking for something in return. Even if we think we're doing something selflessly, we aren't. Oftentimes taking pride in doing selfless acts takes away the gravity of the action. I think about all these things walking up the stairs into my room. I fall onto my bed and crash, looking up at the ceiling. All I can think of at this moment in time is how hard we all have it.

We as humans don't have a harder time than any other human. All of our problems are simply different. We let our egotistical mindset take over and think our problems are worse than someone else's. I lay there thinking this, and as soon as I started to feel myself nodding off, I got a text. "Who could that be at this hour?" I said to myself, knowing full well who it was and what their intentions were. It was from Alexa. She wanted to meet outside my house. Why she showed up at the most inopportune times, I will never know. I put my snow jacket and snow boots on and went outside.

I saw her standing right next to my mailbox, staring at me, her deep blue eyes piercing the veil of snow. I walked up to her and asked, "What are you, crazy or something? Why did you need me now? It's almost eleven thirty P.M."

She smirked as if she knew something I didn't, then replied slyly, "You see, my dear Watson, there's some fun to be had tonight. We both know the

4

'Snowflake Ball' is coming up soon. Well, what I propose is that we start to plan for what we're going to do to spice it up."

She said those last three words with a wicked smile on her face. Any other person would call her beautiful, and this whole scene was surreal. With the snow flying around us and blanketing the streets. Covering everything in a sheen of white fluffy snow. However, I was wise to her tricks and schemes, knowing that she was really the Devil. The whole tone of this conversation was ominous, not magical in any sense of the word. I invited her in to talk about what she wanted, and we went up to my room.

I closed the door and turned to her, saying, "So what kind of crazy concoction of a plan have you whisked up this time, Sherlock?" Keeping with the Sherlock Holmes theme. I half expected her to light up her tobacco pipe as she spilled her evil plan to me.

She winked and said, "Well, what I wanted to do was sneak in while it was being set up. Then maybe find where they were controlling the stage lights for the dance and hijack them that night."

I thought it over, turning it around in my mind, then finally asked, "How do you plan to do all this?" I knew there was something more to it than just using the lights for some fun, but that would have to wait.

An evil grin on her face grew as she said, "That's where you come in, Ryan. You distract the person manning the light and sound booth, and I sneak in and lock him out."

I looked at her, surprised she'd actually thought this through. I decided to go along with it, "Sure, I'll give you the help since you're begging for it, Alexa," I smiled back smugly.

She walked past me saying, "Good boy, I knew you would, Ryan. You're always so dependable. See ya tomorrow." With that, she was gone. Like a tornado, she crashed in without warning, destroying everything and dissipating seconds after she was done.

She left quickly and went home, leaving me only one text saying, "Good talk, 'Watson'", with a wink at the end of it.

I was worn out from all of today's events, remembering school and all the work I had to do. I lay down on my bed, exhausted, wanting to just fall asleep and never wake up. I stared up at my plain white ceiling and watched the ceiling fan turn as my eyelids got heavy. I slowly started to fade out of consciousness, drifting off into the dream world. Sleep was the only thing I needed after this busy day.

Nightmare 1

I woke up in a cold sweat. I looked around, seeing vague images of my room. However, it was very eerie and off-putting. I felt a chill go down my spine. I rolled out of bed staring at the clock, it was 12:44 A.M. That was only a minute after I had fallen asleep. Strange, it felt like I was out for way longer. I lay back, staring up again, trying to fall back to sleep. All of a sudden, I remembered everything that had happened that day in vivid detail. It had begun with me waking up and getting started for the day. I saw through my own eyes, looking like I was staring through binoculars. It was a weird experience, and also terrifying to me. What was happening? That was all I could ask.

I wake up staring. Getting ready for school, Friday mornings were always the best mornings. Just eight hours stood between me and the weekend. I looked at my clock. It was 6:21 A.M. I got up, showered, and went to my car. I was one of the lucky kids, my parents had an old car they let me use to get to school. That meant I didn't have to walk through the horrible Maine snow. I got to school and met up with Alexa. She was already talking to her friends. I walked up to her and said, "How's it, hangin' nerds?" Alexa's head span, and she winked, replying with, "Great, what about you, Mr. Jock?" It was funny because I was nowhere near a jock. We laughed it off and started to walk to our classes.

The day flew by with everything going smoothly and regularly. I always hated my classes so I couldn't wait to sprint out those doors with Alexa following. It was up until now that everything was normal. Even though everything seemed real, as soon as I got out of school I blacked out, and it was nighttime outside and snowing. That's when I knew something was wrong. I started to walk to my car, but it wasn't in my usual spot.

I looked through the complete ice and snow-covered parking lot and it was dead quiet. This was unusual even though I lived in a small town, it was never near empty or quiet. The darkness consumed everything as I kept walking away from it towards my house. I ran down my street and each streetlight died as I passed it. It was horrible running in the snow, but the darkness kept gaining on me, getting closer and closer to me each step I took. I ran into my house, and my bad knee started to hurt. With each step I took closer to my room, it hurt worse. I climbed up my stairs with excruciating pain in my right leg, finally reaching my room. I opened the door and slammed it shut as I fell on my knees. I looked down, and my right leg was glowing in a pulsatile fashion. Each pulse hurts worse than the last. I got into my bed and fell asleep as the darkness crept into my room engulfing me.

Chapter 1

I woke up in my bed terrified of that nightmare I had just had. It seemed so vivid and real. It felt like it couldn't be so realistic, and it scared me beyond any fear I'd ever felt. I wasn't scared in general; I was scared of the lucidness of the dream. Usually, I forget everything in the morning, but when I looked at my right leg I winced as if some pain still lingered in it, which it did. I sat up and rubbed my leg that had hurt so much the night before and tried to convince myself nothing weird was happening, it was just a "nightmare".

I walked downstairs, each step hurting with the pressure placed on my right leg. It started to numb up some, however, it still hurt pretty bad. I walked into the kitchen and the amazing smell of eggs, bacon, and hash browns hit my nose. I instantly smiled and stopped thinking about the pain in the bliss of the amazing aroma surrounding me.

I walked into the kitchen and said, "Mornin', breakfast smells delicious, guys." My mom turned from her position at the stove and gave me a big smile as my dad sat in his usual place at the table. He was drinking black coffee and reading his phone as he usually did in the mornings. I feel it's strange how phones had done that, replacing newspapers almost completely. They replaced almost everything. It was like a crazy multi-tool that's always with us.

They both smiled at me, and I grabbed a glass and the orange juice. My dad looked at me and said, "How'd ya sleep? You were gone last night when we walked into your room. You just mumbled a few words in your sleep. Was it a good dream?"

It was far from good, and for that matter, it was far from a dream. It was the worst sleep I'd had in weeks, but I couldn't say that. I didn't want to talk about it, so I just responded with, "Yep, it was a great sleep. I'm fully rested and ready for today. Hopefully, it's a relaxing one, not a crazy one. But you know how Alexa is, she'll probably show up out of nowhere." They laughed in agreement with the statement I'd just made.

By the time they'd finished laughing, we all had our food and drinks at our table ready for us to devour. I was really hungry for some reason. Maybe it was because of that dream. Could dreams have that big of an effect on us physically and mentally? I thought this to myself as I ate as if I hadn't eaten in weeks. I finished and thanked my mom for breakfast while walking up the stairs back to my room to get ready for the day. I grabbed my clothes and hopped into the shower to freshen up, because I'd been sweating a lot last night and reeked. I guessed that "nightmare" did a number on me.

I got into the steaming shower with warm water falling onto my back. It was heaven, the only real escape I had from life and everything in it. This was my sanctuary, the water hitting my head and neck curing all thoughts of pain. All I felt was the warmth of the water, and the sound of it hitting my neck and the walls of the shower around me. I finished showering and got out of the safety and warmth of the fog. I grabbed my towel and dried it off as I heard a rock hit the bathroom window softly. I put on my neatly folded clothes from the counter as I heard rock after rock hit the window. I knew full well who was throwing them, but I didn't dare peer outside for fear of being hit.

So, I hurried downstairs and got my coat on, saying farewell to my mom and dad before exiting. I got out to see the same stunning blue eyes greet me and bid me to come closer. Alexa was standing there, and she smiled a welcoming smile, then greeted me saying, "Hi there, you clean up nice. Didn't know you had it in you."

I smiled back softly and said, "Pfft, I always look this good. You look like a real girly girl today. I've never seen you wear so much make-up. If I didn't know better, I'd think you were trying to impress me."

However, I felt that there was something suspicious about how dressed up she was. She blushed softly, making it seem like she was doing it for me, but something was still off. I decided to push those thoughts out of my head and I asked her, "What do you have planned for us today? Something fun I hope?"

She smiled her normal sly smile and said without hesitation, "We're going to drive to Portland, Maine. I've always wanted to see Old Port, haven't you?"

I thought it over and said, "Yeah, I have. Actually this is perfect, I needed to get out of the rut I was in. So, it looks like we're going to Old Port. Let me tell my parents I'll be gone until tomorrow night."

I walked back in and told my parents where I wanted to go. They were very lax parents and only gave me one warning. "Don't do anything dumb," they said. Then they gave me an extra forty dollars for gas since I had the money for the hotel already saved up. I ran upstairs quickly, grabbed my backpack, and filled it with a change of clothes and my notebook and pencils.

I walked back outside with my bag, and Alexa flashed a big smile, having known my parents for so long she knew they had said yes. I gave her the thumbs-up and got into my car, throwing my backpack in the back seat. She got in and I asked, "Wanna drop by your house so you can get the stuff you need?"

She replied with a glance that said, *You read my mind.* So, I started up my car and we were off. We drove to her house. She hurriedly got out and ran up the steps to her door. She was gone about fifteen minutes, and came back out sprinting down the steps and got into my car. She threw her stuff in the back seat, and we were off on our four-ish-hour drive to Old Port. This was the first time she and I actually did something big. But the whole thing seemed a little off. I didn't know how or why I knew that there was something wrong, but I did. Maybe it was because Alexa had proposed the idea, but I knew this wasn't some innocent trip.

I did want to believe it was just a fun little trip to one of the most amazing places in Maine. But something in the back of my head just wouldn't let me trust it. While I was thinking, Alexa was slowly falling asleep. She'd always been like this in cars, or anything moving really. It always put her straight to sleep, no matter how much coffee or any other form of energizer she'd had. I always found it curious how such an energetic, crazy person could fall asleep in an instant from being in a car. Anyways, I started to think of all the things to do in Old Port. I really wanted to go out to the beach. I had never been to a beach, even a lake's beach. I also wanted to see the sunset over the water for the first time. I thought that would be a perfect scene for my stories.

I sat there driving for hours, while my companion was sleeping, sweetly smiling. I thought to myself that she seemed so normal like this, but I knew better. Through her facade, I knew she was just as strange and manipulative as the Devil himself. I sat there thinking, still wondering what we should do about our weekend. I felt extremely excited to visit Old Port. I'd never been out of my hometown with my family. So, it was amazing to get to see the rest of Maine. My world was getting two hundred times bigger. In my gut, I couldn't help thinking there was something wrong.

Alexa woke up softly yawning and looking up at me and said, "Are we there yet?"

I looked back down at her and smiled saying, "Not yet, sleepyhead."

After that little exchange, she lay back down and passed out. I finally realized why she had invited me and none of her friends. I knew Alexa had always had feelings for me. But I never thought she would be so bold as to outright do something like this. I got an eerie feeling thinking that I would have to act differently around her so as to not hurt her.

Somehow, I wanted to believe it was much more innocent than that. In the back of my mind, I thought about something that seemed to be very odd. This was purely the fact that she hadn't told me her plan. She always told me her plan, no matter what it was, even for dumb things like how she would sneak out of a class. This one detail bothered me, she didn't tell me anything except "Let's go to Old Port." How naive could I be to trust her so blindly when I knew what she was capable of?

I suddenly thought that this was not a romantic city date but some sinister plan. I thought all of this as we neared the end of our drive. We were still two hours off, but that seemed close enough to me. So, I stopped to get gas

11

at a little station, and as soon as the engine went off, Alexa's head jerked up. It was like she had just heard a gunshot. She stared at me saying, "Are we there now?"

I responded with, "Not unless you want me to leave you at this gas station in the middle of nowhere. Anyway, I'm going into the store to buy water and some gum. Do you want anything?"

She shook her head, and with that, I walked into the convenience store. I grabbed two bottles of water and some generic gum and walked up to the clerk. There was no one else around, even the station was dead. Looked like this place didn't get a lot of business. The girl working the register was very upbeat while ringing my items up. She had hazel eyes and chestnut brown hair that softly came down into a bob. She was a little shorter than me. I got lost thinking all of this as she said, "Okay, hun, that'll be six dollars fifty."

I grabbed the money out of my wallet and handed it to her, smiling.

She took it, handed me the bag, and said, "Have a good day, darlin'."

I walked out to the car and handed Alexa one of the bottles of water. I knew her too well, she would've whined to drink from mine because she was, "Dying of thirst." So, I got her one, and she knew I would too. She flashed her devilish smile again saying, "Aww, always so considerate of me."

I shrugged and said, "I just didn't want you whining to drink some of mine later."

She took a sip and put it into the cupholder. She lay back down as I turned the car back on, falling instantly asleep to the soft hum of the engine. Her hair fell softly around her face as the sun hit her just at the perfect angle. She looked like a goddess from a painting. I couldn't help but smile softly while thinking this, then I focused back on the road. It was amazing how the sea air pushed the pine trees back, bending them to its will.

Each needle of the pine trees swayed with the cross breeze being dragged inland from the sea. I rolled down the window and could taste the salt in the wind. I couldn't believe that the stories were true. All the myths seemed to give way to reality. The sun was at high noon, casting light over all the land. Today was perfect, slightly overcast but very sunny. I continued to think about what Old Port might look like. I imagined it like a big bustling city from the movies. In my head, I saw businessmen rushing around on their phones, and tourists taking pictures all over the place. I imagined street magicians and musicians alike all supplying shows and trying to make a living. I imagined that the restaurants were full of important and high-class people.

I got pulled back into reality with another cute yawn and a tugging at my sleeve. Looks like someone's awake and wants my attention, I thought. Alexa said, "Ryan, why are you always so deep in thought?"

I looked at her confused about how to answer. I finally said, "Well, my mind just kind of drifts off when I start to think. Then it finally gets to the point where I forget about my surroundings."

She looked back at me, mulling the information over in her head, and lay back down. I suddenly felt a sharp jolt in my right leg. I looked down for a second, and it was pulsating the light again. However, this time it was just in my head, I was making it up because the pain was back. I ignored it, and it got somewhat worse with every thirty minutes that passed. We passed a sign saying ten miles to Old Port. I got excited that it was around less than ten minutes with the speed we were traveling at. I smiled as I saw the buildings peeking over the hill and continued to drive.

Alexa was still sound asleep. I decided to let her sleep for a bit longer. I knew how she got if she was woken up even remotely earlier than she was ready to be. We finally crossed the threshold and I laughed softly. I'd finally made it to… somewhere. I wasn't in my tiny hometown anymore. I got off the interstate and rode on the highway for a little bit. I had been looking for the hotel that Alexa said she had booked. But my mind started to wander. I thought about the beach and the city and everything that was going to happen. I was so excited to take this huge step out of my comfort zone and into the world. This is it, I thought to myself. I'd made it to a big city, and I was ready to enjoy myself no matter what Alexa did or didn't have planned.

Chapter 2

She had booked us a hotel called The Press Hotel, Autograph Collection. It was really nice compared to the motels I'd seen in movies. Her family was rich so I kind of expected some extravagant place. I woke her up as I pulled into the parking space. She was so excited, if she had been a dog her tail would be wagging and her ears fully erect. I could see the intensity in her eyes. She had been waiting so long for this.

She finally said softly, "Are we here?"

I replied with a laugh, saying, "Yeah, we are, sleepy."

I got out and went to the back of the car and grabbed our backpacks. Alexa got out of the car and walked around it lazily. As if she were some kind of sloth. She yawned as we walked up to the front desk. A real snooty man in very nice dress clothes walked up from behind the counter.

He said, "What are you kids doing here?"

I replied snarkily, "We have a reservation."

He looked shocked at the fact two kids could afford to stay there. He asked for my name, and I gave it to him, and he quickly regained his composure and apologized. A bellhop that was no older than me had walked up and taken our bags, if you could call two backpacks bags.

We went into an elevator, and I knew Alexa had dropped some cash but I didn't expect a top-floor room. We went up to the highest floor of the building. Apparently, Alexa had spent a huge sum of money and even got us the Honeymoon Suite. I was so surprised, I shot her a look that said, *How the hell did you get this money?* She just shrugged and smiled her evil smile at me. I knew there was no way her parents knew how much she had spent on that room.

I understood why she had only taken a brief time to get her things and say goodbye. It was because she didn't want her parents to find out about the hotel. She'd probably just told them she was going out with a friend for the weekend, and they'd just nodded saying sure, whatever.

Her parents were extremely strict, mainly when it came to Alexa and her frivolous spending habits. I let all these thoughts slip my mind when the bellhop opened the door and set our "bags" down.

He said, "Don't hesitate to ask for anything. We're at your service, love birds."

I was so confused I wouldn't have been surprised if my chin was on the floor with my mouth hanging wide open. Alexa must have figured out why I was confused, and the bellhop had already left us.

I turned to her saying, "What did he mean, love birds?"

She smiled a wicked smile and replied, "Well, to get this room you have to be married. So, I told them we've just been wed. So put this on."

She tossed me a wedding band and I slid it on, confused, but understanding why she did it. Then she put on an amazing diamond ring. That diamond might have been worth more than my car. I knew where she'd got these, and I felt sick. She had stolen her parents' wedding rings.

I knew there was something wrong. Something told me this wasn't the only trouble she would be causing today. I ignored her as she continued to talk about the suite. I really didn't care anymore. I was over it and all the crazy shit she says. I just wanted to sit down and think. I didn't want to listen to her evil plans for the weekend. I was just tired.

All of a sudden, she slugged me in the arm because I was ignoring her.

"Ow, that hurt," I said as I jolted back to reality.

She smirked and said, "You deserved it. How could you ignore me?"

I shrugged and said, "Well, I have been thinking about what we should do. You know, while we were here."

She seemed to chew that over, and then realized she hadn't planned to do anything. She gasped as she realized she didn't have a plan. She went silent, starting to think about what we should do.

I broke the silence saying, "How about we go to the beach after we have dinner?"

She smiled and thought it over, then finally said, "Sounds good, you're smarter than you look and act."

We both laughed softly. I pretended to get upset saying, "I'm the dumb one? You're the one who always needs saving from plans she doesn't think through."

She smirked and sniped back saying, "My knight in shining armor."

We both laughed, and I sat on the couch looking at restaurants. Alexa sat down with me, staring at them as well, like they were from some alien planet. I ignored her, pointing at things she didn't know about.

I drifted off into thoughts about what was going on. I was finally on my journey. I needed to get myself out of my rut. I didn't know if it would be better or worse to get out of this rut. But we all need to keep moving on. The people that stay still get left behind by society and everyone else. It's sad how we do that. We just leave other people who aren't as advanced as we are behind. I know one day that I might be the one getting left behind. I really didn't want that to happen, so I'd decided to get a change of scenery. I was hoping this would help get me out of my bad mood.

All of a sudden, my right leg started to hurt until I was lying down on the couch, unable to move it. Alexa sat next to my head in a panic and said, "Ryan! What's wrong?"

I responded saying, "My leg. I-I can't move my right leg."

She started to softly rub my right leg. I felt slightly better, seeing her so concerned about me. I lifted my right leg onto the couch with my hands, and the pain started to slowly fade away.

I told her, "It's okay, I'm better now. Sorry, that happens sometimes, but never like that."

She stared at me, scared of what had just happened to me. Then tentatively replied, "How long?"

I looked down and said, "For a long time. To be exact, about a few years ago."

She looked in shock as if upset that she had never noticed it before. I lay there gradually regaining the movement in my leg. She softly combed my hair with her fingers. It was soothing. I lay there and my pain drained away way faster than normal. She finally spoke softly in an angelic voice, "Why did you never tell me?"

I shrugged and replied, "It's not that big of an issue. It's only been acting up recently."

She smiled sweetly. This was weird. She was normally a huge pain. Always badgering me for answers. However, there was a change in her mood. She was calm, something I would've never expected from her. I lay there feeling like I could fall asleep with how soothing she was. My eyelids started to get heavy. I was dog tired, I had just been driving for over four hours.

I told her, "Hey, I'm gonna go lay in the bed and go to sleep. Wake me up at around six-ish so we can plan dinner and go out. My treat."

She replied with a small nod, and then I walked off to the room and fell asleep.

Nightmare 2

I suddenly felt the same pain as I had the night before. Right as I woke up, I saw a cloud of black smoke start to vanish. I started taking small breaths, scared half to death. With each tiny exhale I made black smoke come from my mouth. I slowly exhaled one final time, and it ended. I continued in awe, just breathing, but that was it. It was over. I was so confused, until I saw where I was.

I looked around dreamily and was terrified. I was back in my room in the exact position I had been in when I woke up last night. All the emotions rushed back, and the fear consumed me. The darkness had gotten me, maybe that was why I was breathing black smoke. I looked at the clock and it was blinking at 12:00 as if it had been reset. Which was weird. I hadn't reset it when I had fallen, had I? How could that even happen?

I got out of bed and walked to the door cautiously, ready to try to wake myself up as soon as I felt anything was wrong. I walked into the hall and down the staircase, hearing my parents talking. My dad was worried. But about what? I had no clue really.

I quietly snuck out of the living room and outside. I figured it would be better to not interact with the imaginary pictures of my family for now. I saw Alexa standing at my mailbox, waiting for me. She said, "Tell the truth." She said this over and over. I walked up to her to touch her but then she was instantly gone. However, her words "Tell the truth" rang through my head constantly. I didn't know what I could've been lying about.

There was a dark feeling in my chest, a real heavy feeling. I saw a little faint wisp of light floating off in the distance. I kept hearing the words "Tell the truth" running around my mind as if Alexa were standing next to me saying them. The wisp was at the end of my street, and it started to float towards town as I walked slowly towards it. Then instantly the words Alexa had said got louder and louder as I got closer to town. My right leg started pulsating like the night before.

It hurt as I continued to walk down my empty street. I vowed I would make it to the wisp. I couldn't let the darkness now creeping up on me consume me again. I didn't know if the little light could save me, but it was worth a shot. I started to run. With each step I felt like I was running on a treadmill with a steep incline.

My legs burned. The light flashing from my leg hurt worse and worse until it crippled me, and I fell to the ground unable to move anymore. I was lying on the ground crying from the pain, and then everything went black. I couldn't breathe.

I felt a smack across my face. I rubbed my cheek and noticed Alexa lying down facing me. I was curled up into almost a ball, clutching my leg, what it seemed like I was doing in my sleep. Alexa had a worried look on her face and said, "Ryan! Are you okay? You were crying in your sleep and wouldn't wake up when I tried shaking you. You just kept crying and clutched your leg. I was terrified."

I replied sleepily, still waking up, "I was having a nightmare. They've been really vivid these last two days. They've seemed to have left me with physical side effects of my body hurting afterward. It's okay, I'll live though. Don't worry, Lex." She hated it when I called her "Lex".

She made a snarky reply, "Are you six? Nightmares? Really? That was more like a night terror. Tell me what has happened in them."

I told her the stories of how they both ended horribly, seeming like I had died. She thought it over in her head and smiled, looking at the clock. It was time for dinner. We were starving because we hadn't eaten that day. So, we got up and I put on nice clothes and so did Alexa. She put on a cute evening gown that suited her very well. She asked, "Where are we going to eat? Did we even decide on a place?"

It was my turn to surprise her. I smiled widely, saying, "It's a secret I know of, a place my parents told me was perfect. I think you'll love it."

Then with those as our final words, she smiled, and I opened the door ready to go out on the town. I took her to a little place called Grace which was a former church. However, it was refurbished and now was a five-star restaurant. My parents went here for their anniversary last year and they said the cuisine was amazing. We walked in. I knew a person who managed the floor staff of the restaurant. He was one of my old friends who moved out here when he graduated.

He had gotten Alexa and me an amazing table in front of a gorgeous stained-glass wall. It was of "Mary and baby Jesus". The colors were so vibrant you would've expected it to have been made that year. There was not a single spot of dust as the last light of the sun drifted in through the colored wall. Raining a small rainbow on our table full of deep blues, vibrant greens, bloody reds, dandelion yellows, and a color I can only describe as violet.

We sat down, and our server was incredibly fast in walking right up and taking our drink orders. I got a coke and Alexa got an Arnold Palmer. An Arnold Palmer is an iced tea-lemonade hybrid, and Alexa's favorite drink. He came back with our drinks and bread, and we ordered a starter for the table. We decided to try something new, Deep Fried Foie Gras.

Foie Gras is a French delicacy and is a duck that has been fried, in this case over some nice bread, usually baguette. The waiter came back holding it and set it down for us to share. Then we ordered our real food while he was still there. I ordered a Grilled Black Angus Hanger Steak, and Alexa ordered the Miso Marinated Monkfish. They both sounded delicious.

I knew Alexa would love this place, not only were historical monuments one of her favorite things, but she loved seafood. This place was known for its fish preparations. We finally got to dig into the flakey and perfectly cooked Foie Gras. It was a perfect hue of gold with an amazing-smelling garlic butter sauce dripping off the top and onto the bread, making my mouth water. We gorged ourselves eating all of the Foie Gras.

Our meals came out and we both just stared wide-eyed like little kids on Christmas morning. The waiter set them down, and they were cooked to perfection. My steak had been seared and blackened exactly to my liking. The aroma was indescribable; it was just the essence of deliciousness. I cut into it, and the marbled steak was red and juicy on the inside and with it came some stunning potatoes.

I scarfed it up and so did Alexa. We had starved all day and deserved this. After we finished destroying our meals, we sat back, both full to the brim. Alexa smiled and asked, "How? How did you know about this place? Let alone get us in without a reservation."

I responded slyly, "I've got my connections, you know that. I'm glad we came on this trip, Alexa," I said to change the topic because I was glad we had done this. This trip was something I needed.

Alexa replies softly, "I'm glad we did too, Ryan. It's amazing to get to spend time with a great friend like this."

We both got a little shy even though we were "married", at least we were pretending we were. If you saw us wearing those rings and having a candlelit dinner like that, you'd have assumed we were married too. I paid for the dinner, and we walked out into the frigid winter night.

Chapter 3

The sea breeze was refreshing and blowing through my hair, softly swaying my shirt with its force. I looked back, and Alexa was holding onto my arm as we walked. The atmosphere was amazing. Old Port at night was beautiful. The slight glow from the streetlamps and the loud fun aura surrounding all of the restaurants. We walked down the cobblestone streets feeling like we were in medieval London.

It had a magical feel like we had just gone back in time. In one minute we were in the middle of Old Port. We walked from store to store through the town. We passed a store called Bliss. It was some sort of women's boutique. Alexa stopped and stared in through the window.

I asked her, "Why are we stopping?"

She said with excitement in her voice, "They have the boots I wanted. The designer boots. The Frye Company Harness 8R Black Boots. I've always wanted a pair."

I stared at her in wonder. I'd never seen her wear boots. She kept staring at the boots like she was going to die if I pulled her away from the window.

I told her, "Why don't we go in?"

She smiled and stared up at me like a little kid, giving a slight nod. We walked into the store and were instantly greeted by a beautiful girl.

She smiled at us and said, "Welcome to our store. If you have any questions, don't hesitate to ask."

I said, "I think we know what we want."

She smiled sweetly, replying with, "What would that be?"

I looked at Alexa and gave her a nod. She looked at the girl and asked her to get the boots she talked about in the window. The girl walked into the backroom, looking for Alexa's size, and came out with a box. Alexa tried the boots on and loved them, then she made a face at me as if begging me to buy them for her. I had saved a lot over the years so I could spare the money for her.

She always did a ton of things for me, so the least I could do was help her out, like always. I smile and handed the girl my card, and she rang the boots up and gives us a nice bag to carry the box in. Alexa was so happy she couldn't wait to go and try them on. I had made her promise to wait till we went back to the room to put them on.

I looked at my watch and realized we had been out for around four hours. At this point it was almost 11:00. The night wasn't over yet. I wanted to go to one more place tonight before we left the next day. We walked hand in hand while going to the place I wanted to go to. This place was the Portland Pier.

I turned to look at Alexa while we were walking and said, "How come you wanted to do this trip with me?"

She looked at me with a sad expression and finally spoke, "I just wanted to hang out with you. It's always fun and I thought this would finally get you to tell me."

She had a tough time getting the last words out, and finally looked back to where we were walking, ignoring that it ever happened. She looked sad even while carrying her new shoes. We got to the Pier and walked to the end of it, staring at the moon. It was a full moon that reflected off of the water, making it seem the sky had been duplicated.

I asked, "What were you going to say?"

She looked pained to respond but did so with tears welling up in her eyes, "I want you t-t-to t-tell m-me the t-t-truth. I've noticed how you've been acting. Ryan, you can't hide things from me. I know something has been up these past few years, you haven't been hiding it well."

Those words cut my heart. I couldn't believe that I wasn't hiding it well. I'd never told anyone about the accident. Not once, so for her to have seen through all of those lies, I couldn't believe it. I guessed she'd always known things about me that I hadn't even known yet.

I was visibly shaking, and she noticed, grabbing me to steady me and bringing me back out of my mind. I pulled out my notebook and wrote something in it briefly. It was weird how I hadn't been writing lately. I had blamed it on the nightmares, but it was something else. I was busy. For once I didn't have time to write.

I was always so alone because I wanted to be, so I had copious amounts of time to write and not be bothered. I though about this and looked back on the events of the last few days. Everything was so much fun. It really was, otherwise, I would've written more.

Alexa stared at me and said, "Ryan, please can you just show me? Tell me the truth for once. You've lied so much this past year and the one before. Please, tell me."

This plea I couldn't ignore. She was my best friend. I had to tell her at least part of it, to give her piece of mind.

I responded slowly, and my voice suddenly seemed dead as I spoke, "OK, let's go back to the hotel and I'll tell you." We walked along the road towards the hotel. Alexa seemed a little more lighthearted now. She was smiling and whistling while we walked. I was surprised at how late everything stayed open. It was like it had just gotten dark two minutes ago even though it was 11:30 P.M.

We admired the city because neither of us had been out of our town that often. Everything seemed so big and bright here comparatively. Alexa even started skipping. It was strange to be holding hands with a girl skipping. We made it to the lobby, and she immediately stopped, and we walked in slowly.

As soon as we walked in, the flood of lights hit us and we both were a little dazed at the change in lighting. We walked past the front desk, holding hands to keep the facade of us being married, and the snooty man smiled at us as we walked. We got into the elevator and made it to the room.

I unlocked the door, and as soon as it was shut Alexa was badgering me. She stared up at me, begging me to tell her. I sat down on the couch, and she sat next to me. I smiled, and she stared, ready to take in all of the information.

I started to tell my story about what had happened those few fateful years ago. My dad was a construction worker for a big company. He had been assigned to that town and we'd been there since I was born. He would often go to the edge of town. He had been building a library a good distance off of the town for a private donor.

I would always play on the site as a kid. The only other people I remembered being on the site were the workers. I also remembered hanging out with Alexa and Heather. But at that point, it started to get a little hazy. I had no clue why I couldn't recall, but I just couldn't. At that point I started to forget a lot of stuff, I think. That was the problem with not having a good memory. I couldn't remember what I was supposed to remember.

I lied to my friends when they asked about past events, pretending I knew. Slowly I drew inwards, stopping a lot of communication with people I once cared about. The one person I kept in my life was Alexa. She never gave up on me no matter how hard I tried to hide from everyone.

On the outside, I seemed extremely outgoing and confident. However, I was hiding deep in the recesses of my mind, not wanting anyone to get in. I wanted to be forgotten about. I didn't feel happy doing things I once loved.

I finished telling her my story, and she softly held my hand and rubbed my back. Especially when I got choked up at parts because it was hard to remember. It hurt me to even think about those events really. She saw how this visibly hurt me. She looked at me with soft eyes and I knew I was fine. I was surprised she had stayed around after all I had done to push everyone out.

She smiled softly saying, "I told you. You can always tell me anything. Just no more lying. You've been lying for too long. I need the truth. I stuck by you because we're friends. We've been friends since we were kids. I could never let you turn yourself into an recluse."

I laughed, in complete shock. I had done this to everyone. I asked, "How did you know you could reach me? I guess you never did, huh? That's just how you are. You would never have given up on me. I'm just lucky to have someone like you."

We sat there awkwardly after just saying these things. We both realized how much each one of us mattered to the other. I hugged her softly. I could tell it shocked her. This was the first hug I had given anyone who wasn't my parents since the accident.

She regained her senses and hugged me back tightly and started crying. I rubbed her back, now it was my turn to comfort her. It'd been so long since we had actually hugged, or even shared a day like today. We used to do these things all the time before the accident. The shock must've brought her back to those days.

I said, "I-I-I'm sorry."

She responded with, "Shhh. It's okay. All that matters is that things will go back the way they were."

I sat back down and laughed a little to myself. She sat with me, and then we looked at one another, smiling. I was dead tired, and I needed to sleep.

I said, "Hey, you want the couch, or should I take the couch? I'm tired today. It was a busy day of driving. I need a good night's rest."

She smiled sweetly and said, "Why don't we stay in the same bed like when we were kids?"

I looked back in shock and said, "Because we're not kids anymore."

Looking down, she sounded dejected when she said, "I just wanted it to be the same as it used to be."

Well yes, I did share some things with her. It could never go back to the time before in my head. It just wouldn't be possible. She must've noticed what I was thinking about.

Then she said sharply, "You're taking the couch then."

It was settled, she walked off into the bedroom, and I set up the pull-out couch. This hotel room was huge and had beautifully painted walls of white and gold. I noticed all of this now as I was lying in the pullout bed. I stared up at the ceiling covered in newspapers.

I was tired, my eyes felt heavy as they explored the room lazily. I tried to keep looking as each blink I took was longer than the last, until I fell into a deep sleep.

Nightmare 3

I woke up lying on the cement. I could hardly breathe. I then started to cough up this black viscous liquid. I kept coughing it up as if it was coming from my lungs. Every time I'd heave it hurt worse until I finally coughed it all up.

I noticed the wisp again and my leg pain had somewhat subsided. It was nowhere near as bad as it had been the other two times. I thought this as the wisp started to float back towards me. It came to me almost as if telling me to follow. I just wanted to stay there.

I stood up, and it floated all around me until I started moving. Then it flew towards where it wanted me to follow. This was strange in my mind. I knew none of this was real, but everything seemed so real.

I walked towards where it floated, which was my town. It was dark like night, but the sun was still in the sky. I looked at my town in surprise. It was dead. Not empty, but dead. The buildings were run down and almost turned into rubble. There was an eerie aura surrounding it.

The cars looked as if they had been abandoned in the street for years on end. It was so strange, I guessed that explained why in the first dream my car wasn't in the lot. But how was Alexa the same in the second dream?

So many questions, and no answers in sight. It terrified me. I didn't know when I was. Yes, I said when. That's the only explanation, I knew where I was, I didn't know what time I was in. It felt like the future, but there was one thing that couldn't be explained and that was the sky.

How was the sky pitch black when the sun was out? I thought this while walking with the wisp. It started towards the edge of town, and I followed closely. In an instant a flash of light hit my eyes, blinding me. It was like someone turned on a lightbulb in a pitch-black room. I was dazed.

I started to try to walk again, and the light pulsed again, stopping me from moving. My leg pain started to grow exponentially. Each step felt like a semi-truck was running into my right leg at sixty-five miles per hour. I kept walking as the pain kept doubling.

The darkness around me started to encroach on me, growing closer to my head as I walked. My right leg all the while was flashing light like crazy, and the wisp was gone.

I tried to cry out for help from my wisp friend who was leading me somewhere.

But as soon as I opened my mouth to say something, the darkness went into it. Everything was so thick I could hardly close my mouth.

I could see the wisp floating in the distance as if it had heard my call. It was just watching me at this point. It was useless, nothing could save me from this. I felt like I was going to die from this. Everything felt so real, the suffocation felt like I would really die.

All I could see was the outlines of trees in the darkness and the wisp watching me. Taunting me. It seemed as if it felt bad for what was happening to me. However, it still didn't want to get involved.

I hadn't even known if it could help me but it felt like it could. It was light, and isn't the light supposed to beat back the darkness, I thought to myself. Then the darkness finally did it and everything went black.

I couldn't see anything; I couldn't say anything. I was just there, with a crushing weight on my right leg and left arm. It hurt horribly, and all I had on my mind was the pain.

Each second, I stayed there suspended in the blackness, I wondered how I was alive. Nonetheless, I was alive. I knew I had to fight to beat this darkness. But it was too hard. Everything ended, there was nothing more. I wasn't even there anymore, it seemed. It was all gone. Nothing was left, not even me. All that I saw was a vision of a girl. I hadn't known her ever in my life, but yet I was seeing her. Then everything went black.

Chapter 4

Everything was black as I opened my eyes slowly. Then my vision came back to me, and I had a splitting headache. I looked around the room the same as when I went to bed last night. I lay back down and stared up at the ceiling. I knew Alexa was still there because she couldn't leave. She didn't drive well, based on the same reason she couldn't stay in any moving vehicle. It's because she would fall asleep at the wheel.

I had watched it before. She fell asleep while driving to school one day. Thankfully, I was in the car to keep us from crashing, and I drove the rest of the way. Anyways, she couldn't drive on her own. Especially not for four plus hours, so I knew she was still here.

I cleaned up my bed area and folded the pull-out couch back up. I walked into the bedroom, and Alexa was passed out. It looked like she had been crying last night. She was still holding the pillow she must've cried into. There was a huge stain on it from her make-up. I sat down next to her and softly rub her back.

She didn't wake up. However, she just murmured something in her sleep. "Tell the truth. Please… Don't just walk away," was what she murmured in broken sentences. I frowned. Was this because I didn't want to go back to the way things were before? Sadness overwhelmed me as I thought to myself that I was what caused her to feel so down.

I whispered in her ear, "I'll tell you the truth someday. I promise."

She woke up with a devilish smile on her face, as if she had planned this. With a smirk, she sat up. I was still shocked. I'd thought she was out like a light. I shouldn't have been so dumb. I knew she was a really light sleeper at night. The only time she slept deeply was in moving vehicles.

"I got you. I knew you didn't tell the full truth. I knew it, Ryan. You can't hide things from me," she said.

"Like you could ever figure out what I was hiding. You're too dim to think that hard about something, Alexa," I said, laughing like we were back to the old days.

"I'm gonna shower, so get out, Alexa, unless you want to watch me," I said as I grabbed a towel and put it in the bathroom.

"Maybe I do," she said with a wink, and her evil smile again.

Gone was the vulnerable sweet girl of yesterday. Back was the callous witch that I'd come to know.

"H-h-hey, don't say those things, get out," I said nervously. She blew me a kiss and gave me a sly wink as she walked out. She loved to mess with me. I hated how she knew me so well.

I got into the shower and let the warm droplets of water hit my back. The steam cleared my sinuses and I felt relieved. Everything ached. From what? I didn't know. How could a dream physically hurt me, I asked myself. I looked down at my legs, and on my right leg the scar tissue was bulging.

It was like a fresh wound again. I didn't understand how this happened, or was happening to me. Each night it seemed to get worse with the progressing dreams. There had to be some sort of explanation. Something I could blame this on.

I washed myself, and my leg hurt as I softly brushed the loofah against it. I finished and got out and wrapped a towel around me because it hurt my leg too much to dry it off regularly.

"So, there's the scar." I heard a voice from behind me. I turned around to see Alexa staring at me. I instantly tried to cover up in shock. At least I had a towel wrapped around me before I got out of the shower.

"Alexa, why are you in here? Give me a real reason, not just 'I wanted to mess with you.'" I finished saying this, and she stepped into the bathroom.

"I wanted to see if you at least gave me some form of the truth last night. Looks like you definitely did. That scar is horrible." With that, she walked out.

"I'll let you get dressed and I'll talk more," she said from outside the door.

I did feel bad about not telling her the full truth. But I wasn't going to start now. I couldn't tell her the full story. She seemed to be okay with the fact that my original story was truthful. I pulled out my notebook and started to write.

The Lion Who Wanted to Reach the Moon

There once was a lion who wanted to reach the moon. He was alone. He had been separated from his pride when he was young. He walked over the desert sands for days on end, always towards the moon. He knew that every day the moon would rise again, and he would in turn follow it.

He kept walking, getting thirsty on his trek when he came upon a spring. This spring was isolated and alone. The only thing there was a snake. This snake came up to him. He was not afraid of a small snake and walked right past it.

"Hey, what are you doing?" the snake said.

"I'm going to the moon," he replied curtly.

"Why?" the snake asked inquisitively.

"Because it's always been there for me," he replied.

"Okay, well if you climbed a mountain, you could get closer to it," said the snake.

The lion roared and thought this over for a bit. The snake continuously spoke, trying to get him to keep talking.

"Thanks," said the lion after finishing his thought.

The snake didn't want the lion to leave her, so she climbed onto his back. He didn't care so much and just kept on walking over the soft cool sands. He walked closer to the mountain as the sun started to rise and then decided it was time to sleep. He would climb the mountain tomorrow. As the glimmers of sun beamed over the top of the mountain the lion lay down.

He gave one roar, looking up at the sun, and fell asleep. The snake curled up around him, and also fell asleep in the warmth of the sun.

I finished writing this short start to a story. Then I realized this was the first time in a while I had actually written something like this. I looked down at the book in my hand and slid it into my back pocket as I walked out of the bathroom.

"Took you long enough, damn."

"Hey, it takes time to look this good," I smirked, winning the conversation. She didn't have any comeback to what I just said, which was weird. Usually, she was very quick on the uptake. I laughed and sat down next to her.

"You should shower too; we have a long ride ahead of us," I said.

"Okay, but no sneaking around like I did to you," she replied with an evil smile.

I sat there and turned on the TV, and some show on a history channel was on. It was some weird thing about aliens. I ignored it as I went deep into thought. This change of pace definitely helped me a lot. It's amazing how we've gotten so comfortable in our position in the world. What is also wonderous is how we can reach "stability".

Stability is different for each person. It's a matter of perception. You can't force anyone to have the same perception as you. But we end up manipulating people into seeing the same view as us.

This happens all of the time. It's mainly seen in the politicians or the best of our public speakers. They're able to grab onto an idea and convince hundreds, thousands, or even millions of people. Not a lot of people see what's really going on when this is happening to them.

When we're manipulated well, we end up thinking all of the things being told to us are what we already thought. Even if our ideas were completely different before we were convinced. I find it amazing how perception can be so easily and masterfully manipulated.

I finished thinking about this and stared at the TV again as it changed to a documentary about World War Two. Alexa came out fully dressed and with our backpacks. She smiled and held out her hand as if asking for something. I looked down at my hand and realized I was wearing the wedding band still. I had forgotten about it completely. I put it in her hand and grabbed our bags from her.

"Ready to go, Miss?" I asked.

"You know it. Get us home before dark," she said with a wink.

We walked out of the room. I made sure we had everything and indeed we didn't forget a thing. I looked back at the grand hotel room full of white modern furniture and smiled softly.

I later remembered fondly the time we spent in that room. Even if it was for such a short time, it had a deep and meaningful memory tied to it. That was me finally giving some of the truth I held deep inside away. My chest felt so much lighter as if I had lost a twelve pounds in weight that had been holding it down.

As I thought of this, I finally noticed that Alexa has grabbed my hand. I assumed it was to keep up the act of a married couple as we left. So that the snooty man wouldn't bother us as we walked out.

"Bye, hope you two had a wonderful time," said the snooty well-dressed man.

We nodded and smiled as we went out to the parking lot, where Alexa had gotten my car valeted. Man, were her parents (mainly her dad) going to be mad when we got home.

The brisk morning breeze nipped at us incessantly. I felt my teeth clattering in my mouth, which was a sign I was shivering. The weather in Maine during winter isn't the nicest. It was so cold it felt like we would freeze if we didn't get to the car faster.

We rushed over and made it just in time to not have to amputate any fingers or toes due to frostbite. Then finally I unlocked the car, and we got in. Again, we threw our backpacks carelessly behind us. I put the key in the ignition and turned on the car. With a vroom, it whirred to life, and that meant I could turn the heater on.

With the heater on and everything situated, I drove out of the parking lot. Proceeding down the same road we had driven on when coming to Old Port. I looked at the city. It was cold, so no one was out and about this early. However, the breakfast places were full to the brim.

I stared at them as we drove past. How could there be no one walking around outside but the restaurants are so full? I asked myself. True to her nature, Alexa had already passed out next to me. She never was good on road trips. She always left the driver alone.

At least it brought me back to the past. Like when we would ride in the car with our parents to places, she could barely keep her eyes open. The trivial things like that reminded me that some people don't change that much. It was refreshing that she had stayed relatively similar to how she had always been.

I got lost in thought, thinking about how we constantly change. It's weird how we always change, adapting to each new situation. We change in a matter of seconds, including in our reactions. We could react one way to some news told to us by someone. But react the exact opposite when someone different tells us the same news.

We genuinely want everyone to like us. Even when I do this, I say things to make people happy. We say things that people want to hear rather than what they really need to hear. I find it troubling as most people do, to tell the truth all of the time. Somehow it seems harder to tell the truth to people than it is to lie to them.

I think this is attesting to how we are as humans. We make up little lies to "save" people's feelings. We do these things partially selflessly but partially selfishly. I say this because we tell little lies to help people and make them feel better, but also to avoid being seen as a "bad friend or person".

We like to take the easier route rather than the one that could provide pushback. The saying most people live by is to choose the path of least resistance. This saying is both helpful and hurtful. It just depends on the situation it's put to use in. A lot of situations people use this in are incorrect in my opinion.

I snapped out of thought when I heard a tiny yawn come from Alexa. I gazed down at her as she lazily opened her piercing blue eyes and shut them again. She smiled as she slept, I wondered what kind of dream she was having. At this point, we were partially done with the trip and were driving through the woods of middle Maine.

The trees stretched along the sides of the road like fences, forcing you to stay on course. It was almost noon now, as I looked at the dash, seeing the 11:47 A.M. flashing. The sky was a deep blue with a ring of clouds starting to slowly swallow it up.

I began to wonder if it would snow on us. That would be horrible for driving. I already had to worry about black ice. Snow would make it even harder to tell what was ice and what wasn't. The clouds seemed to envelop the sky, with a dark gray finally covering the last shining rays of the sun.

Everywhere was suddenly much darker than before. I had always loved cloudy days, but on a day like this it would only cause trouble for me. I was torn on whether I should be happy or not because of the snow. I looked down at Alexa, sleeping like a baby, wishing I was her.

It started to snow as we hit the final leg of our journey home. It was a beautiful flurry flying around in the semi-strong winds. I watched as each snowflake floated slowly down only to be picked back up by a gust of wind. I had never seen anything of this nature before.

I poked Alexa's cheek saying, "Hey, sleepyhead, wake up. It just started snowing, your favorite."

She rubbed her eyes and sat up quickly as if the snow would just stop abruptly. She was like a child and smiled wide as she watched the snow dance around the sky.

"Thanks for waking me. I would've hated to miss this," she said.

"Anytime. I know you love the snow, so I wasn't about to let you sleep through it," I said.

She was too busy looking at the snow on her window to realize I had said anything. I smiled wondering how a girl could be so evil and so innocent in the same body. Maybe she had two people inside of her, controlling her every move. I wondered, smiling softly. I had just realized we had finally reached our town.

She was too distracted in her childlike wonder to notice anything, so I just drove us to her house.

When we got there, I got out and gave her a big hug saying, "Thanks so much for the trip. It was exactly what I needed."

She hugged back tightly and said, "No problem, but I won't stop until you tell the truth."

Those words rang in my head as I waved goodbye and got back into my car to head home. I got home and rushed up to my room before I could be questioned by my parents. I closed the door and sat at my worn mahogany desk, ready to write.

Chapter 5

I sat there staring at the desk and the paper I had just been writing on. I scowled at it as I felt I could've done better. I crumpled it up and threw it into the trash. I sighed heavily and looked up at the ceiling, leaning back in my chair. I just wasted so much time, it seemed.

It felt like an eternity as I stared at the clock. It blinked at me at 8:54 repeatedly. I was so mad thinking it over now. I sighed sadly at the clock and finally calmed down. I thought I was just hungry and realized I hadn't eaten since last night. That's why I had written so badly just a few hours before.

I got up and heard my stomach grumble. It sounded like a hissing snake. All I could hear in my mind since I stopped writing was "tell the truth". I sighed, wondering how she knew. Those words hurt my brain, making me wonder if I should actually tell someone.

I felt like there was venom in my veins. I could feel the poison in my mind, hurting me as I thought deeper. I thought about the accident, and it hurt me. That was the sensation of poison coursing through my body. Making me feel weak and insecure. I kept hearing her words, "Tell the truth". How? That was all I could ask as I sank to my knees out of my chair. I stared at the ceiling, begging for an answer.

She broke me down; she always was that way. Alexa was like a leech that wouldn't let go of me. I couldn't get her off of me. She was too slippery. Every time I was close to pushing her away, she snuck her way close. Using my stone wall as an opportunity to get close instead of finding a way around it. She was clever, every time I let my guard down, she would get closer. It was a tiring battle that it seemed like I was losing.

That was the one thing she did well. She was persistent and never gave up when she set her mind to something. I seemed to be the opposite. I was always trying to give up and run away from my problems. She faced every challenge head-on with strength until she won. I admired and hated her for that.

I lay down flat on my back, and wished I would just sink into the ground and disappear. But I wasn't lucky enough for something like that to happen. Life would never stop reminding me about the accident, and would continue to torture me.

My eyelids felt heavy, and I could barely keep them open. I lay there wishing to not sleep even though I was so exhausted. I couldn't go back to that dark world. I tried to stay awake with all my might, fighting the sleep back. But it was useless. I was so tired I couldn't avoid it.

I had to return to that world no matter how much I hated it. Every time, it got worse, I lay there thinking about the trip. I thought of Alexa and tried to get her to save me. Yet my pleas for help hit her image like a stone wall. I was stuck there. I had no choice; it was time to go back. I drifted into the dream world.

Nightmare 4

I floated there looking back exactly where the last one ended. The girl stood there facing away from me. She was incredibly beautiful, just from seeing her stature. She was tall, around my height, maybe a few inches shorter. I was six foot three, so she must have been at least six feet tall.

She had long flowing chestnut brown hair. It was slightly curled and wavy. Everything was black but she was illuminated in a bright light. I was confused about who she was. Then the moon faded into existence. I finally saw what had been irradiating her.

Her skin was a faint white and the way she stood exuded power. She turned the instant I thought this and looked at me, dead in the eyes. Staring through me with her emerald, green eyes. The moon's light reflected within them was a terrifying yet exhilarating sight.

She walked closer to me, and the world started to shine back to life with each step. The grass was a vibrant green hue. The sounds of the forest I had disappeared in started to exist again. I couldn't believe everything would come back like that; it was truly a shocking sight.

She stepped once more and kept her eyes locked on mine. I stood there, or at least I thought I was standing, who knows anymore? I could probably fly at this point. I tried to avoid her eyes, which were burning with intensity. I was terrified I couldn't speak. She got closer to me, and I looked down, and the ground was underneath me again.

The world glowed a bright blue. It blinded me. I couldn't see, I closed my eyes tight, assuming I was gonna die. Then something amazing happened when the strange girl disappeared. I was now standing back in the forest at night with the wisp floating around me. It seemed almost sentient, like it was happy to see I got out of limbo.

I reached out for it, but it floated away and led me through the woods. I continued to walk through the convoluted path it took. Going deeper and deeper into the woods. I was in excruciating pain with each step. My knee began to hurt worse and worse. It finally stopped dead, and so did I. The next thing that happened, I dropped to my knees at the sight of it. Then it all went black.

I woke up lying in a ball curled up on the floor. I had my legs pressed against my chest. My right knee was jamming into my ribcage. I was sore and hurting. I didn't understand why a dream could do these things to me. I looked around my room and could barely get on one knee. The clock said 7:43 A.M., it taunted me, saying how long I had been trapped in that horrible world. These nightmares keep getting worse, I thought to myself.

I stood up weakly, and I felt the full force of the pain in my leg. It was horrible but I had to walk with it. I couldn't do anything else. There was no way for me to just be like, "Eh, pass on the pain thing." I couldn't just give in either, so I stayed up.

I realized today was Monday. Good thing I had a late start this semester. I didn't have to walk in till around 9:20 A.M. I smiled and the pain started to fade finally. I started to see what fun things I could do to get out of my rut.

CHAPTER 5

I walked out my door to go to school and looked around at the scene.

It was bright and the snow glistened as it melted away into big puddles. My car was clean and had some snow sitting on top of it. I turned to my right and fell on my ass. What was standing there not making a sound was Alexa. She was smiling her devilish smile.

"Hey, why're you always sneaking up on me like that?" I groaned, wishing to not see her today.

"What's the fun in just walking up and saying hi to you? Nothing, that's what, if you saw me, you'd have run for the car," she said with a smirk.

She certainly wasn't wrong. I would've gotten out of there faster than The Flash. I looked at the ground and stood up, brushing the snow off of me. She grabbed my arm holding me hostage and dragged me to the car.

"What's this about now?" I inquired.

"I didn't want you running away. I know you'd never shake me off and potentially hurt me. So, I did the only thing I knew to get to talk to you and that was this," she said, pointing at my captured arm.

I really didn't want to talk to her today. She must have sensed that. For some reason, she had perfect clairvoyant abilities. I was still shocked; she must have really needed to talk to me. I wondered what about. She snapped in front of me as if she had been talking the whole time and was scowling.

"You gonna daydream all day or listen to me?" she asked, upset.

"Sorry," I said.

"Anyways, as I was saying, I need to talk to you. We both know the Snowflake Ball is this week. I really want to do this so we can be remembered," she said happily.

"Why's being remembered so important to you? I'm sure no one will forget you. How could anyone even do that? I envy everyone who hasn't met you." I laughed softly at that last part.

She frowned and thought it over.

"This town won't remember me if you won't remember me," she said matter of factly.

"If you choose to forget me, so will the town. Then I'll know I didn't leave a big impact. Hell, I wouldn't have even made a small impact if that happened," she said, on the verge of tears.

She took this really hard, I could tell. I could see the pain in her face. How could the most beautiful girl in my school and possibly the town be so insecure? I wondered. I had to respond, but I didn't want to remember her.

"Look, Alexa, I won't ever forget you. No matter how hard I would try, you'd always pop back up. Just like now, look at how many people I pushed out. I couldn't push you out. Also, look, I'm talking to you, that's more credit. I rarely talk to anyone anymore," I said calmly.

She stopped crying, looked me in the eyes and said the words I dreaded. "Promise me."

She knew I had never broken a promise. I couldn't do it. A promise was a huge commitment for me. Every promise I made I would stick to. My mind and heart couldn't let me break one. I didn't want to promise her because that meant I couldn't forget her. The last thing I needed was something to remind me of home.

"I promise, Alexa, I will never forget you," I said weakly.

That seemed to be enough for her. She had gotten me and she knew it. I started up the car and drove us to school. I thought it over, maybe it was a good thing I'd remember her. All the good things that happened to me when I was in that town were because of her. I just didn't want to get close to her and burn her. We didn't talk for the whole drive.

I pulled into the parking spot in the junior lot. Then got out and looked at Alexa who was asleep as usual. I poked her and woke her up.

"Hey, we're at school, sleepyhead," I said.

"Aww, so sweet, waking me up," she said with a wink.

I walked through the lot, and she followed right behind, catching up to walk with me.

"Rude, not waiting for a lady," she said.

"You're hardly a dainty lady, Alexa," I replied with a smirk.

She slapped me on the arm softly and I laughed. We walked slowly, we got there around half an hour before we were meant to. I stared at the school with hopeful eyes. I missed normality. Alexa could tell and smiled, looking up at me.

I rarely showed most of my emotions, especially happiness. What can I say? I was hopeful for a new day. Finally, my refresh was going to begin. We walked into the center of the courtyard, or "quad" as it was called. The leaves on the trees had long since died. Snow covered the ground and reflected the sun shining upwards.

I walked through the snow, kicking it out of the way. I stared up at the sun and bathed in its glorious light. Nobody seemed to be walking outside today. This was normal because the school is connected one hundred percent by indoor hallways. So, there was no reason to want to be outside in a horrible Maine winter.

But I liked the snow. It was refreshing to me. Most people hated it, including Alexa, but I loved it. The snow was so beautiful to me and amazing. How each individual flake would never repeat put me in awe. It was so amazing to me because all over the world there is snow. But to think that out of all of those places, it is almost impossible that a snowflake had ever been the same. Blew my mind.

I also liked the aesthetic of the dead winter trees. It was a pleasant change. Most of Maine was covered by pines or something similar. So, for these trees on campus to actually lose their leaves and stay like this was nice.

"Hey, dummy, think fast," I heard Alexa say as I ducked, anticipating the snowball.

But Alexa had planned for that, and I was hit dead in the cheek. I was hit by a slight feeling of ice nipping my nose. My cheek burned slightly from the freezer burn.

"No fair, I wasn't ready, Alexa," I said sorely as I dodged another snowball.

"You're never gonna win this fight if you don't throw any back," she said as if she were taunting me, even though it was just true.

I grabbed a ball of snow and threw it back at her as I jumped out of the way of one of hers. It hit her square in the shoulder. It had gotten all in her hair, right on target. I laughed loudly and kept ducking hers. The score was one-one. I assumed we were playing best of three, typical of our snowball fights.

"Hey, you got something in your hair," I teased, smiling wryly.

She looked at her hair and shook her head, trying to get the snow out. She was furious. I had messed up "Ms. Popular's" hair. She started throwing an onslaught of snowballs my way. I dodged most of them. She was an unbelievably bad shot most of the time, which I used to my advantage.

I ducked behind trees, hiding from her fury. She was really mad, or pretending to be, and I couldn't stop myself from laughing. She was so serious about dumb little things like that. I grabbed up another snowball and peeked around the tree and she was gone.

That was weird, I would have heard her if she had gone somewhere else. Wouldn't I have? I wondered, then I heard a whistle from behind me. Clever girl. She had gotten me while I was distracted, laughing, she was flanking me. She laughed an evil laugh and threw the last snowball. I had lost and accepted it. But something was different about this snowball.

It was way bigger than all of the others. Then I realized what she had done. What a shady thing to do. She had put a rock in the center of this one. I could see how tightly it was packed too. This was going to really hurt. Then it hit and I fell to the ground hard. All of a sudden everything went black.

Chapter 6

"*Is he gonna be, okay?" I said as I walked with the nurse who had just picked Ryan up.*

"What'd you throw at him, Alexa?" she asked.

"A snowball with a rock in it," I replied sheepishly.

"Really, Alexa, why? I know you get out of hand sometimes. But this is excessive. You knocked Ryan out cold. I hope you didn't do any damage to him," she said, sounding disappointed in me.

We walked to the school infirmary, and he just lay there asleep. Then he stirred and woke up suddenly, gasping for air.

I looked at the sky, trying to catch my breath. Wait. Is that a ceiling? I thought to myself. I slowly looked around, surveying my surroundings. Then I saw who was sitting there, seemingly terribly upset. It was Alexa, who was looking down with a sad expression on her face.

"Umm. Why the long face?" I said.

"I'm sorry I hurt you," she said in a sad tone.

"It's no problem, I'm not hurt too bad," I said dizzily. My center of balance was a little off after that hit.

"I know but I still feel bad," she said, looking like she had this morning. She was sulking and wouldn't look at me. I found it funny how she was so worried about me. The girl who never cared about anyone or anything cared about me.

"Cheer up. We got out of class. That's one of your favorite things, right?" I smiled softly, still lying there.

"Since when do you care?" She had gotten her attitude back.

This was the Alexa I knew. The one from this morning was strange and vulnerable. That wasn't who she was or had ever been. It didn't suit her. She was an extraordinarily strong individual. I knew even strong people needed breaks once in a while. I thought this was my way of giving back to her over those past years. I got up weakly and almost fell. I was fine though, at least in my mind I was. Alexa caught me and then pushed me off of her and laughed.

"You think I'd be caught dead helping you? I know you can walk. Quit pretending," she said, smiling.

"Well, look at you, this is way different from like five minutes ago. Welcome back, Alexa," I said as I patted her head.

She hated it when I touched her hair. So, I did it anyway, and she kept swatting my hand off of her head. Each time I'd keep patting her head. We walked out of the infirmary and went to our classes. Luckily, I had different classes from Alexa this year.

I got into my Algebra 3-4 class and sat down at my desk, trying not to disrupt the class. Of course, I didn't. I was one of the quietest kids in the school. Which had been the exact opposite a few years back. But that was a sore subject, so I just ignored it. I got my work out and my teacher just rambled on about nothing. As it seemed to me most math teachers did.

I just kind of drifted off into a daydream because I couldn't focus on the teacher. Whatever he was teaching I could relearn from the book. I started to think about today. It seemed impossible that these things were happening. But the change of scenery brought back my spirit, so to speak. It's amazing what a vacation can do for a person. Even such a minuscule one.

Why had Alexa been so strange today? Did she feel she was losing me? If she had me to begin with. These were tough questions to answer, at least for me. I guessed when we get used to someone and the way they act. When they do something, you perceive as out of character you think something's changed in them.

We do that all the time. If we look back at our past, we will see how we judged people. Even the people who claim to not be judgmental, at one point have judged someone. When people try to say they aren't, I think that means they're ashamed of it. But we shouldn't be. Humans have always judged one another since the dawn of our species. It's just a natural reaction because we all have likes and dislikes. So, we often judge the things we dislike about people.

People say that you're a bad person if you do certain things. Well, if you look at it this way, we all have been bad people at one point. By each individual's definition, a bad person is a person who is doing or has done things we determine to be terrible. My logic is that we have all done and said bad things, so we have all been bad people.

Another thing I think about often is how much we think about the past. We look at the past so frequently that we miss the present. In my opinion, it's fine to look back and remember events fondly. But if you are constantly trying to go back to a point in time, you're wasting more of your remaining time. I say that we should live the years of our lives to the fullest. Because who's to say when the good old days were? You should live like you're still in those days, not pine after the past.

The bell rings and snaps me back to reality. I walked outside, and it was snowing. I loved the snow, if it wasn't already obvious. I stood and watched all of the flakes fall one by one. Then I got hit by a snowball from behind my back. I turned around to see Alexa's face bright red as she stared at me and laughed.

"Didn't you get in trouble for throwing those already today?" I said.

"Depends, are you still mad about it?" she said.

"Nope," I replied.

"Then no, I didn't." She smiled slyly.

We walked together to my next class and were silent most of the way. She wasn't herself today. Most of the time she was all talkative. But at random times she can be the exact opposite. She just stared at the ground. Maybe she felt bad because she had hurt me today. But usually, that wouldn't be enough to get her this quiet. It was an eerie silence.

I didn't hear any other noise from other people, like I had gone deaf. I feared I had until we bumped into a girl who was hurriedly running down the hall. I heard a yelp for help as she fell to the ground. I barely managed to reach out in time to catch her. She didn't even care that she had fallen; she was more worried about her work. Because when she started to fall, she dropped all of her papers.

I crouched down to help her pick everything up. Then I noticed who it was. This girl was someone I knew, but from where? The height, eyes, and hair color, all of them seemed familiar, but how? I was surprised I had noticed all of this because this was completely out of character, for me to recognize someone.

She gave a faint smile and said, "Thanks for catching me."

"No problem. I'm surprised my reflexes were that quick," I responded, smiling.

"I need to go thanks for the help." With those words, she was gone in an instant.

Alexa was staring at me and smiling, which was weird. I didn't trust it, and more importantly, I didn't trust her. She had given me plenty of reasons to not trust her at all. I stared at her for a second and then shrugged it off and started to walk. Everything was so surreal the rest of that day I didn't know what was going on. The last bell rang, and I sprinted out of school. Alexa barely caught up to me to drive her home.

I drove her home, and everything was quiet as usual. I couldn't get that girl out of my head. Alexa was asleep, lying on the seat stretched out. It wasn't a long drive at all. Yet she stayed true to her nature and passed out as soon as we got in. That girl was so familiar, I couldn't tell where she was from. It was stuck in my head as I got to Alexa's house.

"Hey, sleepy, time to go home," I said, leaning over and poking her.

"Five more minutes," she said sleepily.

"Nope, you gotta go, I'm kicking you out," I said.

"Fine, be that way, Ryan," she said while waking up and grabbing her bag.

She got up and opened the door. Then she was gone like she hadn't even been there to begin with; she had just disappeared. I drove home and I was really ready to go home. I couldn't sleep. Not even if I tried. I wasn't tired at all. On top of that my legs were still sore from sleeping curled up in a ball like that.

I just thought about the day's events. What had even happened when I got knocked out? I wondered. Who was that girl? So many questions and no answers. I stared at the road as I drove, thinking these things. Why are there never any real answers to some questions? It was so strange that I realized that so late. Some questions you can just never answer. I pulled into the driveway and got out of the car.

I walked up the stairs and opened the front door. No one was home. I could tell by how the garage was still empty. Also, nothing was cooking. That was a dead giveaway because they were always cooking food. I swear that they should have been chefs instead of what they currently did. I always joked with them about that. They never did anything else, or at least from what I knew.

I didn't really care what they did, it's not like I was their keeper or anything. It was not my job to worry about their every move. I went up to my room and opened the door. I couldn't think as I walked in and lay down. The thing that clouded my mind was that girl. Who was she? I kept thinking the same thing over and over.

"No, that can't be her," I said out loud to myself.

It couldn't be the girl I was thinking of. It just couldn't have been her, right? I tried to ignore that thought and started to think about how I could know her. That was way more confusing than anything else I thought back into my past. I tried to see if I'd ever seen this girl or even talked to her just once. I couldn't think of anything at all. How was this possible? I'd met everyone in that town. Or so I thought. This mystery girl was worrying me now.

I texted Alexa, "Hey, did you know that girl I helped today? I can't remember her. I've never met her, which is weird."

She didn't respond for like five minutes, but what she said confused me no end.

"Not once have I ever seen her face. I know everyone in this town, but she definitely isn't someone from here. She's new but no one has moved out. Which makes it impossible she's here, right? Are there any new buildings going up? Ask your parents."

47

When she said that I couldn't fathom it. They didn't mention anything about new construction, did they? How could this girl be here? Even if she were to have moved in, there was no place for her to move. Where did she come from? Why was it my first time meeting her? I assumed that today must've been her first day, which would have explained some of the papers. She must have gotten catch-up papers today.

But the questions still remained: who was she and why was she here? I racked my brain, thinking about how she could have seemed familiar. If this was the first time Alexa had seen her. Then there was no way for her to be familiar to me. It seemed now that it was a calculated fall she had done. I wondered how she hadn't seen us when she was walking down the hall. She wasn't even walking in our direction until she saw me, then she bumped into us. Also, she seemed hurried like she didn't want me to get a good look at her.

Something was off with this girl, that much was true. I lay on my bed now, staring up, thinking about this girl, when I heard a knock on my window. I turned to see snow on it. I guessed it was Alexa again, so I walked over to it. I looked down to the yard, yet no one was there. Whoever it was had either run away or just disappeared, I'd say the first. I suddenly had a sense of déjà vu. This had happened once before. Then my leg started to ache as I sat there. Like a memory had just jump-started the pain in me.

I had to sit on the bed because the pain was so crippling. I was cold and you could see the steam from my breathing. This was weird because the furnace in my house was on. I was hit with a wave of terror, like something horrible was about to happen. My skin looked pale compared to the normal tan. I could barely move my leg. The pain was so intense. It felt like someone had strapped five tons of bricks to just one of my legs.

It got colder and colder in my room, and I couldn't do anything. I couldn't even get out. I was too weak to move. It felt like I had stepped back in time to a memory, but which memory? This was creepy, everything seemed familiar yet changed slightly. This was "normal" for dreams but not real life. I knew I was awake, not asleep. Right? I didn't even know that much anymore. Everything seemed superficial, like it was all cheap fake remakes.

This was very supernatural, that's for sure. I couldn't tell if everything around me was real or another dream. It scared me knowing that I even had to question reality. Nothing was safe for me in this world, that was the horrific realization I came to. I looked up at the ceiling, and it was the same ceiling my room had always had. Nothing changed, just felt way cheaper or like fake knockoffs.

This was a weird feeling to have, but it was the only one I knew at this point. Because that couldn't have been reality. I had forgotten about the pain in my leg by this point. Honestly, I thought I would freeze to death. I was shivering to keep my body warm. I couldn't do anything but sit there as the room got colder and colder.

Then something strange happened. I heard Alexa's voice from outside the window. Everything started to warm up slightly. I could hardly walk but I went to the window. I opened it, and there she was, standing in the yard.

"Hey! Where'd you go? You saw me and just walked back into your room while I was talking," she yelled loudly up at me.

"I'll come down, wait up for me!" I said and went downstairs.

Chapter 7

I ran outside. Man, I was glad to see her. I'd just had one of the worst experiences of my life. What had happened would probably haunt me for the rest of my life.

"Hey, weirdo, where'd you disappear for like ten minutes?" she said mockingly.

"Umm… Long story. I'll have to tell ya it one day. But for now, I'm just glad you're here," I said, smiling softly.

I honestly felt she had saved me from whatever that was. I was so confused about what had happened. I just decided to ignore it and see what Alexa wanted.

"So, what'd you want anyways?" I asked.

"I needed to talk to you. I'm really sorry for today," she said sheepishly.

"No worries, I know it's just how you are." I smiled weakly.

"Well, what I wanted to talk about is the plans," she said shyly.

"Yeah, what about them?" I asked.

"Well, we should set them up so they're getting ready for the ball tomorrow. Pick up all the stuff we'll need," she said, and with those last words, she ran off to her house.

She was so weird. Why did she always have to do that? Right after she finished her sentences, just jump up and sprint away. It was annoying. I wanted to tell her what happened so badly.

I recollected all of what had just happened to me in complete awe that it had even happened. I probably looked like a freak, staring at the snow while doing so. After I wrapped my brain around it somewhat. Then I walked inside. When I went up to my room, I felt a strong urge to write, for some reason.

The Lion Who Wanted to Reach the Moon Ch. 2

The lion woke up with the annoying snake still on his back. He walked during the night to try to reach the moon climbing the mountain. He climbed higher and higher as the snake slept. At some point during his climb, the lion looked back and saw nothing. The snake was no longer on his back. She must have left while he was climbing.

Then he heard the loud screech of an eagle. He looked all around for the majestic bird. Yet there was nothing around him. Then a single feather fell from the sky as he looked around, confused. The noise of flapping wings grew closer. It was an ominous sound. Hearing such a loud flap so close to you. He roared in answer to the screech the eagle had let out.

Still, he did not see the eagle, but he saw what the eagle had left when he reached a small break. It was a corpse of what he did not know. He walked up to it tentatively and was a little scared of where it had come from. He stared at the creature, wondering what it had been, then there came a call from behind.

"What are you doing? Eat," said the voice.

"What is it? Why did you give this to me?" said the lion softly.

"It doesn't matter who I am. Just know that I have given this to you. Remember I will need a favor one day too," the voice said again as it faded away.

The loud sound of flapping came again as another screech was let out. This time the lion shook with fear. He roared softly as he ate, thankful for the food. He hadn't realized how hungry he was until he saw the food. The lion was starving and ate the whole meal, leaving nothing but the bones. However, hunger was not his only trouble.

The lion was also very cold now. The higher he had gotten on the mountain, the colder it was at night. He was so determined to reach the moon, he had ignored the cold. Yet now it was nothing to be trifled with. He started to shiver from the frostbite that was currently developing.

He roared and started to keep climbing. But each step had gotten harder as his body seemed to freeze up. The lion walked and fought with all his might against the cold, making almost zero progress. He felt like he was fighting a losing battle.

The lion finally looked up and asked, "Why does it have to be so cold? Moon, why do you make this so hard?"

As he said this, something seemed to have heard him in the cosmos. He looked at the sky once more, still chilled to the bone. But something strange had happened. There were little flickers of light. That light was coming off the horizon, lighting up the sky slowly. The sun was rising, and with it came warmth.

The sun slowly rose higher into the sky, and, as he watched it, he roared again loudly. The sky was filled with a red and orangish glow, with pink sprinkled throughout the sky as the sun danced to its position. He watched this spectacle happily, feeling safer from the horrible cold on the mountain.

Suddenly there was more warmth than ever. The lion felt so much better and was ready to lay there. He sat in the sun and bathed in its glorious light. This warmth healed him and reinvigorated his motivation. He had not been ready before, but with this reassurance he was ready.

The sun finished its slow ascent into the sky. It was as if the sun had heard his pleas to the moon.

"Thank you," said the lion proudly.

"You're welcome," the sun seemed to wave back with that message.

So, the sun had heard him and was listening. He was glad to have someone or something on his side. He lay down in the sun and took a nap.

I closed my notebook and finished with the chapter I was working on. I was happy with it. To be completely honest with myself, it had been a while since I was truly proud of my writing. But the trip had reinstated my confidence in my writing, making me feel stronger.

I looked up at the ceiling, and then remembered that Alexa and I needed stuff. We needed materials to be more exact, to do what she was planning. It wasn't too much that we needed. Mainly music and voice recordings were the main things she needed.

I texted her, "Hey, want to meet up?"

She took a while to reply and said, "Sure, but where?"

"I don't know, you pick, Alexa."

"I always pick, Ryan. But let's meet at the usual spot." She ended the conversation with that.

I knew where she wanted to meet. We used to go there all the time as kids. We used to walk into the woods and hang out by this abandoned mansion. We thought it was haunted but didn't care much. This mansion was around one hundred years old. Some old rich person from the 19th century had it built but never used it. It was fully furnished and just really run down.

The paint was chipping off the walls and the wood was rotten. It had water damage on almost all of the floorboards. The ceiling leaked, but when it rained it was mostly dry. It was well-insulated, so it didn't get cold in the winter. It was a nice place for kids to hang out.

Anyways, we'd been going there for around seven years. We found it and thought we were incredibly lucky. This was because almost no one was ever there. I smiled and got on my coat, walking out of the house. Alexa hadn't said when to meet. But one thing about Alexa was that when she said to meet it always meant right away. It was never to meet at some later time; it was always instantaneous. I knew she would probably be waiting for me.

I turned around the corner to get off of my street. Then I saw something that made me stop dead. It was more of the person doing the thing that made me stop. It was that mystery girl walking down the street. It was strange that something so normal would be so weird to me.

She was walking very hurriedly, carrying groceries from the mart. She always seemed to be in a hurry. The thing that was weird was that it looked like she was almost running. This was impossible in the current conditions. Snow was covering everywhere, blanketing the whole town. Yet she was still moving amazingly fast.

This girl was very odd indeed. I cataloged this in my brain and decided not to stalk her. I would never live it down if Alexa found out I was stalking her. Even if I was doing it for *research.* I felt a little shocked at seeing this girl in the first place. I thought she was a figment of my imagination. This was because no one knew who she was, not even Alexa. But Alexa did see her, so that meant she was real.

I was thinking all of this while walking in the opposite direction to the strange girl. I looked up and it was cloudy. It was the kind of cloudy that was pretty and somewhat menacing. It was a very weird omen, especially after seeing that girl like that. I don't really believe in higher powers affecting us. I also don't agree with superstitions. I think they're somewhat dumb.

Making up reasons for things we can't explain is a weird concept. However, I guess we've been doing that since the beginning of time. We as humans have always been finding ways to explain the unexplained. I think that's an amazing quality of human nature. Do I fully believe it redeems all of the other qualities? Not really.

I thought about all these things as I reached the edge of the woods. I looked up once again, and it seemed as if it was going to snow. Yet nothing happened. The sky just shifted its shade of gray. Alexa was probably already at our spot and waiting for me. She was always faster than me, at least athletically. Apparently, she was also always one step ahead of me mentally. She could predict what I had hidden from her so easily.

It was an oddly charming quality she had. I think the thing that made it charming was that while she did know what I was hiding, she never forced me to do things I didn't want to. I rarely wanted to share, but I think that was part of her strategy to get to me. She thought that if she never rushed me, I would tell her sooner or later. It seemed like it was working. It really did.

I had wanted to tell her so many things, but I kept them inside. Thankfully, I still had my judgment. I didn't know how Alexa would respond if I were to tell her. The thing I really didn't want was for her to give me any shit for being "crazy". I knew that would be the word she would use to describe me.

I walked deeper into the woods and finally the sky opened up. It was snowing, man did I love snow. I looked up and spun like I was still a child. I wish I could go back to those days, but I knew that it was better to focus on the future. So, I would never waste some of the remaining years of my life. I looked around and noticed how close I was.

I ignored the snow for now and walked up to the house. Then I heard a strange sound like the cracking of a branch, ringing out through the woods. Things carried in the silence of the woods, so there was no way of telling where it came from. Then I heard a loud scream from behind me. I jumped;

I was so terrified I almost jumped out of my own skin.

I was shaking as I slowly turned around to hear a loud laugh. It was Alexa, she was standing there red in the face, cracking up. She must've thought that was the best practical joke of all time.

"Don't wet yourself 'Dane Cook,'" I said in an upset tone.

"Hey, that one was good. I got you. I got you. Why are you so easily scared? Huh, Ryan?" she said mockingly.

She loved to mock me and take shots at me whenever she got the chance.

"I don't know, maybe because it's the middle of the creepy woods. Also, not to mention it's snowing, making visibility next to nothing. That explains why I was so scared," I said, getting more angry with her.

"Geez, don't get your panties in a bunch, bud," she said, mocking me again.

I opened the door, and didn't care if she followed or not. I walked in and lay on the couch with leather soft and malleable from years of wear and tear. I let out a loud sigh, finally setting all of my tension free from my body. Alexa loomed over me and gave me a devilish grin.

"How's it going? Sorry for scaring you..." she said, almost seeming actually sorry.

But I knew the truth, if I accepted the apology, she would be like, "I wasn't really sorry, dummy." So, I just lay there and sighed again as the couch creaked from her sitting on it.

"Hey, you're too heavy for this couch, Alexa," I said, laughing softly.

"Umm. You're the 'fatty'. I'm not the hefty one here," she said softly.

"Sure, sure I am, Alexa," I said with a wink.

She smiled, and realized I had accepted her apology. I knew that this was her real way of apologizing. She was always a weird girl. I sat up and propped my back up with the armrest.

"So, what are our plans?" I said.

"We can do that later. I want to talk to you," she said very seriously.

This wasn't like Alexa; she was usually always upbeat. She was never the serious type. I didn't know what she needed to talk about. But all of a sudden, my leg started to hurt. I didn't know why it did now. I winced with pain clearly in my face.

Alexa looked concerned but I couldn't hear her as the pain slowly grew. It hurt worse and worse with each passing second. Alexa softly massaged my leg as she tried to convince me everything was going to be okay. At least, that was what I thought she had been saying. Yet the pain still grew. It was a horrible recurrence, but it showed no sign of stopping soon.

The room got a little darker. I thought I was about to pass out. Everything went dark except Alexa, it was just me and her. I could see the concern in her eyes and the fear they harbored. I didn't want her to feel that fear. I didn't want to feel this fear myself. It was a horrible feeling of no control over anything.

She kept rubbing my leg, and tried to keep me awake as long as possible. I didn't want to leave her scared like this. I couldn't do that to her and to myself. Who knew what would happen between now and when I woke up? Certainly I didn't, and I wanted my control back.

All of a sudden, the pain just went away, and I heard clearly what Alexa was saying.

"I want to talk about that strange girl. The one we knew nothing about today. I have some big news I found out about her," she said in an exhausted voice.

Chapter 8

That really got my attention. I stared at the hole in the ceiling, my leg still numb. She just looked at me, and probably thought I'd died. I let out a deep sigh, not wanting to talk or even move at all. I wanted to hear the news, but to tell the truth I was scared. I still didn't know if I wanted to know the real truth about our mystery girl. Meanwhile, Alexa was staring down at me with slightly concerned eyes. I looked up blankly and met her gaze.

She kept talking but I couldn't hear the words. I was so out of it. I could hardly focus on her, to be completely honest. Staring at me, she shook my arm. I think she realized I wasn't listening, finally. That brought me back to reality. I couldn't ignore her forever. I knew that much.

"Did you hear what I said? Have you even been listening to the news?" she said, a little upset.

"Sorry, after I finished that little episode everything kinda went out of focus," I replied meekly.

"Well, anyways, before whatever that was that interrupted us, what I had been saying was that I found some things out. I've been looking into this girl and who she really is. What I found out was, it's a little weird that you didn't know her. She's the daughter of the CEO of the construction company your dad works for. The question is why she's here," Alexa said.

I was in shock, all I could ask was, "Wait, you mean the girl that no one knows is the daughter of the CEO?"

"That's what I just said, didn't I?" she responded snarkily. "Can I continue?" she asked inquisitively.

"Yes," I said dejectedly.

"Okay, so as I was saying, this girl is here because of her father, right? That's what I thought, but no, she's not. For some reason, no one knows she came back to live with her father again. She used to go to this all-girls boarding school in Massachusetts. Now she's back here, and rumor is that she got kicked out. I don't think she got kicked out though. The way she acts is odd. I would never pick her out as a bad kid. So, I took the liberty of looking up her school life and grades from her previous school."

"Wait right there. Did you say you hacked into the school's database and took her records? That's illegal, Alexa." I said this with disbelief, this was the kind of thing that I had to save her from when she got in trouble.

"Well, anyway, what I was getting at is that she didn't get kicked out. She left on her own. She had all A's and B's back at that girls school. That's what is so weird about it. Well, that was all the news I got, so do you have anything you want to add? I think you should talk to your parents about it. They're bound to know something about it, Ryan." She finished this without skipping a beat.

I was left wondering what I had just heard. Not only had Alexa done something highly illegal and dangerous, she found out a lot about this girl. But, wait, she didn't get her name? That was weird. I thought back to her talking, and she never mentioned the girl's name. I thought how weird this was when I felt a snowflake hit my nose. Maybe one of the windows is open, I thought. Alexa was just staring at me, waiting for me to absorb all of the information she had just laid on me. I sat there and stared back.

"I should ask my parents about her. I don't know how they'll take it though. I never really ask about other people. Maybe they'll be happy. Who knows, all I know is I need to find out who this girl is," I said while staring at nothing in particular. I had just said what was on my mind really.

Alexa nodded in agreement. We were both very intrigued by this strange girl. With that, we both sat there thinking thoughts of our mysterious girl. I wondered who she was and why she really came back. It couldn't have been because of how amazing it was here because it was not. It also couldn't be because of the people because this town was just as friendly as any other town. So that left the question of why she was here. Was she here for me? No, that would be way too narcissistic for me to think. She couldn't be here for me. She wouldn't even know who I was.

Yet for some reason, all I could think back to was her bumping into just me. That was a long hallway, and she didn't just turn a corner and run into me. It seemed almost intentional, the way it happened. Like she knew what would come next. It was eerie how Alexa could predict that I was hiding things from her. I did not need another weird clairvoyant girl in my life. But there was some strange pull she had, some aura about her. That just held me in, and I couldn't stop thinking about this girl.

At least now I knew who she was, sort of. But I didn't even know her name. I knew whose daughter she was. I sat here thinking, and Alexa had just lain in my lap. I wondered what my parents know, that was all I kept thinking about. They had to know something, right? Alexa and I sat there for around two more hours, just brainstorming and talking. Finally, at around seven o'clock we decided to start walking home. It was a silent walk. We had been talking for so long that we needed some silence.

Reaching town, I noticed it was dark. The sun had set around two hours before. It was strange that the woods had seemed to be lit up before. I thought this but decided to not question why the woods were light but here was dark. It was like we had gone from a sunny slightly cloudy day into darkness. This was with almost no transition at all. It was like someone had pulled a thick curtain across the previous bright blue sky.

Alexa hadn't seemed to notice this, but I had. I couldn't stop thinking about it. She just kinda walked slowly, like a sloth, dragging her feet with each step. We had finally reached the corner where she had to leave. We said our goodbyes and walked our separate paths to our own homes. I walked into my home ready to question my parents about this strange new girl. I wanted to see if they knew anything about it.

Something was off. I got an unmistakable eerie feeling when walking into my house. Like someone else was there, but not my family. It was a very ominous feeling. I walked in and put my bag by the door just like normal. Then I walked to the entrance of the kitchen. My parents stood there talking to someone.

Some big burly man I had never known was standing stock still, talking to my parents. Mainly my dad. My mom was just there holding his arm. This man was dressed very nicely in a suit and tie. The very air around this man seemed to be completely erased wherever he moved. I knew that this was impossible, but he wasn't very nice looking. He was very... how would I put this? *Menacing.*

They all just barely noticed me and stopped talking. It was like I had seen something I shouldn't have. Then this immensely powerful man walked hurriedly out of the room. He didn't stop speed-walking till he was out of the door and in his car. Wait. Something was familiar with the way he had been walking. It was like I'd seen someone walk that way before. Was that who I thought it was? He was the CEO of the construction company.

I now had renewed faith that my parents would definitely know something about this girl. Even if what had just happened was sketchy, I had to trust my parents, right? I walked up to them, and it was like I hadn't seen them in days. Probably because I hadn't really. I was always in my room or out with Alexa when they were home. So, I really hadn't seen them for the past four or five days. I guessed that would be weird to some people, but not me. That was just how my family was. I stopped thinking about this and finally decided to question them.

"Who was that?" I asked. "Why was he here?"

"He's the CEO of the construction company. As for why he was here, he just needed to talk with your father," my mom said.

"Hey, I've got a question. Do you know if he has a daughter?" I asked inquisitively. "Do you by chance know her name?"

"He does, how'd you know? Also, why do you need her name?" My mom answered my question with a question.

"I just wanted to know, I suppose. Well, do you know her name or not?" I asked again.

"It's Heather. That's so weird that you ask. You never ask about others, especially not girls. Well anyways, yeah, her name is Heather," she said, somewhat concerned.

"Thanks, Mom, love ya. I'm going up to my room. I'll make myself something to eat. See you two later." With those words, I dashed out of the kitchen.

I ran up the old creaky Maine staircase and sprinted into my room. I slammed the door shut right as I crossed over the threshold. I had so much new information to process. My parents are being weird and acting strange. There was a new girl that has just appeared in the town out of nowhere. Then on top of that the Ball was coming up.

This was trouble. Everything about these new people was off. It was weird. I stared at my oak desk and smiled at my pen lying there. I looked at it and saw the word "sleep". Come to think of it, I hadn't really slept in a day or two. That was odd. Maybe I just... I don't know. I guess I was so curious that I could hardly sleep. Maybe that was why everything had been so off. I hadn't had a good night's sleep in forever, it seemed.

While thinking this, I decided that I should probably take a nap. It was not normal to stay up so long without being fatigued. So, I lay down on my bed, and a wave of exhaustion washed over me. It was crazy, like all of a sudden, as soon as I hit the bed, I felt the need to sleep. Whereas a second ago I could've run all the way around the block. I had no way of knowing why I was so tired, I just knew I was.

I fought to keep my eyes open for a few seconds to try to turn off the light. But my struggles were all for nothing. Try as I might, my arms and body wouldn't listen to me. They just wanted to shut down and make me sleep. I didn't want to leave the light on, but I guessed it didn't really matter. Within an instant, I had fallen asleep. I was at the mercy of the dream world now.

Nightmare 5

I was now back in the woods where I'd been before. I stared at the building in front of me. As I did, a huge fire of emotions burned inside of me. It was like my whole body was burning down. I felt horribly sad, seeing this sight. I was shaking almost to the point of tears.

I took a step towards the destroyed building. But it pushed me back. I got removed from where I was standing. I was now facing the woods, and the wisp was long gone. It was no longer lingering around me. But I heard a faint whistle coming from behind me. I turned to see the strange girl. The same one from school. It was Heather. I stared at her as she walked, whistling. She looked younger now. Like, younger than me.

I looked around and realized I was shorter too. I was the same height as I had been in 7th Grade. This was really scary now, how was I younger? I didn't feel younger. I felt a slight breeze brush my knees. Wait, my knees? I looked down and I was wearing shorts. This was way weirder than any of the others. Yet it was definitely not as scary as the others.

I heard the whistling getting louder like the girl was walking toward me. I turned again to see her walking right up to me. It was like she didn't even see me. But I noticed her. She was staring right at me. But not really at me, more like through me. It was so strange. I knew this look. I'd done it before, and I did it a lot really, at least recently.

Soon she was right next to me. I watched her move closer and closer to me. I couldn't move as she walked past me. I tried to reach out to her to talk, but I couldn't do anything. Then, all of a sudden, she disappeared. The world had lost all sound as if I had gone deaf. I looked around, trying to see her, but she was nowhere to be seen.

It was eerily quiet. I took a step forward and still heard nothing. I walked towards a tree to see if I could make a sound. I picked up speed, getting even more terrified I'd never hear again. The woods were dark and ominous. Then I heard something, but it was very, very faint. If you've ever taken a hearing test, the sound was a little quieter than the quietest beep in the test.

The sound kept repeating in my mind. It was like people were talking to me and I could just barely make out a word. The voice kept talking and repeating over and over. It got louder and I could make out exactly what it was saying.

It was saying, "Face it, Ryan. Face it, Ryan. Face it, Ryan..."

What do I need to face? I asked myself. I heard it get louder and louder. Until it was like this woman was yelling it in my ears. I could make out the gender of the voice now. It was definitely a woman's voice.

Then suddenly the screaming stopped completely. But something worse happened and my leg started to hurt.

"Not this again," I said, irritated.

I was tired of this. I just wanted answers. Every answer I got just convoluted all of the other things happening. It was like the truth was buried in a pile of lies. Then my leg hurt worse and worse as things started to fade. The world started to fall away from me, getting darker to an almost blackness. It was so dark I reached out to try to save myself. What happened next had me completely stunned.

As I was reaching out, a hand grabbed my arm. It was a girl's hand and the darkness kept creeping in on me. But then this girl pulled me to her, and then the moon shone again. It illuminated the girl. The girl was Heather. She stood stock still, holding me close, and I could see again. I was saved.

Then the light faded but she was still holding me. But it got darker and darker, and after that she vanished.

Chapter 9

I woke up on the floor. Man, that was some violent dreaming, I thought to myself. I didn't want to face what was happening, to be honest. I just wanted to fade into the background like I always do. I was exhausted even though I had just woke up. This was getting to be a normal that I didn't like.

I seemed to be having these dreams every time I closed my eyes now. I couldn't escape them. It was horrible, tormenting my every thought. I wanted to just run away from life. Everything was so complicated now. I was beginning to think nothing would ever be normal again for me, and that hurt.

I guessed my life hadn't been that normal before, but it was normal to me. People are always so quick to judge. They seldom get to know the person before they judge them, and it sickens me. We preach equality but we fight to be similar to one another so that we're liked. Society has been called a rat race for many reasons but it's so much lower than that. Rats have basic respect for one another and never degrade one another by appearance. Not many animals put another down based on looks. But they let the animals with differences live together in harmony. The weakest even get to live with respect until they die.

Humans have no respect for one another. Even if we do have respect for others, it's only for people similar to us. Okay, okay, I'll step off my soap box for a bit. I just really dislike how we pretend to be all PC (politically correct) and polite when it is just a facade.

We are progressive and want to be very progressive. But a lot of our progress right now is moving backward. We definitely act like we're moving forward and the smarter of us are manipulating us into believing just that. Yet in reality, they're just dragging us backward.

I was ready to go back to normal at school. Honestly, I got up hoping I could go to school today. Then suddenly I got a call on my phone from Alexa. I ignored it for a bit and got ready. But the ringtone kept playing. It actually took the whole ringtone, then I read the message she'd left.

"Ryan, I need your help! Urgently no time to explain. There's more to the story I found out that will chill you to the bone," the message said.

I thought to myself, Wait, really? There's no way this can be real, surely something must not be that bad. Alexa sounded like she was terrified. I ran downstairs and hurried to see what was so wrong.

"Hey guys, can you call me out of school today? Alexa had an emergency she needed me to help her with," I yelled back at my parents as I dashed out the door to my car. I got into my car and slammed the door and started to drive to Alexa's. I was so worried about what was going on. I didn't even know why she had called, but I knew when she was panicking. But when she called me, she was hysterical. She wasn't just slightly worried about something.

I got closer to her house. All I thought of was her and the conflicting issues that surrounded this topic. I thought of Heather's dad weirdly rushing away. I thought of how every time I saw Heather in real life, she was in a hurry somewhere. Overall, I just tried to wrap my head around the news that could break even Alexa down. She was normally the more "let stuff roll off my back" type of girl. So, for her to be this scared was off-character.

I pulled up to her snow-covered driveway. I pulled up on the side of the road and ran up through the snow to her door. I knocked on the door normally, which took all of my power to do. Then Alexa opened the door still in her PJs. Her face was fraught with worry.

"Get in, quick!" she screamed quietly.

"Okay, calm down, Alexa."

"Thank god you're here, Ryan."

She slammed the door shut as I walked in casually. She stared at me and then threw her arms around me before I could even take my coat off. I felt trapped in a blanket as she squeezed tighter. She pinned my arms to my sides, then let go and stared at me with tears in her eyes.

I looked down, and could tell she was really upset with whatever was going on. I didn't want to say anything along the lines of "It'll be okay" because I didn't know if it would be. I refused to lie, I'd never lie really. The only times I lied were out of necessity. She kept sobbing and I felt bad because it made me sad to see her crying.

I connected with her, and it had been a long time since I'd done that. I understood how she felt. I had those feelings almost all of the time. She let go and hurriedly rushed me to her room. She then stood in front of me and showed me her phone. I could hardly make out the article she was showing me on account of her pale shaking hands.

But what I could make out almost made me fall where I stood. It made me sick. "Lendinbrisk, a small town in Maine, is being redeveloped after years of stagnation." This was horrible. This meant a lot of people were either about to lose their jobs or our town was about to get way bigger. Both were really bad, but I thought back to the first time they tried this and failed. That memory hurt.

"This explains why Heather's back," I said.

"You didn't read it all."

"What do you mean? It's just an easy remodel."

"No, not just that the company's going under."

"But it said it was being repaired after years of stagnation."

"That article was from 2011. That was seven years ago, Ryan."

"They just quoted that reporter at the beginning then?"

"Yes, Ryan. But the next part says the town's construction company is going under. What was once a powerhouse is now crippled. Around sixty-seven percent of the people in the town work for the construction company. But it's going out of business if nothing turns around soon."

"That can't be."

"It is. Ryan, our parents are about to be out of their jobs."

I stared at the floor in disbelief. Just another weird, horrible thing that was happening. How could so many bad things happen and not a single good one? How could this be happening? We could lose our house; my family was on the brink of losing everything.

Alexa walked past me, deep in thought, and sat in her chair. She turned to her computer and looked something up quickly. She turned around to face me and showed me the screen.

"See?" she said in a sullen voice.

"Yes, I know the development stopped mysteriously in 2011. So what?"

"Why did it stop, is the question, Ryan."

"I don't know," I said, wincing as the pain in my knee returned for a split second.

"I'm going to get to the bottom of this, Ryan. With or without you. I need to find these answers. I can't just let this go."

"I can't either, Alexa. This ruins everything for both of us. If our parents, both sets, get fired we lose everything. The house, the cars, just overall everything."

"I know we lose a lot but I'm gonna find this out if it kills me, Ryan."

"I've got your back, Lex."

"Good, then go to the library and check out these stories for me."

"Okay, see ya soon, Lexi."

"Bye, Ry," she said. I thought to myself, Man, it's been like six-seven-ish years since we used those nicknames.

I grabbed the list from her and went out to my car. All of a sudden, a cold gust of ominous wind hit my chest. I looked down at my car's front windshield and it had a sticky note on it that hadn't been there when I got here.

The note said, "Meet me at the library. I know what you know. I know more than you know. Meet me there NOW!!!"

I stood there in shock for a second. The note didn't have a line identifying the author or anything; it was just some person. I went to the library not because of the note but because Alexa needed me to. I told her I would help, and some sketchy notes weren't gonna stop me.

I started my car and heat it up. I loved the warmth that would've been my deciding factor of where I would move to. I drove through the snow-covered town and reached the library. I walked up to the doors of the library and saw another note hidden from the public eye. I wanted to ignore it, but my curiosity got the best of me.

I grabbed it and looked at it. It said, "Hey, yes you. Ryan, come to the back. I have all of the things you came here for. I have all of the information you would ever need. From ~Doesn't Matter"

The first thought I had was, That's cocky. To sign it with that. Plus, how did whoever this was know exactly what I was here for? It did also mention me by name, which made chills run down my spine.

I walked around the library to see the stack of stuff Alexa wanted just lying on the floor tied up with a string. But the person was nowhere to be seen.

"Hello?" I said cautiously.

"Is anyone here? Show yourself. Why are you playing with my head like this?" I yelled.

No one had responded though. It looked like all of this was fresh but there were no signs of life. No people, no footprints, and there weren't even any animals around. It felt like I was in hell or something close to that with time standing still. Now that I thought about it, if anything I'd say it was more like purgatory than hell.

I stood there as a wave of cold washed over me despite that I was still in my coat and pants. I decided to forget whatever was going on and not tell Alexa about what was happening. So, I just ran to my car, hopped in, and started it up. I drove along the icy road somewhat fast, almost spinning out twice. I wanted to get back as quickly as I could because I was scared for Alexa.

I parked and ran up her steps and opened up the door.

"Hey, Lex, are you still here?" I yelled as I ran up the stairs. Her parents were long gone before I came back, so I had no fear of them catching me.

"Alexa?"

Still no answer. It was dead silent.

"Lexi, this isn't funny. Where are you? I'm really worried." I opened her

68

door, and she wasn't there.

"Alexa. This isn't funny, quit joking." I fell to my knees, begging that this was all just some joke.

I was on the verge of tears when I heard a sound. It was a slight snicker, but I heard it. I turned around and Alexa was standing there holding back a huge laugh.

"That wasn't funny."

"HAHAHAHA, sure it was, Ryan."

"No. It wasn't. I was worried about you."

"Why? Nothing has happened since you left. It was kinda cute the way you came in yelling for me. Wait, why were you yelling again?"

I couldn't hide this from her. There was just no way. Not with how I'd made that huge scene. I had to confess what had happened when I went out.

"Okay, so when I went out to my car, there was this note. It scared me a bit, but I thought it was a joke. Then when I got to the library there was another note that told me they had gotten all the stuff you needed. That note also told me that they knew everything you and I wanted to know."

She stood there thinking about it for a bit.

"Who could it have been?" she said.

"I don't know, Alexa, that's the issue here."

She thought for a bit more, then said, "Well, one of the few people it could be is Heather. But how could she know what we were talking about, especially to get everything we wanted for us."

"I thought you were a genius, Sherlock. Why are you asking me?" I said softly.

I was scared I didn't get to find out who that was. I wanted to know who it was more so than what had been happening in the town. It had to have been Heather, right? All I could do in reality was just assume that it was.

I stared at the floor, thinking, hoping, wishing the answer would just appear there, and I would understand everything instantly. Alexa walked up to me and poked me on the chest as she went to sit at the desk. I walked up with the books and DVDs in my hand. I set them on the desk, still tied up like they had been. She stared at them and was visibly confused.

"How did you tie them so perfectly?"

"I didn't. Whoever that was in the note did," I responded softly. All Alexa did was stare at me, confused.

"Ryan, no one else ties bows like this." She pointed to it, it was double knotted just like how I always did it.

"Wait. It couldn't have been me, Alexa. I swear," I said while crossing my heart.

This was getting weirder by the second.

She was just looking at the strange anomaly.

I thought of the possibility of me actually doing this, but it didn't seem likely. Then Alexa interrupted my train of thought.

"Then who did it, Ryan?" she said.

"I don't know, Alexa. No one was even near it when I went back there," I said shakily.

"But it was someone who knew exactly what we needed, right? How is it possible? Ryan, was someone listening to us while we were up here? Everyone we know is either working or at school." She was getting louder by the second.

"Calm down, Lex, we'll find this out somehow, I promise, but right now let's just look at what this person gave us. It looks like all the stuff you asked for, so let's just see it," I said trying to keep my blood cool.

We had so many questions and no answers.

Chapter 10

I cut the string off the books and DVDs and pulled the book out from the bottom. It was a log of all of the construction workers and what happened from 2009 to 2011 when the construction mysteriously stopped. It looked as if someone had taken four spiral notebooks and mashed them together into one big one.

I started to read from early 2010 to when it stopped in 2011. This was a weird thing for the library to have. Then I thought of something and looked at the sides and front and back. This wasn't the library's. It had no tag for returns.

"Alexa, look at this. It's not from the library."

"What do you mean?"

"I'm saying that this is someone's personal property. Not the library's book."

"There's nothing to indicate that, Ryan. Wait, no way, it doesn't have any markings on it. You're right... But who could have this?"

"Here, hand it back to me, let me keep reading. You read the book about the history of our town up till the present day," I said as I took my book back from her.

I read all of the entries, but nothing was out of the ordinary from these guys' point of view. One said, "We've been focusing on building the new library recently. Kids seem to like coming to visit the complete part of it. We tell them they can't stay but they just sit and read."

That was weird. Why would they just allow the kids to stay in a construction zone? They must've been really nice. As I thought about this a small rock hit the window. But only I noticed this rock, Alexa just sat there reading intently.

"Hey, Lexi, I heard a rock hit the window, should I go and see what it was?"

"You just want to get out of reading, Ryan."

"No, a small rock hit the window. I'm gonna go see who threw it. I'll be back later, keep reading. I'm following whatever that was no matter how far it runs."

"Okay, Ryan, but be back by like nine-ish for dinner so we can talk over what I found. Got it?"

"Yep, nine is the time to be back. Got it," I said as I dashed out the door.

Alexa yelled something at me, but I didn't hear it. I ran outside, and there was a person. It was a hooded man or woman. I couldn't see their face, and that was the point, I assumed. The stranger turned to me and revealed a little of its face to me. All I could see through the shadow was a mouth. It smirked at me as if this was what they had expected.

"Who are you?" I yelled.

"You'll find out soon enough," they yelled back and started to run from me.

No way was I letting this person beat me. I chased them as they slipped around the corner of the house as if they were a shadow. They were fast but I could last. Most would be getting winded from sprinting, but not me. I've been a runner all my life. My lung capacity is amazing. I chased the hooded person, but when I turned the corner to see the woods they were gone.

I thought they had escaped me, but the wind acted up, blowing their cover away, and I saw them hiding behind a tree. I ran up and grabbed the robed person by the shoulder. But when I looked at it the cloak had just been nailed to the tree to trick me.

I looked around and heard a burst of boisterous laughter from whoever was playing with me. It was all around me, surrounding me. I felt I should just succumb and accept defeat at that moment. Then out of nowhere, I heard a twig break loudly as if someone ran over it. The laughter immediately stopped. I knew I had whoever this was. I chased the sound and saw the person trying to run through the woods, dodging the trees perfectly. But their shoes kept getting caught in holes hidden by the snow.

I knew these woods like the back of my hand and sprinted over every hole and crevice that would potentially slow me down. I was gaining on the person fast. Then out of the blue, the stranger stopped and turned around, giving up.

"I wanted this facade to last a while longer," the distorted voice said.

"Well sadly you failed, now please tell me what's going on."

"I guess I should start by letting you hear my real voice." The distortion stopped and the real voice shone through. It was the sweetest voice I'd ever heard. This girl was an angel. I was sure of it.

"Wait. I know that voice," I said, walking closer to her.

"Yes, we met briefly once before, Ryan."

"Well then who are you?" I said, racking my brain for who she was.

"Man, you don't remember me at all? Harsh. It's Heather, of course."

I walked up to her, and she took off her hood. I stared into her emerald, green eyes and she smiled broadly back at me. I felt a strange feeling of déjà vu. But I hadn't met Heather till just recently, so this couldn't have happened, could it?

"Earth to Ryan. Hey, you always get lost in my eyes, huh?"

"I'm sorry, I was just thinking of something. It's almost like this has happened before, like me and you in the woods like this."

"That's because this has happened before, Ryan. A long time ago."

"What do you mean, Heather? I've only just met you."

"But you haven't just met me, Ryan. God, you don't remember anything, do you?"

"That's impossible," I said as I tried to hold onto my sanity.

I tried to think of meeting her before, but nothing came up. Then abruptly she interrupted my train of thought.

"I'll tell you in time, don't worry."

"When will that time be?"

"Soon. For now, let's go to that special place we used to hang out." She said this then started to lead me somewhere.

The route got familiar. It was the same place me and Alexa had been not but a few days ago. It was that house still covered in snow, and still as creepy as ever. My leg started to feel like a dead weight as I approached it. I kept walking through it, trying not to show Heather how bad I physically hurt.

It was going to overwhelm me soon. I couldn't keep my feelings in for long. I would pass out as soon as I made it inside if I kept this act up. We walked up the steps, each getting harder to manage as I finally stepped in the door and threw myself on the couch in relief.

"What's wrong with you? You're that tired now after a short walk? You sprinted after me for twelve minutes and that tiny walk winded you?"

I just looked at her and shrugged as I rubbed my leg.

"No, don't tell me, Ryan. Please don't say it's still happening."

"What do you mean?"

"You know what I mean, Ryan."

"No, I really don't, Heather."

"Fine, be that way, Ryan. But we need to talk so just try not to interrupt me."

"Okay, okay. I won't interrupt you, Heather, just tell me what's going on."

"Buckle up because here comes some heavy story."

"I'm ready."

"Believe it or not, we met a long time ago. Actually, to be exact it was around eleven years ago in 1st Grade. Well towards the end of it anyways. I was new in town because my dad had just moved us here for the construction company. I was shy, so usually we didn't talk or hang out when Alexa was around. She hadn't even known I existed. She just ignored me and never really ever talked to me.

"But I hope you can try to remember me and you finding this house. We actually found it in the same situation that just happened. You were at Alexa's house in her room, and I wanted to talk to you. So, I threw the rock at the window knowing you'd come out. But I saw Alexa come with you, so I ran. I tricked you into walking to a tree where I had taped my jacket to sneak away. But I stepped on a branch while leaving and you caught me. The same way as before.

"Except for the time you caught me back then you hugged me and said, 'You can't keep running, Heather.' I remember trying to run again and you caught me as we saw this house in the distance. We saw no lights on and knew that nobody was there. So, we went in and sat here the same as before and talked. That's all I feel like sharing now, Ryan, but we'll talk more about the past later." She ended this abruptly and softly took my hand in hers.

I felt her heart pulsing through her veins. Those memories must have been so vivid for her. I thought about them later, and slightly remembered it, and it made me smile and wince as a sharp pain hit me right away.

"Why are you back then?"

"Because I couldn't stand knowing you were possibly going to forget me. Ryan, we were best friends. You promised me you'd remember me forever. That promise is always on my mind."

"Then it must hurt to know I don't remember so much."

"It does but I know it's in there somewhere. You were always so strong, even when my mother died, you never let me cry. You've always been there for me."

"Wait. Your mother died?"

"You don't even remember that much? Ouch. Did our time mean nothing?"

"No. I'm sure it did, Heather, it's just that a lot has changed. I've lost a lot of what I used to remember. All I remember is Alexa and the friendship I had with her. I slightly remember you and it slowly comes back with each story I hear. I'm sorry I can't remember you as vividly as you do me. Our friendship was incredibly special if all of this is true, which I feel it is." I ended this thought by squeezing her hand even though I didn't remember her. If this was all true, then she must have been really special to me.

She started to tear up, I assumed because of how little I remembered. I decided that it made me sad to see her beautiful green eyes sparkle as they welled up with tears. I hugged her close to my heart and softly stroked her hair to calm her. It felt oddly familiar, like I'd done it many times.

Heather grabbed onto my shirt and held it tight. She must've remembered too. She felt like I remember even though I didn't, but I didn't want to be the one to rain on her parade.

"I assume you missed this?"

"I did but I'm much stronger than I was before," she said with a smile.

I looked at my phone and saw it was 7:46 P.M. Not too late, just getting close to when I should be back. Heather saw this and frowned; she knew what that look meant. It meant I had promised Alexa I would be back at some time, and it was fast approaching.

"Ryan. I have so much to tell you and remind you of. I hope one day it will be enough to stop the pain you're in."

"What do you mean by that? I'm not in any pain at all."

"Yeah, sure, Mr. Tough Guy."

I laughed happily and smiled at her. There was something different between the way she talked and the way Alexa did. They could say the exact same thing, but Alexa's version would always seem more harsh, or intense would be the better descriptor.

"It's getting late, isn't it, Heather?"

"Not too late, it's almost eight but that's not too late. I know why you say that, Ryan. You promised Alexa you'd be back at some time."

"Yes, I did. Sorry to cut our time short but she kind of freaks out whenever I'm late. I had a fun time hearing your stories of the past and remembering them. But sadly, we should probably head out."

"She's always had you on a tight leash, ever since we were little."

"That's the truth. The only time she didn't was in middle and early high school. I was so popular that we were always hanging out with other people, so she wasn't as controlling." With that, I stood up and helped her get ready to go.

"Let's get going, can you walk me to my house first? It's much closer to this place than hers and you can walk the normal streets to her house again much easier. It's a win-win." She said as she gave me some adorable puppy dog eyes.

"Yes, what kind of friend would I be letting you walk alone in the dark woods."

We started walking and she grabbed my hand. She probably didn't want to lose me. It was so dark out that you could hardly see four feet in front of your face. The snow didn't help the visibility much.

We walked in silence the whole way back to the road because we both had so much to talk about, and learned that if we got back to the normal roads, we'd have to stop the deep conversation abruptly. I smiled as she lightly lifted our arms up and down in a swinging fashion. She was really like a little kid.

We got to the street and said our goodbyes. We unanimously decided to text one another later, so I got her number, then I was off. I walked up the street and it felt like I was being watched. It was so off-putting that I started to fear what would happen. I started to worry and decided it would be better to run there rather than walk slowly.

I thought of something as I walked towards Alexa's house. That was, I should have asked Heather if she had given us those books. She had to, right? If not her then who? I dropped this as I made it to Alexa's house and walked through the front door right before it hit nine o'clock on the dot. Perfect timing, I thought to myself as I smiled and said hello to Alexa's parents, and walked up to her room to meet her.

"Hey, did you miss me? Hopefully not too much."

"Where have you been, mister? You made me worry." She said this with a sad expression on her face. Which did not suit her at all.

Chapter 11

I looked back and gave her a smile knowing it'd cheer her up. She loved it when I smiled because nowadays they had become few and far between. She just kind of frowned when she saw it. I didn't know what I did, truthfully.

"Don't think you can talk your way out of this. I was seriously worried. You didn't take my calls or even look at my texts." She finished saying this, trying to stop her voice from breaking.

"I didn't get any texts or calls, Alexa." I said this and showed her my phone. She stared in disbelief at the lack of anything to do with calls or texts.

"How?"

"How what, Lex?"

"There's no way that you didn't get even one text."

"Yes, there is, because guess what, I didn't get one."

She slumped over, defeated. However, she let out a deep sigh which meant that she was secretly relieved that I didn't just ignore her. I walked over, grabbed my phone back and smiled.

"See? Nothing to worry about."

"I guess you're right," she said begrudgingly.

"Well? What happened while I was gone? Did you find something out or just miss me?"

"Read this." Then out of nowhere, I saw a book hurtling towards me as I quickly grabbed it from the air.

"What's this?" I said as I looked at the book's cover.

In bold it said *The Truth About What Happened*. It was a strange title, but the truth about what? I opened it to the first page and it was blank. Then I got to the next and it started to talk about the construction that was here a few years back.

It went in-depth into how everything going on was always up to code, so it didn't make sense for there to ever be any issue. I continued reading and it was all the stuff I'd heard before, nothing new to the story at all.

Then it said something that caught my eye. "One day during mid-August things took a turn for the worse. This **event** stopped construction completely and had people leaving in droves." What could have happened that caused such a big operation to just abruptly end? I asked myself. Then it just started to give the old facts that we already knew.

"What was the event?"

"No one knows. Not even the writer of that book. The truth? My ass."

"Do you have any theories, Lexi?"

"Nothing comes to mind. Why?"

"Then what was the point of having me read that?"

"You don't understand, do you."

"No, I don't."

"Look at who wrote it and when it was published."

I looked down to see the words "By Heather Greenwich."

"No. This can't be... Can it?"

Alexa just stood there in silence.

"Lex... Are you telling me that, Heather? The Heather that I know authored this book?"

"Yes. God, Ryan. You read the author's name, didn't you?" She said this emotionlessly.

"Lexi, what's wrong?"

"Nothing."

"Okay, then I gotta go home, it's getting late." It was almost 11 P.M.

"Be safe. Please text when you're home."

"Will do. See ya later, Lex." With those words, I left her room and walked to my car.

I turned on the engine and saw that something was on my dash. I swear it wasn't there before. It was a sticky note. How it got in there I couldn't have even begun to guess. I was too tired from all the craziness to think. So, I just picked it up and read it without trying to look too much into it. It said, "Don't worry, I'm always here. You know where to go."

I didn't want to even try to decipher that, so I pushed it into the recesses of my mind and stuck the sticky note back on the dash. The drive home was uneventful, nothing noteworthy really happened at all.

I walked into my house and was surprised to see all of the lights out. I walked toward the kitchen and saw a faint blue glow coming from the living room. I obviously assumed it was the glow of the TV, so I walked in. Sure enough it was but my parents were asleep on the couch. I decided to wake them up and send them to bed.

They kind of mumbled something but I couldn't really hear it, so I just ignored it. I walked into my room after getting ready and jumped onto the bed. I stared at the ceiling, thinking of today. What did Heather really know? Why would she keep hiding the truth from me? My mind wandered to many different places. Like what was going on with Alexa when I got back? She seemed mad.

I thought this while sitting up because I couldn't sleep with all of these thoughts running around. Alexa almost made me feel guilty for leaving, like I had done something wrong. But I hadn't even done anything. She could've just come with me but for some reason she hadn't. My leg hadn't acted up for a long time. I felt sorrow, for some reason. It was as if I remembered something horrible. But I didn't know what it was. I lay down feeling sleepy out of nowhere.

Nightmare 6

I opened my eyes after closing them and was no longer in my room. Wait... I was just in my room. How am I in the middle of the woods? I looked around and saw Heather facing me. I must've fallen asleep. It was the only explanation I could give for the miraculous change of scenery. I walked towards Heather as she stared down at me. She didn't flinch but instead smiled as I got closer to her. I took each step carefully so as to not trip.

I got a few steps away from her and she winked at me. Then out of the corner of my eye I saw a shadow run behind a tree. It had to be my imagination, right? It was just a dream anyway, all in my head, right? As I got closer to Heather, she almost seemed to fade away slightly. I kept walking towards her. I was so close I could just reach out and touch her. I tried to and failed. My hand seemingly went right through her. How was that even possible? I guess a lot of things in my dreams seemed impossible. She just flashed a bright smile at me as I stood there dumbfounded.

Then suddenly the world started to blur around me as if I was running at some insane speed. I look around me and I just saw tree after tree flash before my eyes. Where was I getting moved to? My leg started to hurt again as we approached where we were meant to stop. I could tell we were slowing down, nearing our destination. The woods got eerily quiet as I got closer to my ending point. Gone were the happy songs of birds and the sweet clicking of squirrels and chipmunks fighting over food. This was an ominous, almost dare I say evil place. I was put down at my destination and almost immediately fell to the ground.

The impact of my landing on top of my hurting knee was too much for my legs to bear and they almost instantly gave out. I looked around to find myself facing that same decrepit library. The same that the wisp not three nights before had teleported me away from. I was stronger now, so it made sense to take me back to it. At least, I thought I was. My leg was hurting less than it had the first time I arrived here. I was ready to see whatever the dreamscape wanted me to. The library was familiar. But now it looked more like something out of a horror film. The paint was chipped and covered in moss and mud. The windows were dirty and tinted yellowish-brown from the years of sun bleach and dust.

The building looked as if the slightest gust of wind were to blow past it, then the building would surely collapse. I couldn't get away from this building, it wouldn't let me leave. I tried to walk back to the woods, but I just couldn't. It was as if there was a barrier pushing me. I sucked up my fear and walked into the building. Each step amplified the pain in my leg. I kept pushing forward towards the front desk where a librarian would normally sit. But this was a dream and there was no sweet lady to greet me. There was nothing but cobwebs covering all of the things around me. Then something happened and a loud crash rang out making me fear the glass was breaking. However, the sound wasn't a shatter, it was a clang of metal hitting concrete. This sound made my leg stiffen and I fell to the ground from the sudden change. The light started to fade around me, getting darker and darker. I was being swallowed by shadow.

All of a sudden, a light in the distance grew closer. I called out to it, thinking that my wisp friend had returned to save me. But it wasn't that friendly glowing wisp that I used to know. It was a dark red now as if it had been angered. It came closer to me, each foot it gained made my skin burn more. I stared at it, challenging it. The wisp did not like that it grew bigger and burned brighter than before. I yelled at it, "What do you want from me?! Why...? Why did you have to choose me?" The wisp makes no sound, just floats closer.

I was on the brink of tears. I couldn't ever get away from the emotional stress. Even in my dreams the stress and fear followed me everywhere. There was no escape. I should just give up on this struggle. But something in me told me I couldn't. I stood there watching the light get closer and closer with no response.

Then a voice came out of the wisp, "Ryan, you need to face your fears. This will not end until you find closure." What could it mean by that? Also, wait. That voice. I knew that voice. It was from a long time ago. It sounded as if it was a little kid's voice. Then everything went black, and I could no longer move.

I woke up in my bed terrified. I couldn't keep dealing with these dreams. I stared up at the ceiling, not wanting to move. I just wanted to lay there forever, doing nothing. I never wanted to move or talk to anyone again. But you know what? That was not me. That was not the Ryan I was. But that was who I was now before it was different. I used to be happy, proud, and confident. I got up and smiled. I wasn't going to let this hurt me. At least, not openly anymore.

As people, we can pretend to be happy better than we can actually be happy. I know this because we all want to be what we think is "polite". In all honesty, politeness is in the eye of the beholder. We all perceive things differently so something that may not offend you and you might see as polite could completely offend someone else.

Perception. It all comes back to that. Every situation you're in and how it affects you is based on your own perception. No other person will perceive the information given to them the same as you do. We all interpret things differently. It shows us that we are similar, and also very contrasting as well. Our personalities are all different, and on top of that no one sees you the same as someone else. You could have people who like you and see certain aspects of you. But on the other side of that, you could have people hate you for the seeming lack of those same aspects the others liked you for.

These facts are hard to completely understand and talk about. Yet here we are talking like this and trying to grasp this very alien concept. I should step off of my soapbox. I hope whoever is reading this can at least try to understand me and what I'm saying. What we all want in life is acceptance, and I haven't found mine yet. At least not from what I can tell. I lay there writing this in my journal and realized I hadn't added to my short story recently. I guessed I hadn't had anything noteworthy to add to it.

I should have something else to add later, I thought to myself as I stood up. I felt a sudden rush to the head because of how fast I had stood up. I ran to the bathroom shower and got ready because today was gonna be a big day. I knew it would be, too. How did I know? I couldn't really say, but it was something I could feel. I grabbed my backpack after I got dressed and got in my car as fast as I could. One weird thing I will say I saw as I ran out was that my mom and dad weren't up yet. Normally they were up at five A.M. having some crazy debate about what had happened in the news the day before.

I had to ignore this and get going to school. It was only seven A.M. but the roads were covered in snow, so I needed to be safe. I drove carefully there and stood in the parking lot looking around. It was almost time for the first bell, so where was everyone? The parking lot was empty... I went into the school because the doors were unlocked like they should be, to welcome the students back to another day. This had been really weird recently, with things like this happening on a consistent basis. Whatever, this doesn't matter, was all I could think. I started walking down the corridor for my first-hour class.

I opened the door to find that the class was empty, but my teacher was standing there. Mr. Reynolds, my economics teacher, was my favorite teacher of the day. But something seemed really off with him just staring at the papers on his desk.

I walked up to him and asked, "What's happening, Mr. R? Why is no one here?"

"Nothing, Ryan. It's just empty today."

"Why?"

"Because it's teacher prep day. Why are you here?"

"When were we notified of this day?"

"Like, eight-ish days ago, weren't you here?"

"I was... Um... I must've been tuned out. I'll go have a good day, sorry for bothering you."

That was weird. I swear that there was no announcement saying we'd have a personal day today. I guess I should have just believed him and walked out and gone home. But why were my parents gone too? That was an odd coincidence, right? Maybe I was thinking too much. I did that a lot, sometimes I should have just let it go. But for some reason, I never could, so I decided to investigate.

Chapter 12

I ran down the halls and sure enough, the teachers were all in classes, but no students were there to occupy them. I sprinted outside and instantly worried about Lex and Heather. My parents being gone was weird but neither of them had texted me that morning. So, I texted them trying to get a response, but nothing happened. That was weird because Alexa was always quick to respond to me. Heather just got here so I hadn't talked to her in a while. I ran over to my car and got into it, turning the key to start the heater. The warmth flowed over me like rushing water, relaxing my nerves. I drove to Alexa's house while trying to stay calm. When I got to her door just before I knock on its rough wooden surface, I heard sobbing.

"Lex? Is that you?"

"Ryan, they're gone. They're really gone."

"Open the door, let me in."

Slowly the door creaked open and I ran into the entryway and knelt next to her.

"What happened? Alexa?"

"I woke up and no one was here. Then to top it all off I lost my phone so I couldn't call or text anyone."

"What do you mean, gone?"

"I mean that it was like they had just disappeared. I went into their room, and it was bare, nothing was on the walls. They didn't even have clothes in the closet. It was as if they had just disappeared," she said, getting into hysterics again.

85

Softly I tried to comfort her and rubbed her back as she sobbed onto my shoulder. She told me all of this. She'd had a very bad time with abandonment.

When she was little her parents left her with her aunt and said they'd be back. However, they didn't come back for two years after they said that. Imagine trusting your parents so much to just let them leave on the promise of returning. This event destroyed her. I couldn't imagine how she felt right now. Sometimes we tried so hard to understand someone's feelings when really, they just wanted you to listen.

"Ryan... Ryan... Ryan...! Hello? Come back, p-please?" She said this trembling.

"I'm sorry, I zoned out. I'm not one of the best of friends, am I?"

"Shut up, you big dummy," she said, smiling.

"What's with that smile?" It looked bittersweet. She had tears streaming down her cheeks, but her mouth was wide, and smirking as if to say, *That's what I needed.*

"Ryan, let's go find them."

"Okay, but I have to make one more stop before we leave."

"Fine. Let's just hurry up."

We both got into my car after Alexa had cleaned up. I turned the key and the engine started kicking. I started driving, but to where? That was for me to know and Alexa to find out. I knew she would detest this if I told her. I needed the support though if we were truly going to solve this. I got to the house I thought was right and ran up the steps. I got to the door, and it opened as if whoever was on the other side knew I was coming.

Out came a burly man around six foot five. He leered at me with disdain. Again, I met Heather's father, this time he didn't run off. He stood there and didn't say a word, but in his stare, I could feel the blood lust. It was as if he thought that even speaking to me was a waste of his time. Suddenly he walked off, and from behind him came Heather. She smiled, probably happy to see me again.

We got into the car, and Alexa stared daggers at me. I could feel the anger in her gaze. But I just smiled and shrugged at her as if to say, *Why so mad?*

Then she spoke. "Ryan, why did you go get Heather?"

"Because I felt like she would be instrumental in helping us solve the problem at hand."

"Well, I guess you could be right. How's it going, H?"

She always called Heather "H", and Heather hated it. But this time she just seemed cool and collected. She had really grown since the time she had left. I looked at her, worried about the response, and she just smiled and winked at me slyly saying, "Our secrets are safe."

"Pretty good, how about yourself, Lex?"

Alexa was obviously caught off guard and couldn't even respond to it. She was almost seething with anger. The last time these two had seen each other was a horrible combination of hate and anger. They had ended on a bad note, so to speak. Alexa and Heather always had a rivalry with one another. I had no clue as to why they were such big rivals, but they were. Then, the day Heather was leaving town, Alexa took it one step too far.

Flashback to when the three of us were 11

Alexa yelled at Heather, "Good, no one will miss you. Especially not Ryan. Nobody ever really liked you; they just pretended."

The venom in those words cut Heather to the bone.

Then came the rebuttal from Heather, "Alexa, I always hated you. You always thought you were the smartest person in the room. You're just a pathetic worm feeding off the fear of others. You're scary, Alexa, that's why people shy away from you. You aren't some 'God' like you think you are. I'm glad I never have to see your face again. Goodbye, Ryan. I hope I get to see you again one day."

End

That day a lot was said about both parties involved. Sadly, this created a divide between the two even deeper than before. It looked to me as we drove in silence that the hatred was still shared between them. It hurt me to know two of my best friends could hate one another so much.

Breaking the awkward silence was what I had to try to do so I said, "Hey, girls, where do we think we should look first? Wait, we haven't even told Heather what was wrong. Okay, so, Heather, we found out that Alexa's parents were gone. It was as if they vanished into thin air, their clothes were gone, and they didn't leave any information at all."

"Sounds like they were smart," Heather retorted.

"Heather, I know you two have your differences, but please can we be civil for one minute? Alexa is really hurting right now. The last thing I want is for us to not be able to find her parents."

"Ugh, fine. Ryan, I think I might know what happened. I'd need to check the logs from my dad's work."

"We can't get in there, Heather; those don't help here."

"But we can," she said, twirling a brass key around her fingers and holding up an ID badge with her name on it.

"How did you get those? I swear, if I get in trouble because you stole from your father..."

"Don't worry, they're mine, read the tag, it's my badge. Also, the key is just to the filing cabinet."

I settled down and kept driving. We now had a destination. Alexa was lying down asleep. A small frown crossed her lips. She was dejected and hurting. I felt so bad I knew Heather would make her mad, but I also knew that we needed her information.

"Hey, why's Alexa asleep?" Heather said, breaking my train of thought.

"Oh, she sleeps whenever she gets into a moving vehicle. She's always been that way. I feel bad for her, this must break her heart."

"Why? Do her parents matter that much to her?"

"No, it's just that they had abandoned her once before. This must be like a sick and twisted déjà vu to her."

"I never knew that about her," Heather said with a tint of compassion in her voice.

"She likes to act tough so she can't be hurt by other people. She believes if she can push people out and not let them close, she won't feel abandoned. But she also has a fear of being alone," I said with a bittersweet smile. Looking at her face, I could see it was crestfallen with the latest information she had just gotten.

"I understand those feelings. I've had them myself; the fear of loneliness consumes you."

After that, I had nothing else to say. It was hard to respond with anything comforting. That was the second time I had lost my voice and couldn't help. I hated this feeling, the feeling of helplessness. It's a feeling we all have a few times in our lives. Where everything seems completely out of our control. I feel that it can happen at any time. The worst is when it happens, and you can control the scenario but don't because it feels like you are incapable of helping.

A tear grazed my cheek as I thought of the cold reality. If we couldn't find Alexa's parents, she would give up. I'd lose one of my best friends in the whole world. I knew her now and I knew her when she lost them the first time. She shut me out and never spoke to me. She became muted and often would not show up to school. This reality hit me like a speeding bus. Honestly, if I'd had a choice between the two, I'd have taken the bus.

We approached our destination and, as we did, I saw something weird dart into the woods out of the corner of my eye. I pulled into the parking lot and tried to push whatever that shadowy figure was out of my head. I shook Alexa awake and we all got out and walked to the door. There was a mechanical lock with a red light and a sleek plastic scanner. Heather walked up and winked back at me as she slid the card through the scanner. We waited, and the light flashed green, meaning we were in. The three of us walked in like we owned the place.

The office was exceedingly high tech looking for some small construction company. They had modern art hanging on the walls and brand-new computers at every desk. I looked at each one and it seemed to be locked up like Fort Knox. They had a screensaver that required a password and then from what it seemed they'd still have to put in their credentials to be checked.

We got to a big corner office in the back of the room, which was where I assumed her father worked. Heather slid the card key through another scanner, and it blinked green and then flashed red slowly. Heather looked back, shocked, as if to say that that had never happened before. Looks like we'd tripped the silent alarm. Heather then gestured for us to run, so me and Alexa sprinted out, only to be caught by the security.

They grabbed us and walked us back to where Heather was. I looked at Heather angrily. Nothing ever goes right, it just all gets ruined in the end. It's funny how we blame fate for everything that doesn't turn out our way. Because nothing bad that happens to us could be caused by us. I thought of this staring at my feet, then I felt the jab of a baton to the gut. I hunched over, the wind knocked out of me. That caught me off guard, that's for sure.

Alexa and Heather immediately knelt next to me and started rubbing my back. I looked up to see the security guards laughing. One wasn't much taller than Alexa. One had a hood over his or her face and the other matched my height, or at least that's what I assumed. I was easily stronger than they were, but they had the weapons, so all I could do was scowl.

"Ryan, are you alright?" Heather asked in a worried tone.

"I'm fine, don't worry. Nice cheap shot, buddy," I said, still fixated on the one who hit me.

"You weren't listening, kid, so I did what I thought would make you listen." The shorter one was snickering at me. The tone of the voice was not too gruff but very feminine. I had to assume that this one was a woman.

"Let me go, I'm the owner's daughter. See?!?" Heather said, throwing the plastic into their face.

"We don't care who you are, darling. You could be the president and I wouldn't let you go till the boss got here," said the taller one with a deep husky tone.

I started to listen and soon realized we'd see the big hulking mass walk in that was Heather's father. I did not want to see him. If he saw me with his daughter, I would be dead for sure. While it was obvious that she left with me, it didn't look good that we were in his office.

They locked us in the office, and we sat there trapped, waiting for the "boss" to appear. Heather slumped down to the ground, defeated. She frowned and wondered why her dad had taken her access away. There was never a secret between the two but today she had been blocked for the first time. She looked so confused and hurt. Meanwhile, Alexa was looking at the window and glass, eyeing it suspiciously. I could tell what she was thinking. Just by the mischievous look she had in her eyes, I could tell she was wondering if she could or should break the glass.

I decided to walk over to Heather first.

"Hey, how's it going, Heather?"

"Why??? Why would he block me? Ryan, what did I do to betray his trust?" she said, quivering with fear.

"I don't know, did you disobey him recently? Maybe it's not you he distrusts."

"What do you mean?" she asked with a quizzical tone.

"What if he doesn't trust me? He knows we have been spending time together recently. What if he thought I was trouble and blocked you to be safe?"

A frown was plastered on her face as the truth hit her.

"He doesn't trust me around you. He thinks I'm some dumb puppy following you around. That's why he made us leave in the first place," she said, seething with anger.

"Wait, what do you mean?" I said, confused.

"He thought I was in love with you. He took me away the first time because he had thought you would be in trouble. He thought you'd ruin his perfect little girl."

"Wow. I never saw that coming."

I try to grasp a concept so foreign as I sit down next to her. I put one hand on her back and rubbed it softly, shushing her. She started to calm down, and I felt her back start to relax. I could tell the tension was leaving her, and she was back to the same girl she was before.

As I got up to leave, she grabbed my hand and looked at me strangely. It almost felt like a look of longing or love. I shook that off because there was no way Heather could really love me. It was almost funny to think about us together. I grabbed her hand and we pulled apart like our normal handshake and walked over to the resident crazy person Alexa.

"Hey, Lexi, whatcha thinking? How to break out of this joint?" I said, laughing as I did.

"What's so funny about that? Hmm? Smart guy?" she said, frustrated.

"Calm down. Lex, you know we can't break bulletproof glass."

"Yeah, but we can break regular glass," she said, picking up a chip of glass.

"How did you get a perfect circle of glass off of that?"

"With this," she said, holding up a glass cutter.

"Where'd you get that, Lexi?"

"On the desk, god, these idiots didn't even check the room before locking us in here," she said, smiling as wide as possible. I high-fived her and then gave her a big hug. I was glad she was still the way she was. I couldn't imagine her losing that spark she'd always had.

"I'll get Heather because we're breaking out of here," I said, walking over to Heather.

Chapter 13

I reached Heather, and she was just staring at the ground thinking.

"What's up, doc?" I said, imitating Bugs Bunny.

"Nothing, just thinking about some things. I think I know where Alexa's parents went," she said, frowning.

"Why is that bad news?"

"Because where they are will be hard to reach fast. I found the vacation day ledgers and they were marked."

"But why was Lex left behind?"

"One problem at a time, Ryan."

"Well, Alexa is breaking us out right now. So, let's get over it and help her," I said, helping her up. We walked over to Alexa slowly and watched her.

I then took the lead and went to help stabilize the glass hole she had cut out. It was big enough for a person to fit through, that was all that mattered. I caught the glass cut-out as it fell into my arms.

"My knight in shining armor," Alexa said in a raggedy tone. She was upset-sounding and breathing heavily.

"Ladies first," I said to them, and they both hopped out the window and started to run. I jumped last and chased after them, holding out my keys, and unlocked my car. We jumped in, and I booked it out of there. I stared at the trees, looking for the shadowy figure. I saw a glimpse of it and strangely it looked like an animal. But not a normal forest creature, this was something else. I had to ignore it and keep driving.

"Where am I going, guys?"

"To my house. Now," Alexa said, seething. I didn't know what had upset her so much but whatever it was had really rubbed her the wrong way.

I drove carefully there, still trying to be fast without making us swing into a snowbank or a house. The tension in the car was palpable. I pulled into Alexa's driveway, and she jumped out of the car, slamming the door. Heather and I followed.

She left the door open for us and was sitting in the kitchen staring at some papers. I walked up to her and tried to calm her down by softly grabbing her hand.

As I did, she hissed at me, "Let go. You've done enough as it already stands." I frowned and stepped back. What had I done that was so wrong? Comforted both of my friends when we were captured. Then she kept staring at the paper as if the interaction had never happened.

"What are these papers?"

"Instructions, Ryan."

"For?"

"Me." Alexa was still terribly upset, and I could hear her voice shaking.

"What's wrong, Lexi?"

"Everything, everything is wrong, Ryan. How could anything be okay?" she said, starting to cry. Meanwhile Heather was staring, watching the whole scene wide-eyed.

I walked up to her and started rubbing her shoulders, saying in a soothing tone, "Everything will be fine, Lex. Don't worry, I know it's hard to believe but you can trust in me. I don't want to speak for Heather, but I think you can rely on her too. We're a group of friends and there is no changing that. We fight, we make up, we're like a family but we never leave. Got that?"

"Got it," she said, smiling softly. I wiped the tears from her eyes and beckoned Heather over. We both then embraced Alexa, and we all stood there for a while in the calming warmth.

"Friends forever," I said, breaking our hug and holding my hand in between us. Then my two friends finally got along and put their hands in as well.

"Friends forever," they both said and that was that. The bond had been made and I doubt we'd break it anytime soon. We sat down together at the table and started to read the instructions. At first, they made no sense. I started to drift off and want to write. It had been a long stressful few days. I took out my small notebook and a pen and wrote.

The Lion Who Wanted to Reach the Moon Ch. 3

The lion woke up and walked his way towards the peak. He tried with all of his might to get higher and higher.

"Hey, dummy. Yoohoo. Buddy, quit daydreaming and talk to me," said the snake in his ear.

The lion had almost forgotten the obnoxious thing on his back. What a life that would be, he thought to himself.

"Yes?" he said, his voice booming and echoing against the rock surfaces.

"Have you reached the sun yet?" she hissed happily.

"The moon," he said, disappointed that she had forgotten.

"Yeah, that, did ya make it?"

"Does it look like we're at the top of the mountain?"

"No."

"Then there's your answer," the lion stated coldly.

They walked in silence for a few peaks. The lion could hear the snake snoring from time to time. He then came across an owl sitting on a tree branch. The owl was timid and didn't make the first move, which was fine by the lion. He was tired of talking and just wanted to relax. Then he thought about talking to the owl. This was strange because he'd never wanted to talk to anything or anyone else before. But this owl felt familiar, as if he had seen it before.

"Hello, how are you?"

"G...good," she whispered.

"Why are you up here?" he asked.

"This is my home," she said softly.

"So high on this peak, why?"

"Because I prefer to be alone."

"I feel like I know you."

"You do?"

"Yes, it's a strange feeling," the lion said loud enough for the sky to shake in

response.

The sudden shaking of the sky caused the snow accumulated in the clouds to fall in droves. The owl made a gesture as if to beckon him into her home. He walked over, curious as to why she would be so nice. He got into her home of a giant dead tree, and it was warm. The tree surprisingly fit his whole body, but he was pushed up against the bird and the snake was resting on a branch.

"Nice place you have here."

"It's not mine, I just found it like this. It was a good nesting place so I chose to stay maybe a little longer than I should. Anyways, what is a lion doing on top of a mountain? Especially during the middle of the night like this?" she asked tentatively.

"I'm going to reach the moon."

"Why?"

"Because the moon is my friend and it's always taken care of me."

"Oh."

The snow outside suddenly stopped.

"Thanks for helping me. But now me and this annoying snake must be on our way."

"You're leaving so soon?" she said in a sultry tone.

"Yes. We must go. I need to make it to the top of the mountain. You are very welcome to tag along if you'd like," the lion said jovially.

"No. She can't. I don't know why but something tells me that she will try to sabotage us," the snake hissed into his ear.

"Have faith," he said back to the snake.

"Fine, but I don't like this," she whispered again, and lay back down.

"I think I'd like to join you on your quest. I can scout the best path for you to go on too," she said.

"Thank you very much, and until we need that you can ride on my shoulder," he said with a smile.

The lion, now with two passengers, continued on his journey. They were uncomfortable to carry but at least he had company. The lion started to climb the rock face again, making it up three or four more ledges before reaching a clearing covered in snow. It was freshly sprinkled without a print or hint anyone else had *been there.*

He stepped into the snow, and it froze his paws. He had to think of some other way to get across this clearing, he thought to himself. The moon was about to go to sleep for the day. He saw the pinks and oranges caused by the sun's tendrils whipping over the edge of the globe. He watched the snow and kept wondering what to do. Then something strange happened, when the moon waved goodbye and danced behind the earth once again.

The lion watched the snow and as he did so it seemed to slowly disappear. The sun's beaming rays were erasing all that had happened during the night. The day had begun anew.

"It's strange, isn't it?"

"What is?" he was answered by both girls.

"How the sun erases what happens during the night. It's like when each new day begins the things that happened during the moon's reign slowly get pushed into hushed whispers. It happens every day, things that happen during the night stay hidden in the shadows of the moon."

"That is strange. I've never looked at it that way," the owl said.

"Always so preachy. You never just let anything happen," hissed the snake with venom.

The lion shook off her rude comments and walked into the middle of the clearing. The snow was gone, and he wanted to rest his legs. He sat there taking in the warmth and preparing for the journey to come.

"Hey, Ryan! Hello?!?!" shouted Alexa.

I was shaken awake from the writing trance I was in.

"What's up?"

"We found out what the instructions meant," said Heather softly.

"Yeah, we found it all, we know what to do."

"Then let's go do it. But first, let's stop by my house. I need something from there."

"What could you need, Ryan? Time is of the essence and all that. We don't have time for you to kiss your mommy and daddy goodbye," Alexa said jokingly.

Then I thought of something earlier. My house seemed emptier than normal. The usual bickering was nowhere to be found in the morning. To top that off, I hadn't gotten any texts from them. Normally if I didn't see them in the morning and left before they'd woke up, they would've texted. But looking at my phone, I didn't have any notifications from them.

"Ryan? What's wrong, Ryan?"

"Ryan, talked to us. Please," Heather begged.

"Your face has gone pale. What happened?" Alexa asked, scared.

"I haven't seen my parents today at all either. Not even in the kitchen. They always wake up early and make breakfast."

"Yeah, that's a fact. I've been to way too many of your family breakfasts to know that they always have it. So what? They might've gone out today and had it at the diner," Alexa said.

"Let's go to the diner then. At least we can ask Larry if he's seen them today," Heather said, offering a solution.

"O... okay. Let's go," I said, shaking.

This was terrifying; they couldn't have just disappeared, right? Of course, they could have, what was I thinking, with Alexa's parents disappearing anything was possible. We ran to my car. I started it and slammed it out of the park. We rolled up to Larry's Diner fast and I spun into a parking spot.

We all dashed into Larry's to find him wiping down the tables.

"Larry! Larry! Have you seen my parents today?" I said, yelling to get over the loud music he was pumping into his earbuds.

"Hmm? What do ya need, Ryan?" he casually inquired why I had just screamed at him.

"Have you seen my parents this morning?" I asked desperately.

"Can't say that I have. But I did serve her father," Larry said, pointing at Heather.

"Wait what?" she said, dumbfounded.

"Yep, sat down and ate but then got some important phone call and dashed out," he said nonchalantly.

We took off running, and got to my car before he could say another word. I kicked it into high gear, and we sped to my house. The drive went by in a blur. I hardly caught any glimpse of the road as I tunneled in on my house.

Almost crashing five times, I finally made it to my driveway, and I parked the car, taking no time to sprint out of the driver's side door and slam it. I burst through the entrance and entered my living room hastily. I ran all through the house calling out, "Mom! Dad! Where are you??!!" to no reply at all. After my psychotic break, I fell to my knees in their completely bare room.

Chapter 14

The girls finally entered the room I was in, finding me a crumpled mess. I was folded in on myself and was holding my knees to my chest. I just wanted to disappear too. Where had my parents gone? Where did Alexa's parents go? This had to be connected in some shape or form. I couldn't think, I just knew that my family was gone, and I was the last one standing. In a way, all three of us had lost our families. Alexa's parents had disappeared along with mine and Heather's father was probably at the center of it.

"Ryan...?" I heard a soft voice whisper to me.

"Hmm?" I couldn't form words.

"It's gonna be fine..." she said.

"How do you know that?" I replied dejectedly.

"I just do," she said firmly.

I looked up and saw the girls huddled around me, but neither of them was talking. Strange, I thought, for sure it was one of them who was whispering to me. Then I felt a tickle on my neck and saw a faint glow behind me. It couldn't be what I was thinking, could it?

It was the wisp. Except I had not been asleep when I heard it. But I did hear it speak. Because Heather and Alexa didn't reply when I lifted my head. They just sat there hugging me. *This has to be in my head, right?* I decided to ask the girls if they saw that thing.

"Hey, guys? Did you see anything weird just now?" I asked in a shaky tone.

"Nope. What do you mean 'weird'?" they both responded.

"Like a strange light. See anything like that?"

"There was a weird greenish-blue glow to the room for a second, yeah, why?" Alexa asked.

"Just making sure I wasn't insane."

"Pfft, good luck with that, you've been looney since we met. I'm surprised you were never sent to a mental institution."

"Thanks, Lex," I said plainly.

I got up and paced around the room thinking of all the possibilities. Then I realized Heather was still kneeling and staring at the ground blankly. It looked like she were frozen in place, or like a robot whose battery just died.

"Yoo-hoo? Hey, crazy robot friend, are you alive? Did you just die? I know you're alive, you responded to me a minute ago," I said, waving my hand in front of her.

I watched her, mesmerized by the stillness of her body. I'd never seen a human being actually that calm and unmoving. I couldn't believe this. Something supernatural must've been happening. I walked up and shook her to try to get her to move.

"Hey! You really can't hear me?"

Alexa came running back into the room. She was holding some papers that looked older than us. It looked like parchment, not normal paper. I stared at her quizzically, wondering what she could be thinking. As if she sensed it, she said to me, "They're like the plans I had at my house but older and for a descendant."

"A descendant?"

"Yes, it says here at the top, 'cannot be done by a descendant. If done by a no-descendant of any age, these pages will disappear.'"

"That's a joke, right?"

"I wouldn't assume so, but it looks super old and important."

"Looks like we're just at the beginning of the strange events, not the end of them."

"That's for sure."

I took the papers from her and felt the grainy soft quality of the paper. It felt brittle as if any tear or start of one would turn it into a cloud of fine dust.

I stared at the pages, but then suddenly my leg started to feel as if it was on fire. I sat down rapidly, feeling as if my leg was about to burn off and I'd have a stump in place.

I touched Heather but she was cold to the touch. It was as if she was a solid block of ice that I couldn't warm up. She looked peaceful yet also menacing to me.

I ran upstairs to grab some blankets to warm her up. Then back down the ancient creaky Maine staircase, I sprinted holding a heating pad and two blankets. With each step I took, another board made a cracking sound. It was as if each wooden step was howling in pain at the force being put on it.

I made it to the bottom to find Heather standing up straight, looking at me with a concerned, calm demeanor.

"Where is Alexa?" I asked.

"Here, who are you talking to?" Alexa said, walking into the hallway, and as she did this Heather disappeared.

"Where's Heather?"

"Still in the same position, why? You look like you've seen a ghost, what happened?"

"She was just standing where you are now, at least that's what I saw. Maybe my mind is playing tricks on me."

"Ummm. Okay? Let's get those blankets and stuff for her," she said with a tinge of disbelief.

"Why'd you say it like that?"

"Like what?"

"You said it as if I was lying or as if you didn't think it was just my imagination," I said, stepping closer to her and walking with her to the next room.

"I do believe you. It was simply weird that you thought you saw her there," she said while helping me cover Heather in the blankets.

I hated that about what had been happening recently. I couldn't trust whether or not anything was real now because so much seemed real but had to be false. It was like this in everyone's life at some point. It mainly happened when we age, and our brains start to deteriorate and cause us to get mental diseases. But sometimes if you have trust issues it could seem the same. The worst part about this was that I could only trust what others said.

Then came a knock on my chest. It wasn't hard but soft and kind. It was Alexa trying to wake me from my deep thoughts. She knew when I got like this it could be dark.

"Hey, Watson. What are you thinking about? It looks serious."

"Ah, 'twas nothing, Sherlock. Thank you, though," I said softly and gave her a light punch on the arm.

Some normal guy I am, right? I think it's funny how we want to fit in and be normal. When you think about it, being different actually is the true essence of normal. People always look at themselves with the harshest magnifying glasses. It gives us this distorted view of what's really going on. It causes us to think everyone is looking at us and judging us, scrutinizing every single detail about us. In reality, everyone is too focused on themselves to even realize what's going on around them.

"Hey, Ryan? You there?" Alexa said softly.

"Yes, what's up? Sorry, I was just lost in thought again. This time not so bad," I said sheepishly.

"Then I'm guessing you didn't hear what I said, did you?"

"No, I didn't. What was it you said?"

"Don't worry about it," she said with a smirk.

"Aww, come on now, I need to know."

Suddenly under the blankets we saw movement, and with lightning speed, Heather was standing back up again staring at us as if nothing had happened. It seemed as if time had just rewound. She was in a similar position but standing and holding onto me instead of us crouched on the ground. I pried her off of me and watched as she frowned.

I gave Alexa a sideways glance, wondering if what just happened was real. She nodded, and that was all I needed as confirmation. I stared back at her as if to say, *Let's just drop it for now. No need to complicate things any further.*

I picked the parchment back up and walked into the kitchen. I stared at the bare walls and felt a pang of pain enter my heart. All the pictures of me and my family were gone, leaving only the square indication on the wall that they had been there. I watched the time on the stove, wishing that I could just rewind that clock and have the entire world just go in reverse. I wanted to go back to that day before this all started. I wished that I could go back to that day in front of my house when everything started to happen.

My heart ached but I had one clue as to what was happening and it was right in front of me. I needed to finish whatever this was and just hope by the end of it everything returned to normal. As I read the instructions in front of me on this old parchment, the importance could not be mistaken.

For a descendant's eyes only. This document shall disappear upon being fully viewed by a non-descendant of any age.

To the bearer of this document, I depart to thee three pearls of wisdom.

1. The location to solve thy problems is already known by thee.

2. A key is hidden somewhere in this location.

3. The smallest light can illuminate the darkest places.

I read this and got zero answers. The location I needed to find I already knew? How could I know where this location was? This paper seemed to only give me more questions and didn't solve any of the problems we had accumulated.

I lay the paper down and folded it up, thinking I should save it for later. I then noticed my notebook on the table.

"Hmm, strange," I said, picking it up.

"What's strange?" Heather asked as she walked in.

"I don't remember bringing my notebook down here. Yet here it is on my table."

"That is strange," she said, looking as if she were deep in thought.

"Well, I think I should write some things down to clear my head. You can go tell Lex. I'll be done in ten to twenty mins," I said as I opened my notebook and flipped to the next page after Chapter Three.

As Heather walked out of the room, she turned to me and gave me a smile and a wink.

The Lion Who Wanted to Reach the Moon Ch. 4

The lion awakened to see the sun directly above them. He started to walk across the huge clearing that was now a lush green from the stark white of last night. He walked up to the treacherous-looking rock wall in front of the trio and started to climb it. He hopped skillfully and gracefully up the ledges on the cliff face.

Much to his surprise as he reached another clearing, he noticed a warmth that he had never felt before. He turned his head and looked past his mane at the two sitting on his back. Neither moved and they just kept sleeping peacefully.

The lion turned to the snake, and she immediately opened her eyes. That was peculiar, just seconds before she seemed to be sound asleep.

"Good morning. I see you have been awake for a while already," she whispered in his ear as she wrapped herself closer to his head.

"Yes, I decided not to wake either of you as I continued our journey," he said warmly.

"I still don't trust her," she said.

"I know, but I don't care," he replied.

The two then fell into silence, no longer wanting to continue a conversation that would always end the same way.

The light around them seemed to turn a bright orange hue. This meant that the moon would be back in the sky soon. As the orange glow encompassed the world, a few more colors seemed to break out and the light glowed radiantly.

The owl stayed asleep and didn't wake as they walked. The climb was beginning to bore the lion as he reached another resting point. It was night now and the frigid air started to settle on the group. The cold made the lion shake softly; the warmth from earlier that day was gone and was now a distant memory.

While he thought this, the owl woke and fluttered closer to his head. She seemed as if she wanted to speak to him, however, she said nothing. She just stood there perfectly still.

"Hello? Finally awake?"

No response came from her.

"You don't seem too good. Anything on your mind?"

Her eyes showed no response; she just sat there staring off into the distance.

This is really strange, he thinks to himself. He wondered why she seemed somewhat 'broken' right now. He knew she was shy, but this seemed to be a level beyond that. The world then became dark as it shifted to night because the moon wasn't in the sky. The moon seemed to have abandoned them.

The lion roared loudly at the sky, angry that he couldn't continue his quest tonight. He decided to lie down for the night and walk during the day again. His anger wasn't at the moon but at the feeling he got today. There was an emptiness he found within him. Before this day he'd had a purpose, and that was to reach the moon, but recently it seemed his mind had been scattered. He didn't know what to do next with his life, but he knew he must finish what he'd started.

"I hope that my purpose returns to me," he whispered under his breath.

Chapter 15

I closed my notebook and grabbed the parchment then walked into the living room. The girls stared at me. Heather flashed a warm smile and Alexa just kept a blank face. This was weird, it was like they'd had a personality shift. One happy, the other now closed off. I walked up to both of them and sat down.

"How's it going?" I asked tentatively.

"Alright," Alexa responded plainly.

"Scared," Heather said with a frown.

"Well, I read the instructions, and they gave me some cryptic information, but I think we should start our search here. Let's look in the attic for a key of some sort." I tried not to say word for word what the paper listed in case it would disappear. How would it hear me? I had no clue, but I didn't know how it could tell the lineage of the reader either.

I guessed that was just the way life is, always one step ahead of us. Whenever you think something couldn't be as complex as it says, life always throws a wrench into your plans. I thought this as we walked upstairs. Alexa walked into my room and Heather went into my parents' room to search, while I alone went up to the attic. I pulled down the staircase and let it down as soft as possible. But it still made a loud creak as it fully extended. I walked up the dusty oak staircase and each step responded to the weight I put on it.

I stepped into the room, if it could even be called that. As I looked around, I watched the dust that I had kicked up float around the room as natural light rushed in from the small decorative window. I smiled, remembering fondly hiding up here when me and my parents played hide and seek. A feeling of sorrow entered me when I realized that those moments were gone. Soon I'd be grown up and I would be going off to college or into the world.

I knew most adults don't think of teenagers as adults, but I couldn't help feeling like one. Sometimes I think of how lucky I am to have had the schooling that I did, of how lucky I am to be loved by so many. The teachers at my high school treated the students as if they were growing up and becoming adults. I'd heard many stories from other kids about how teachers looked at them as children who didn't understand anything. To some degree we were, but to that point when you think about it everyone had childish tendencies. Even the oldest of us give in to impulsiveness.

I thought about this as I looked at the emptiness of the room and remembered the boxes of yearbooks that used to fill this space. Everything that had anything to do with me or my parents was gone. None of the furniture had disappeared, just the memories of me and my family. The room that used to be filled with memories was now vacant.

My life had just disappeared; it was as if I no longer existed. It seemed that something or someone just wanted to erase me. I couldn't understand why it was just me and Alexa who had these issues suddenly. As I thought these scary thoughts, I stared at the wooden floorboards, trying to see if any were out of place. I wanted to cry and let out all of the feelings I had inside. But I couldn't break it down. I had to stay strong for them. I smiled, thinking about Heather and Alexa, two people who cared about me tremendously.

I went to the window and mindlessly observed the outside. I thought hard about where I would know this key was. Every place I imagined seemed to be wrong, but when I got to the final location my leg started to burn. I knew I was getting closer, and so I had to think even harder about the exact location. But that proved to be too difficult, and I had to give up.

I sprinted down the attic staircase and called for my friends.

"Guys! I know where we need to go!" I yelled.

They both ran out of their respective search locations and asked, "Where?"

"The old library."

"How do you know?" Heather said skeptically.

"I can feel it in my heart... and my *leg*." I said the last part under my breath so neither heard me.

"What was that last part?" Alexa prodded.

"Nothing," I said matter of factly.

"Keep lying then," Alexa said with venom, almost spitting the words at me. Then she walked down to the first floor of my house, and I quickly followed her.

"Hey, what's up? All of a sudden you seem to have changed," I said softly so only she could hear.

"I'm just tired of all the lying. I just want the old you back," she said sadly.

"I know you do but things have changed. I've changed," I whispered hoarsely. I didn't want to accept it, but it was true.

A single tear rolled down Alexa's face. She knew it was true. She knew things could never be the same. Heather walked down the stairs and stopped where she was sensing the serious tone of our conversation. I motioned for her to come down as I softly patted Alexa's back.

We all walked out of the door and to my car. The tension in the air was palpable. We got into the car, and I started the engine. As the car roared to life, I sat behind the wheel feeling hollow. A soft nudge on the shoulder brought me back to reality. As it took us to our destination, I drove to the edge of the woods and parallel-parked my car.

The leather seats felt so foreign that I lifted off of them and stepped out of the car. We kept the same air of silence as our excursion into the woods continued. As we approached the site of the unfinished library, I felt the familiar burn enter my leg. I had to ignore the pain even as it continued to grow. We needed that key and an answer to our mysteries.

We continued into the woods and as we ventured deeper the civilized world seemed to fade into the distance. The eerie feeling I'd had before was back but was more intense now. I think we all had the same thoughts about how the next step was a huge turning point in our lives.

As we approached the dilapidated building, a fear built up in my heart. I felt the pain in my leg amplify, but I pushed through it. Each step was more excruciating than the last. We walked up to the front door and stood still.

"Are you ready?" I asked shakily.

"Yes," Alexa replied calmly.

"Sure am," Heather said, but I could hear in her voice she was uncertain.

"Thank you for the help. I can't express my gratitude more," I said in a somber voice.

"Of course!" Heather said happily.

"You know I'll always be by your side," Alexa said softly.

Her tune certainly changed after that car ride. I didn't know what switch flipped for her, but something did, and she was acting much more docile right now. I reached for the handle and so did the girls. It was a symbolic gesture, by opening the door with me they solidified our bond.

I knew that they meant what they said. We walked into the library and the pain was crippling. I could only stumble along and make it to a dust-covered couch. I sat down and the girls did the same.

"How are you doing?" Heather asked, sensing something wrong.

"Is the pain back, Ryan? How long have you felt this?" Alexa questioned me.

"Yes, but it only just happened, Alexa, and to answer you, Heather, I just need a second and I'll be fine," I said this and felt a tinge of guilt. I hadn't tried to lie about how long this was happening. I also didn't want to admit that I wouldn't be fine for a while. But I knew I had to tough it out.

I stood up abruptly after two minutes of rest and started to walk deeper into the library. Alexa and Heather followed behind me, and I could feel their concern as we continued.

I couldn't let this stop me; I could deal with a little pain. I repeated this in my head as we stepped further into this abandoned project. I looked at the sitting area intended for children and adults alike to sit and read the literature they had just pulled off of a shelf.

It was still a confusing mess to me why they had never fully finished this project. I knew I could probably ask Alexa or Heather and they'd both have answers for me. But I didn't feel like talking anymore. I didn't want to keep lying to them, so I knew it'd be better if I just stayed silent.

I thought of where my parents could be and where Alexa's might be. I walked up to one of the tables and wiped off the mountains of dust that covered it. I then cleaned three seats for me and the girls and sat down at one of them.

"Okay, so we should probably look around here. I personally will walk to the back where it is unfinished and look through the basement," I said, pulling out a map layout of the library from Alexa's backpack. Good thing she'd kept that binder full of stuff that Heather gave us.

"Sounds good to me," Heather said softly.

"Sure, thing, boss," Alexa replied snarkily.

We then split into our own separate sections of the library. I walked to the darkest corridor and stepped onto a set of stairs that weren't fully finished. The smell of the wood varnish not being sealed over made me want to vomit. As a result of never being finished, mold had set into the stairs and was making their integrity suspect to say the least.

With all of these factors bouncing around my head, I forced myself to ignore my survival instincts and walk down the stairs. I reached the bottom with the pain in my leg, still feeling as if it had been set on fire. But I had to ignore that as I walked deeper into the cave of a basement. The cement walls had no wallpaper or paint covering them and the surfaces in some locations were rough as if they had never been fully smoothed out. Tarps still lay strewn about the ground as if they had big plans to continue the construction.

The white from the tarps had long since faded into a dull grayish brown from a mixture of dirt and dust. I walked further into the basement until I reached a wall at the far end where the natural light from above had long since faded. I took out my keychain and turned on a flashlight I had hooked on it.

I could only search with the circular light, and decided to look under the tarps at the end of the basement and work backward toward the stairs. The first two tarps I pulled up and searched under hid nothing, but a dull cement floor that had since cracked and now had small natural flowers growing in. However, when I pulled up the third tarp, I heard something clank against the ground. At first, I thought it to be a small key but when I walked towards it there was a rusted iron handle on the ground. It seemed to have been bolted to the ground, and when I walked over to it, I heard a hollow sound ring out from beneath my feet. It definitely had been a latch into the ground. The handle was dug into the cement as if the grove was made just to fit its shape. I then pulled the handle upwards, and up came a trap door.

On the bottom of this trap door were wooden slats. It looked like they covered this wooden-iron door with cement and matched it up with the tile-like pattern they had dug into the ground to hide it. Down the dark hatch was a metal ladder that seemed to be bolted into a wall that lead deeper into the bottom of the library. What would this be used to house? I thought to myself.

At this point, I decided to walk back up and gather the rest of my group. I called Alexa and Heather to me and explained how I'd found the trap door.

"Also, I think we should only send two down into the hole. This way, in case the two don't come back, in twenty minutes the person above will go get help," I said to them with a profoundly serious tone.

"I want to go with you," they both shouted at the same time.

"I know the job of being above ground may be scary since you will be alone, but it is the only safe way to ensure we all get out of here," I said, keeping my air of authority.

"Then I want to go with you," Alexa stated, staring daggers at Heather.

"But he's going to need someone who won't get mad at him," Heather said, almost as if she was trying to instigate a fight.

"How dare you?! What gives you the right to say that?" Alexa yelled at Heather, scowling.

"I see how you treat him; it's been the same for years. You really haven't changed. You're such a child!" Heather countered with just as much force as Alexa, showing that she wouldn't back down. They continued to bicker back and forth at a pace I can't keep up with. So, I decided to interject.

"Girls! We need to do this quickly. Time is of the essence," I stated very calmly.

"Fine... You can go, Alexa." Heather conceded the fight.

"Okay, let's get moving. The sunlight will be fading soon." I climbed down the ladder. As soon as I got down to the ground level, I looked up the ladder and got ready to catch Alexa in case she fell.

As soon as she got down, she looked around and pulled out her phone. I turned my flashlight back on and so did she, and we illuminated the little room that lead to a dark corridor. As we started to walk, Alexa inched closer as if she was afraid of this spooky tunnel.

The walls were the same as up above, fully cement with rough patches and a curved ceiling. The tunnel seemed as if it lead to a bunker but that couldn't be, why would there be a bunker in the middle of nowhere in Maine? As I was thinking this, I felt Alexa's arm brush mine.

"Hey, are you doing okay?" I asked softly.

"I-I'm okay, just a little scared," she said in a meek voice. She stepped even closer to me and was almost pressed against me now. We kept walking cautiously down the corridor and stopped when we heard the dripping of water splashing onto the ground.

Chapter 16

I turned around using my flashlight to look for the location of the sound. There did seem to be no irrigation or any form of pipes nearby. I decided we should ignore it and keep walking. We moved forward around another thirty feet and hit a crossroads. We had three directions that we could go. Out of these three options, two had solid metal doors at the end of them. These two options were the paths leading left and right. The path leading forward, however, seemed to go on for another hundred or more feet, with what looked like no end.

"So, what door feels lucky?" I asked, trying to lighten the mood.

"How about we try left first then right? I really don't think that it's the center," she said softly.

"I swear, if you're wrong and it's the middle one," I jokingly jabbed her softly on the arm.

"I'm always right," she said as she walked down the left hallway with confidence.

"Hey! Don't leave me behind in that spooky tunnel. What if there are traps that separate us?" I said, running to catch up with her.

We walked shoulder to shoulder down the left tunnel, and got halfway to the door when I heard the dripping again. Since I had decided to ignore it once already, I thought I should just keep doing so. We continued all the way down the hallway and made it to the door. The door was painted the same color gray as the cement. It somehow managed to look immaculate despite being so old and having no upkeep. The hinges looked as if they were made of bronze except the gray peeking out behind the brown betrayed its bluff.

There was no way these hinges would hold for much longer.

"Should I try to open it? It looks like it might be locked but I could probably break it off its hinges," I stated in a hopeful tone.

"Sure, try the handle first though, Ryan, then you can try to break it off," she said with a tinge of doubt entering her voice at the last second.

I tried the handle, and the door didn't budge. I shook the handle, and it was stuck. Then I took a quick kick at the hinges which surprisingly made the door jiggle. I kicked it again and it bounced again. Then I set up for one more big kick at the bottom hinge, hoping to break the screws that had been rusted in place. BOOM! As soon as my foot hit the hinge it snapped free from the wall. I barely had enough time to react, and I grabbed Alexa pulling her down by her waist.

We watched as the door swung down above us, but the top hinge held, and we were safe.

"You okay?" I questioned her.

"Y-yeah. Thanks for looking out," she said, panic enveloping her voice.

"Let's go walk inside the room before this door crushes us," I said quickly, getting to my knees and crawling through the opening. I helped Alexa up and got her through it too.

The room was pitch black as we first entered it. I fumbled into my back pocket, trying to grab my flashlight. I felt the cold metal as it touched my palm and recoiled a little, but then quickly grabbed it. I turned it on and shone it around the room. The size of the room wasn't that big; it seemed to be a ten foot by ten foot floor plan. It was perfectly square, which was amazing to look at, but I had a sinking feeling in my body. I looked around to the opposite wall and it was covered floor to ceiling with buttons. There was nothing in this room except immense amounts of dust and a wall that looked to be a keypad with around a hundred buttons that had different symbols on them. Each button was roughly the size of a soda can laid sideways.

As I started to question what was happening, I heard the door slam to the ground, and a tiny yelp came from behind us. I turned to see Heather standing in the doorway. I instantly rushed over to see her and got her away from the two-ton door that was now lying on the ground.

"Hey! What are you doing down here? You knew it would be dangerous if all three of us came down together. What if that door had fallen on you?" I yelled concernedly at her, as I studied her body, making sure she wasn't injured in any way.

"I'm fine though, and it's been fifteen minutes. I was scared that something would happen to you two. So, I came to check out what happened," she said completely calmly, holding her flashlight at her side.

"How did you know we went to the left?" I asked, confused.

"Easy, it was the only option that had a door swinging from one hinge. If I had to bet money that you did that, I would've done so," she stated nonchalantly.

While I was talking to Heather, it seemed that Alexa was staring daggers at her again. Alexa was a lot more standoffish recently. Alexa opened her mouth as if she wanted to say something, but she just closed it silently and continued to stare. I walked over to the wall, hoping I didn't have to see them fight. The hatred that was between them seemed to have grown instead of diminished since this whole journey started.

I felt a pain deep in my heart to know that they disliked one another so much. Walking up the wall to study the symbols helped me push these thoughts out of my head. I noticed one thing that made certain it wasn't a language or numerical values. It seemed to be pictographs like the Egyptians used except with modern symbols. There were no animal-human crossbreeds or ancient godly symbols. Instead, the symbols were composed of brands and logos of companies all familiar to this age of technology.

This was strange. I had never really thought of it being possible to create a language like this using our most popular companies. It almost made me burst out laughing, seeing it, and I hoped the girls found it just as amusing to see.

"Man, if we become an ancient civilization and people ever find this wall, they'd probably think it was just a translation of our primitive language. Just like we did with the Egyptians and Greeks," I said smiling, thinking of some future archeologists digging this up and trying to decipher the "ancient dialect".

"You're right, that would be a fun sight to see," Heather said warmly.

Alexa just kind of shrugged off what I'd said as she continued to study the wall. Then she walked up and tried to push one of the buttons.

"Hey! We don't know what we're doing yet!" I shouted at her.

"I do," she said with no emotion, and she sure seemed like she was right because the button she pressed lit up green. It did seem that like all thing's green meant good and red meant bad. But the big question on my mind was how many chances we got to be right. As well as what happened if we failed. I guess we had no choice but to just one-shot it. Because if we failed and it killed us then that meant we had no chance to do it again. Of course, that was an extreme assumption, but come on, it was a creepy locked room with buttons on the wall, what other assumption was there to make?

As I was thinking this, Alexa walked up and hit another button. Heather gave me a look that showed her concern, and I just shrugged.

"We just have to trust her," I whispered in her ear.

"I know. It still terrifies me what might happen though," she said back quietly.

"Don't worry, I know she'd never put herself in danger, so that means she's right," I said back, trying to reassure her, and myself to some extent.

Heather flashed a face with a frown showing a confusing emotion I couldn't quite comprehend. Was it jealousy, anger, or fear? I had no way of knowing, *I should just let it go,* I thought to myself. I rubbed her arm softly as I walked off to talk to Alexa. Instead of talking to her, I stopped three feet away, noticing she had already pressed roughly twenty-three buttons with each one glowing an emerald green. The light from behind the buttons mesmerized me with their beauty and majesty. To think such a wondrous contraption was made by humans made you question what we couldn't do.

"Heya, how's it going?" I asked Alexa casually.

"Good. Only twenty-seven more to go," she said in a monotone voice.

"Did I do something to upset you?" I inquired.

"No, but she did. She said you and I were to go down. She gave up, yet here she is. She always follows you around like a dog begging for scraps," she hissed quietly enough that Heather couldn't hear.

"Is that really it?" I continued.

"Yes. Twenty more to go," she said, again with no emotion. I sat there with a mixture of emotions, one being confusion and one being awe. I was confused by the relationship Heather and Alexa had and also awestruck by the speed at which Alexa was racing through such a seemingly complex puzzle.

"Fifteen more," she stated to no one in particular.

I began to think about the past and as I did so I realized my leg was still in pain. I had pushed out all of my thoughts about my leg, so I hadn't felt anything till now. It was an amazing feat of the mind that we all possess, the ability to ignore pain when we don't let it occupy our thoughts. The biggest example I could think of is when people get paper cuts on their hands. If you get a paper cut, you feel it sting even though oftentimes you can't even see the injury. The pain of that injury is often minor, but it is discomforting. But the pain disappears faster when you keep doing something after the cut rather than just stopping all activity to deal with the pain. This is the same phenomenon that just happened to my leg.

It's amazing how little we are able to actively control our brain, like pain receptors, or the millions of other small actions it does every second to keep us alive without us knowing, but we can also ignore most pain by not hyper-focusing on it or via chemicals that our brain has our body secrete to dull the pain so we can focus on surviving.

"Five more," Alexa shouted, breaking me out of my trance. I turned around to go talk to Heather, but realized that while I was thinking she had come up next to me. Now she and I were standing side by side watching Alexa complete the puzzle.

Heather leaned over and grabbed my hand softly saying, "Welcome back."

"Thanks?" I said meekly while my cheeks flushed red. I was so embarrassed that I kept going into zombie mode. Then Alexa finished inputting the code, and Heather dropped my hand leaving a piece of paper in it.

Really, notes? How old are we, six? I thought to myself while I folded it and shoved it into my back pocket. Alexa turned around smiling, and as she did so the whole room shook violently. I grabbed Heather's hand, pulled her to where Alexa was and dragged them both to the ground. I didn't know how I knew it would be the safest place, but I did. Because as soon as we hit the ground a giant pillar jutted out of the wall right at head level. But it didn't stop there, it then dragged across the wall.

I shone my light on it, and it revealed two jagged blades on either side of the pillar. It ran the length of the room four times and then slid back into the wall. As quickly as it had started, it was over. I thanked whatever was watching us from above as I stood up, making sure that the room would be completely safe.

"What the hell was that?!?" Alexa shouted with terror, her voice still shaking.

"I don't know but it looked like it was a security measure," I said calmly, trying to be the rock we all needed.

"A security measure for a correct answer?" Heather said in the quietest voice I'd ever heard.

"Was the answer right?" I asked Alexa.

But she didn't have to answer, as soon as I said that the wall of buttons in front of us shook again and a giant door revealed itself. The whole wall seemed to split in half as the ancient mechanism slid the sheets of concrete apart.

"Well, there's our answer," I said, smiling.

"Wait... You want to keep going deeper?" Alexa asked me in awe, as if I was off my meds.

"Of course! We have to find the key, don't we?" I said with a small, forced laugh. I couldn't keep this up inside. I was breaking down.

"Are you sure we'll be okay?" Heather questioned me the same way Alexa did. It was as if they were judging my reaction, trying to figure out if I had been lying or not.

"Yep. We sure will be. Don't worry, we've seen how well my instincts are acting today. I'm two for two on the death-defying stunts," I said, actually laughing hysterically this time. I even knew how dumb that sounded as I was saying it. But I didn't care, we had come too far to give up now.

"Okay… I'll trust you, Ryan," Alexa said softly.

"I trust you too. I know you'll keep us safe and sound," Heather said, smiling.

I sure hoped I could keep that promise. I knew I hadn't told them I'd promised but, in a way, I didn't need to. By believing in this so much, I committed my word and used all the trust they had in me. So, I couldn't break this promise. I was tired of lying.

I couldn't guarantee safety, but I could protect them. Even if I had to sacrifice myself, I would for those two girls. They were the best friends anyone could ask for, no matter their problems with one another they'd never leave my side.

We stood in front of the new door, and as I stood between them, I grabbed both of their hands and said, "We will find this key, and I think I might need a little more paper to fully chronicle our adventures." Those words made me smile and left me with a feeling of true courage. Gone was the false bravado. I was ready for whatever came next.

Chapter 17

We started to walk slowly down the new entrance. The new passageway was remarkably similar to the first one except it seemed to be made of two sheets of concrete. It had no fine lines that sectioned off each part of the tunnel, unlike the first one. It also was as smooth as glass. I felt that the slightest movement would create a huge crack running down the length of this strange hallway. It wasn't a sleek-looking hallway; it was actually quite dull-looking with no shine. But compared to the other two rooms, this one seemed to have been sanded down and then polished with wax.

As we walked, my sneakers squeaked on the ground. It sounded like each step I took I was stepping on a thousand rubber ducks. The noise was loud and piercing, not to mention the echo that ricocheted off of every surface. Then just as it seemed we were making progress we hit a wall.

"Was this here when we started walking?" I said, confused.

"I don't remember seeing a wall this close to the entrance of the passage," Heather stated.

"Me neither," Alexa said, seeming just as confused as me.

"I think we should go check the other two forks of that crossroad," I told them, and got a nod of approval from both. As soon as we turned around, I heard the water splash again. This time it was behind the wall we had just hit. How could that be possible though? I asked myself, trying to search my own head for an answer. It could be an echo from the beginning but if that were true then why hadn't I heard it in front of me first?

This whole thing didn't make any sense. What was I missing? I decided not to add more questions to our excursion and to keep us moving. We made it back to the fork, and this time decided to go to the path opposite the one we just came from.

As we walked down this eerie hallway, I felt a soft presence appear close to me. It was Heather, she was standing much closer than before, but her body language didn't show any fear. It was like she believed what I said more than I did. She radiated strength with each powerful step she took.

As I thought this, a darker spirit seemed to encroach on me as well. I didn't even have to look. I knew it was Alexa. She didn't have the usual mischievous-happy air about her. Instead, she seemed to be hurt. I felt the fangs of her pain bite into my heart, I knew it was because of me. It must have been hard for her to have all of this go on and to have Heather back, ripping her old scars open again.

What Heather didn't know was the pain that Alexa carried behind her confidence. Underneath the sarcasm, she hid so much sorrow and anguish from the past. After that day when we were kids and Heather was gone, Alexa beat herself up for what she had said. She knew she had gone too far, and that knowledge killed her. Alexa was one of the most caring people on this Earth; she never liked to hurt people. But that day something clicked in her, and she said something she couldn't take back. I knew she still felt that pain, and having Heather back seemed to just amplify that.

After the first time her parents left, she used sarcasm as a defense. She hid behind it and put venom into her words to scare off others. She didn't want to open back up. Her heart was closed to others because she feared if she opened it then she'd end up burned again.

I got pulled back to reality when we reached the end of the tunnel and walked into another room. This room was similar to the first one we'd entered but didn't have the symbols. This one had a huge moving puzzle on the ground. It was scrambled up, but you could clearly tell it was meant to be the face of a baby.

"Well, this is unsettling," I said, shaking slightly.

"Yeah, super creepy," Alexa said coldly.

The baby had no hair, but it had some distinguishing features. It had green eyes and small ears. The nose of the child was also rather small compared to the face. As I stood there thinking this, Heather blurted out, "I got this one. I'm good at these moving tile puzzles."

"Okay, we'll just watch then," I said as I brought Alexa back to the entry.

I watched Heather slide the puzzle pieces to the open square as Alexa stared at the ground with a brooding frown. The ground was laid out in a five by five grid with one piece missing from the middle. From watching Heather, I could easily grasp that the way to solve the puzzle was to slide the tiles around until you got the picture correct. However, moving a tile from one corner to another was difficult, requiring multiple slides to achieve the correct positioning.

All the while there was a counter on the wall that seemed to count each move that Heather made. I paid close attention to that detail, noticing she was on move thirty already. I then scanned the rest of the room and saw a number faintly carved into the right wall. That number was eighty-five. This clearly was the maximum number of moves that she could make.

"Hey, Heather, there seems to be a move limit put on you. The limit is eighty-five, and seeing as you're at thirty-four and barely halfway you should be careful. Take a step back if you need to instead of wasting extra moves," I told her encouragingly.

After I said that, Heather looked up dazed and saw the counter. She nodded somewhat then went back to the puzzle, staring at it intently. Her gaze was steely, and she seemed to be thinking about something. But what she was thinking about I couldn't tell just by looking at her. So, I decided not to interrupt her, and as I thought that she started working again.

I turned to Alexa with a concerned face. I could feel the darkness emanating from her. I wanted to say something to try to cheer her up, but no words came out of my mouth. I wished I could just speak my mind to her and help her feel better.

Finally, she noticed I was staring at her, and she mumbled something.

"What was that? I couldn't hear you," I asked.

"Nothing... Don't worry about it, Ryan," she then said something under her breath. But this time I heard it, "Not like you'd care." She clearly thought I had missed it, so she went silent again as she watched Heather.

I looked back at the counter, and it was now at sixty-two, she sure had made a lot of moves in a short time. I then looked at the puzzle and noticed she had barely made any progress at all since the last time I checked. The baby had the top of its head and its eyes in the right place. However, the ears were on the wrong sides and the chin was where the nose should have gone.

Each time she moved one of the tiles you could hear it scrape against the concrete as if in protest. How long had these puzzles sat unsolved down here? I wondered as I walked around the edges of the grid. Heather was now at sixty-eight moves, and she had placed the ears in the correct spot. The final thing she had to do was swap the locations of the chin and nose.

I stood there in awe of her quick and decisive movements. It was as if she knew what the answer was already. Like she had done this before. Maybe she had just played with these puzzles a lot, I thought to myself.

I found myself wondering why puzzles were still an extremely popular activity even in our modern age, where we had the internet, phones, and television always at our fingertips.

With the technological advancements we'd had, you'd think that we'd have more things to do, and the lives of children would be happier. Yet, as technology changes, we stay the same. Our lives had been improved and made more convenient, yet we still dealt with the same problems and social anxiety. We still had bullies, scammers, and liars. Just because technology improved, didn't mean that the people using it did.

As a society, we focus so much on being the most advanced technologically. But we never focus on the people using it. Of course, there are more people using technology for good than there are using it for evil. However, we still have the darkness that comes with the real world. The only thing that changes is when you're online the world is catered to you. If you have the internet, you can live like a king. As you use these websites, they decide to hide opposing views from you. It continues until you are in a false land where everyone agrees with you, and nobody challenges your thought process.

This is a modern sickness. We gain fragile happiness, which in turn makes us defensive and attacks anyone who threatens to shatter it. This can cause huge divisions in nations and even among friends and family. This is the next biggest problem we face as a people. Will we let this powerful tool defeat us? Or will we grow and impose rules for it?

As I thought this, I got a tap on my shoulder and noticed Heather was almost finished. I then looked down and realized I had pulled out my journal and began writing in it. I quickly shut it and put it in my pocket as I looked back in time to see Heather finish.

As she slid the last piece into its correct spot, she turned to us and smiled widely. She was clearly proud, and as I looked at the counter, I saw it was at eighty-four, just one move from the maximum. Then she stepped off the puzzle grid onto the side and the lights above us flashed green.

"I assume that means it's correct?" I said aloud.

"Seems like it," Heather beamed.

"Great job, H," Alexa said, sulking.

"Yeah, you did amazing. I definitely couldn't have done that puzzle," I told her, patting her back.

Her smile only grew as I noticed the flashing had stopped. I heard a loud noise that resembled a metallic screech.

"What do you think that is?" Heather asked.

"I don't know, we haven't checked the center path, maybe there's a door there," I said.

Alexa said something else that was inaudible, but it looked like she agreed. With that said, we walked back to the crossroads and took a right. I noticed as we walked that the water sound had seemed to stop when the screech happened.

"EWWWWWW! What is this?!" I heard Alexa exclaim to my right.

I turned immediately and noticed she was looking at her feet and a dark substance that she had stepped in. I put my flashlight on it, and it was a murky green color. It didn't give off any distinct smell, which was weird. However, this part of the tunnel system was a little more musky than others.

"What is it?" Heather questioned her.

"If I knew that, I wouldn't have said 'What is it?', would I?" Alexa shot back sarcastically.

"Step around with it on there, really quick. Tell me what the consistency feels like. Because it looks like a gel," I stated as I inspected her shoe.

As she walked it made a suction sound as it stuck to the ground and pulled off. It seemed to echo louder than everything else up until this point. The sound made Alexa visibly ill; she looked like she was on the verge of throwing up.

"Okay, that's enough. Here, use this to scrape it off," I said as I handed her my pen.

"Thanks, that was disgusting," she said appreciatively.

"It's probably a mold or some other living substance," I told her, trying to help her soothe her stomach. Truth was, I had no clue what that was.

"You're right. Maybe it's some fungus," she replied, seeming to be calming her stomach.

I noticed that Heather had stayed silent after Alexa snapped at her. It wasn't like her to shy from a challenge issued by Alexa. I looked around and found her behind my left arm as if she were hiding from Alexa. As I turned to her, she shot out from behind me and walked forward, prompting us to follow her.

"Hey, slow down a bit, Heather," I almost yelled.

"Why?" she responded playfully.

"Because I don't want you to be in any danger," I said back sternly.

"And I'd be safer standing behind you?" she replied in the same carefree tone.

"Yes, you actually would. If I step on a trap, you and Alexa would be able to react and jump out of it," I told her, explaining my reasoning for her slowing down.

She seemed to resign right there as she slowly pranced back to my side. Alexa didn't seem to enjoy watching that exchange because she just picked up the pace, forcing me to speed up as well. Her body language showed her feelings exactly, she was clearly upset.

I decided to put my hand on her shoulder as a gesture of peace. I wanted her to calm down and not run so rashly into the darkness. After I did that, her resolve softened, and she seemed to acknowledge that she was overreacting. She didn't need to storm off every time I expressed my concern for Heather. She had to calm down. We were friends and I wanted them both to be safe.

As we continued down this hall, I realized it was longer than all of the other ones. Which was confusing, why would this one have such a lengthy walkway? The other two were around maybe one hundred feet long and this one we had already traveled from what I could tell was at least two hundred feet. Even with the length we traveled, it seemed we still had a long way to go to get to the end of this tunnel.

The flashlight illuminated the walls, gray and craggy. Unlike the extended secret pathway that was clean, this tunnel seemed to be hand-dug. As if a team of people with pickaxes chipped away into this rock wall. It was smooth to a degree, where it seemed an organized team had come in and finished the walls with a sander. Whoever dug this must've been really determined. I couldn't imagine the work it'd take to get this far with manual labor. As I finished that thought we landed in front of a door that was completely agape.

Chapter 18

"It seems the plot thickens, Sherlock," I said, turning toward Alexa.

"It sure seems that way, my dear Watson," she rebutted.

I took the first step into this new corridor. As soon as my foot crossed the threshold, my two friends were right with me. We were side by side now. That was when I understood that I wasn't protecting them by sacrificing myself. If anything, it was selfish for me to force that on them.

I guessed I let my ego get the best of me. I did want to protect them, but I thought the best way to do that now was to just let them be with me. If we went down, we'd do it together. We were friends and a team, I had to accept that and let my teammates help me.

It was funny to think that no matter how prolific we pretend to be, we still fall victim to our own humanity. I thought I was above being egotistical and selfish, but in reality, that thought in itself was self-centered. To them, I put up a front showing a different version of myself. But why did I do this? Why do any of us do this? It's hard to think about and even more challenging to explain.

In reality, we don't have a reason to do this at all, yet we do it all of the time. I think it's just the way we work as social creatures, we try to create a different version of ourselves for each person we meet. We judge them before talking to them and create a persona that we think they'll appreciate.

This mental justification is the same justification we give for lying. When we lie to someone, we try to justify it, and the justification we give most commonly is that we were trying to spare them the news it was that really we had. This isn't inherently bad to do, yet could cause problems in the future.

These small lies are like spider silk weaving in and out of our relationships. And like spider silk when there are only a few lines of it then it is weak, but with a multitude of threads woven together, it is incredibly strong.

I kept seeming to get stuck in my own head as we walked aimlessly forward. After the old, rusted iron door, the walkway continued for a short while. Then it abruptly ended with a solid rock wall in front of our faces. The tunnel after the door was completely different from the rugged rock faces before it. This new path seemed almost crystalline. The flashlight looked as if it were hitting cleavage planes as it kept reflecting and dancing along the walls. The tunnel had many missing segments to it but somehow remained smooth.

As we searched this dead end hoping there was some other secret we could unlock, I found a coin. It seemed terribly old, and I couldn't quite make out the date. Yet it appeared to be significant. I mean, why would an old coin the size of a nickel be down here?

"Hey, I found something," I said up to them as I bent over to retrieve the coin.

"What is it?" they both quickly replied.

"I get the impression that it's an old nickel."

"Why would that be here?" Lex said, perplexed.

"I have no clue. Yet here it is at this dead end behind a locked and rusted iron door, so it can't be a coincidence," I said, turning the coin around in my hand.

"Why is it that this tunnel doesn't have lights, but all the others have them? Well, they weren't turned on until we did a puzzle, but this one doesn't have any light fixtures at all, lit or otherwise." As Alexa said this, I realized that this was strange too.

"You're right, all the others had plenty of unlit light fixtures, but they still had light fixtures. It's strange that this would be the only one to have light fixtures omitted from its design. Especially being the only one behind a huge mechanically sealed iron door," I said, thinking aloud.

I kept on shining the flashlight around, hoping to find anything that would give us any semblance of an answer. I then noticed that Heather again was being strangely silent. This was weird, why was now the time she suddenly became so passive? She'd been this way the whole time we'd been in this maze of tunnels.

I watched her fiddle with the hem of her shirt as she appeared to just stare at nothing. It looked to me as though she was in a trance of some kind. Her face was expressionless as she continued to mess with her shirt. Watching her do this was starting to make me feel unsettled. This place was creepy enough without one of my best friends turning into a zombie.

I decided to walk up and touch her shoulder. But as soon as I got close to her, she woke up. She instantly started to move around again, and looked as though she was pretending to be normal. What had happened to her? What could she be thinking about? I felt as though I needed to keep a closer eye on her. I needed to pay closer attention to detail now and make sure she's okay.

I tried to turn my focus away from her and all of her strange actions and instead concentrate on the coin. However, I couldn't get the image of her fidgeting with her shirt out of my head. Something was wrong, there had to be an explanation. I turned the now warm coin in my hand as if willing it to explain to me what was going on.

"Well, this coin has to be important. Let's look for a place to potentially use it. Maybe there's a secret code on the nickel that we use to unlock another door. There is also the possibility of a slot we have to put this in," I said matter of factly.

"Yeah, you could be onto something there, Ryan," Alexa said with a fake smile.

"What do you think, Heather?" I ask while trying to read her body language.

"Hmm… Wait, were you talking to me?" she asked with a confused look on her face.

"Yes, Earth to Heather, got any ideas where we could use this coin?" I asked her again calmly.

"Well, there is this vending machine in the library. But it's probably not hooked up to anything. Even if it was, the electricity in this place seems shoddy at best," she replied methodically in her answer, leaving the scared and shy girl behind. She was now one of the most confident people I knew, taking over Alexa's space for the time being.

"Unless you have any better ideas, Alexa, I think we should try the vending machine," I said, leading the way back to the library. It wasn't hard to find our way back to the ladder because since we were now on the middle path it was a straight shot back. We walked side by side in the narrow pathway almost shoulder to shoulder. As we walked, I paid attention to the sounds being made. I wanted to know where the splashing came from and what was making it. However, the only sounds that echoed off the walls were the pitter-patter of feet stepping on concrete.

You could instantly tell each of us apart by the sound of our shoes. Heather was happy, almost skipping with sounds only hitting the floor every few seconds. Whereas Alexa was the opposite, having a heavy stomping sound. My footsteps sounded calm and cool, keeping a perfect pace.

Then, as we were about to reach the ladder, I heard the splash again. I spun around so fast you would've thought I heard a gunshot. I gave up on being rational and chased the sound.

"You guys go check the vending machine. I need to find that sound," I yelled back, tossing the coin to my right. I didn't expect it to hit the wall because I knew Alexa was right there, and the coin didn't make any sound, as she caught it she stopped in her tracks. She must've been in shock that I'd put so much faith into knowing she was there.

I had no time to think about any of this as I was starting to hear the noise more frequently. It was coming from the room where Heather solved the baby puzzle. I made it into the room and found the sound, but it wasn't what I was expecting at all. The thing making the sound was a liquid dripping from the ceiling.

It slammed against the concrete, splashing into a wide puddle. I expected to see a pipe, or I really don't know because the sound kept moving around before. This puddle had to have more to it, I knew there was something wrong with it. This ooze was the same color as the thing Alexa had stepped in.

It was definitely organic, that much was true. Nothing about the substance screamed synthetic to me. As I stood there staring at this puddle in wonder, I didn't realized that my friends hadn't follow me. I guessed they either thought I'd be fine or just didn't care about me as much as I had believed. At any rate, I guessed that explained the splashing, however, it didn't explain why it came from so many places. I guessed the echo in these chambers also could explain that and why it appeared to be behind that wall.

I ran back to the middle and back up to the ladder finding that they hadn't waited up at all. There was no protest to me running off, just the acceptance of it. It was dumb of me to run away without them, yet I did do it as some kind of test. It may not have seemed like one, but my intention was to see if Heather would follow me. Because every other time I did something, Heather seemed to follow me, but this time she didn't. It was also a test for Alexa. She never listened to my commands. Even with the initial shock of my trust in her, I would've imagined she'd still have followed me.

Maybe I'm reading too much into this, I said in my head, trying to calm myself down. I climbed up the ladder and up to the library. I casually jogged out of the unfinished basement and into the main room. I was met with two girls looking at a piece of paper on a table. It appeared to be made of the same material as the paper I had gotten at my house.

"Hey, I'm okay. Not that you two were worried about me," I said with a little pain entering my voice.

"You said to go check out the vending machine, and ran off without us. It's your fault we didn't follow you," Alexa said coldly, without even turning her gaze toward me.

"Yeah, you basically told us not to wait up for you, Ryan. Which is pretty out of character for you. You doing okay?" Heather questioned me calmly without looking up from the table.

"You're right... I'm sorry I ran off without you two. Something in me just snapped. I needed to find that sound. Don't you want to know what I found?" I replied dejectedly.

"Sure," they both responded again without even looking at me.

"Alexa, you remember that goo you stepped in? Well, I found a pretty large puddle of it in the baby puzzle room. It was dripping from the ceiling and making a pretty loud echo," I said, chronicling my little excursion.

"I guess that solves one mystery," Alexa said softly.

"Anyways, would you two like to share with the class what you found?" I said, finally asking them to see what they had on the table.

"Oh, not at all, here, Ryan," Heather said to me as I sat down next to her. I could feel the daggers that Alexa was staring at me but at the moment I didn't care.

"Thanks, Heather," I said, leaning closer to her to be able to look at the parchment.

The page in front of me now looked to be a map of sorts. It had a legend in the bottom left corner explaining the symbols we saw. Many of the symbols seemed pretty self-explanatory and didn't really have any confusing pictures. My eyes were instantly drawn to a grove of trees that were behind this building. These trees also had small lettering below them saying, *182 flip*. This was obviously significant and was probably the way for us to continue this confusing journey.

As I pointed this out to the girls, we heard the loud roaring of engines. The sound was unmistakable. There was a group of cars driving up to the old library. I ushered them into a secret compartment I had first noticed when walking in. I slid in behind them and closed the exit behind us. As we sat in this dark little cubby, we heard the sound of boots stomping into the building. The sound of six or seven men walking through the library was unsettling. I then heard the sound of an eighth man walking into the library. These footsteps seemed to silence all of the quiet chatter, so we could only assume this man was important.

I turned to Heather, about to say something, as she held a finger to my lips in a shush gesture. Alexa also frowned in silence as we listened to the man shouting orders. We could hear everything he said.

"Find them. One male and two females. My daughter is among this party. If you should find her first, then bring her to me. If I see one scratch or bruise on her, it's your head. **Literally**." The mystery man barked this loudly, and as soon as he finished talking the scattering of the men sounded throughout the building.

I think I could guess whose father this was, but I didn't want to think about that. I didn't want to think of what he'd do when he found us, namely me and Alexa. I sat there shaking softly. However, in comparison to the other two people in there with me, my soft movement was nothing. Heather and Alexa both had tremors running through their bodies. They obviously were brimming with fear of what would be done to them if caught.

I pulled them both close and wrapped my arms around them. I knew I couldn't protect them if we were found, but I also knew that we couldn't be found. I knew for a fact that we wouldn't be caught. This cubby wasn't on that old map at all, meaning that it wasn't in the original design either. That meant that even though these men "built" this building they didn't know where we were. I held both of the girls in a firm grip, and they seemed to both stop shaking simultaneously. The stillness didn't last long though because as soon as we heard stomping go by our hiding spot, we all started to shake. They seemed to have stopped right in front of where we were hiding.

Chapter 19

I sat there holding them close to me, terrified of what might happen if we got caught. We'd already escaped them once. I had no clue whether we could do the same thing. As we trembled, the knob on the tiny door slowly turned but didn't open. We heard a deep voice boom from a distance.

"Get over here!" the voice shouted to presumably whoever was about to discover us.

"Yes, sir," the person outside the small door replied as we saw the door handle return to its original state.

I rubbed their backs softly as I realized that we were safe for now. As fast as the men appeared, they had vanished. I assumed they had found what we did and were now searching down below. The small compartment we were in was pitch black, and I could barely see my own knees pressed into my chest. The smells of both of the girls in front of me had mixed into a powerful odor. Which was why, I'd guessed, the first man tried to open the compartment in the first place.

We heard the rushing of footsteps in front of the door to our hiding spot again as the men ran into the other side of the building. I thought they were more focused on hiding something than finding us. They seemed to have made sure that whatever we were looking for wouldn't be found. What had we been searching for anyway? We were just following clues to somewhere, but what would we find when we made it to the end? Was the ending to this quest going to be happy or horrible? I guessed only time could tell us that.

"Hey, what do you think they're doing?" I said to the girls.

"Who cares? They're hunting us, Ryan!" Alexa silently shouted.

"They're some group from my father's company," Heather said sheepishly.

"I figured that out from the first comment made by their commander," I replied, giving her a soft scratch on the shoulder to comfort her.

The men walked past the entrance to our hiding spot again. Directly after this, I heard a couple of the cars that had pulled up previously now speeding away. We then heard a much louder booming set of footsteps heading out the door.

He grunted and then yelled, "Find them now! They have the map. If we don't have them all, we could lose everything."

What were they talking about? Whatever we had stepped into was way bigger than I had ever imagined. First, my and Alexa's families had disappeared. Now we were being hunted by a dark organization of men. Was there some kind of treasure being hidden, or something more sinister underneath this building? As I was thinking this, I heard another set of engines turn over and start to reverse out of the parking lot.

"Looks like they're leaving," I whispered.

"Maybe. But we better wait here for a while longer to make sure the coast is clear," Heather replied.

"She's right, we need to stay out of sight and in the shadows for now," Alexa affirmed.

I tried to look for a crack in the door to see if I could sneak a glance at our surroundings. But it was as if this door hadn't aged at all. There was no discernable rot on this wooden door, even though it had been in this uninsulated building for years.

We sat there eerily still for another five minutes until I decided to break our "vow of silence" and open the door just a crack. I looked around and saw no one. Figuring we were in the clear, I opened the door and climbed out. Suddenly, I felt unsteady standing where I was and tried to balance myself on the walls. All of my attempts were in vain as I crashed down to the ground, landing on my side.

"Ryan! Are you okay?!" I heard Heather shout as she stepped out of the cubby.

"Yeah, I just felt really weak and unbalanced for a second," I responded to her calmly.

"Ryan. I'm really starting to worry about you," Alexa chimed in, clearly unsettled by all that she knew about me.

"Really, it's nothing, guys," I replied, trying to hold my composure.

"You just collapsed to the ground out of nowhere. That's not nothing, Ryan," Heather said in a scolding tone.

As I dusted myself off, I made it a point to show them I was fine by hopping on one leg.

"See, if something was wrong with me, would I be able to do this?" I said snarkily.

"We're just concerned for your health and wellbeing," Alexa shot back.

"There's nothing wrong with that. But I'm telling you, I'm fine. I promise," I said while crossing my heart.

"If you say so..." they both replied in unison.

We walked out of the library to see nothing in the parking lot. I sighed a sigh of relief and then began walking around the building.

"What are you doing?" Heather shouted to me.

"Following what the map said," I said back.

"It just had the words *182 flip* underneath a set of trees," Alexa commented.

"That's exactly where I'm going, to see if there's any form of hint as to what to do next," I replied.

We got to the back of the building, and I found a small group of nine trees. I walked through them, and I noticed they had strange symbols on them. Each symbol seemed to be very similar, with each future iteration progressing in complexity. These symbols were different from the first puzzle's symbols, more complex, and looked to be only softly carved into each tree. When I looked at the tree roughly, in the center it appeared to have a combination lock engraved in the middle of its trunk. I rotated the discs and saw that the symbols on the trees were inscribed into them.

"Hey, come look at this!" I shouted to the two girls, who were circling different trees.

"What is it?" Alexa said as she walked up next to me.

"This tree has a combination lock that has all of the symbols that are on the other trees," I replied.

I walked around the clearing to check each of the trees. Which one of these could be the starting point? I figured if we could find the start of this, we could find the combination.

"I think I've broken the code, Ryan," Heather said calmly.

I stepped back to let her step up to the tree. She walked up to the center tree and input the code she assumed to be correct. The tree shuddered and then a compartment opened up lower on the trunk. I stared, dumbfounded.

"How did you do that?" I asked.

"It was simple, each of the symbols seemed to be evolving. Starting with a basic design and then developing into more complex images. The code on the paper said 'one-two-eight flip'. I guessed that 'flip' meant for us to switch the code to two-eight-one. Then I used the symbols from the trees that corresponded with those numbers based on the complexity of the design," she said nonchalantly.

"Good job, Heather," I said in reply.

She figured that out within minutes of us seeing this puzzle. It did seem simple when explained, almost a little too simple compared to the last challenge. I walked up to the tree and stood next to Heather and Alexa to investigate the new compartment that had opened up.

I bent over to look into the new space. It was like a safety deposit box at a bank. The inside walls of the small opening were all metal with a singular ornate key in the middle. The key was standing vertically, placed on a slotted pedestal.

"Is this it?" I said as I reached into the slot.

"Wait!" Alexa shouted at me.

I froze just before grabbing the key.

"What?" I replied.

"What if it's a trap?" she said, with concern staining her face.

"Yeah," Heather agreed quietly.

"Well, fine, you guys, step back and I'll trigger the trap if it is one. But I don't think it would be right after a puzzle like that," I responded.

"Fine..." Alexa said, sighing audibly.

They both stepped away from the tree as I reached inside and grasped the key. I lifted it out of the pedestal, and as soon as I pulled it to me the compartment closed. I turned smugly, smiling because nothing appeared to have happened.

However, the girls didn't return the smile, instead they stared in horror as I heard a sound behind me. The tree was making a sound similar to metal scraping on concrete. I turned and looked down as I got swallowed into the new hole that had been created where the tree was standing.

I heard them scream, "Ryan!" as I slid deeper into the abyss below me.

I flailed my arms around, trying to catch something to save myself. Except the walls all around me were completely smooth, with nothing to grab onto. I slid the key into my pocket to keep it safe. Then I continued to strain my eyes, looking for any place to grab. The darkness enveloped me like in the nightmares, nothing was visible, it was pitch black. My descent seemed to be infinite as I had still not hit the floor.

I looked up to see that the hatch I had fallen into was shut, meaning they couldn't see what would happen to me. I finally accepted that this might be my end because there would surely be no way for me to survive this.

As these thoughts crossed my mind I thought of the girls and all of the good times we'd had. I really was lucky to have friends like them. Why hadn't I just listened to them? They were right. I couldn't believe I kept making the same reckless decisions.

Finally, I felt the crushing weight of gravity throwing me into a sticky substance. My legs were suspended in a weird goo, but I didn't feel any pain from the impact. The substance was somewhat room temperature. I reached in and grabbed a handful of it. It was also very malleable. Fearing something bad happening, I tried to feel around to get my bearings, yet I couldn't grab or touch anything besides the goo below me. It was like there was nothing around me as I flailed my arms around in the vacant space.

The only option I had was to try to dig my way out of the substance. I cupped my hands together, and then started scooping the viscous liquid away from my legs. When I was sure that enough of it was removed from above my legs, I slowly wriggled free. It was difficult to get my footing on the goo, so I slowly crawled over the top of it, trying not to sink. It felt like I was trying to escape the center of a trampoline. Each movement I made sent shockwaves through the substance making it increasingly harder to get anywhere.

I finally reached a location where I felt a smooth concrete pad. The pad was around three or four inches above the goo. I used my upper body to pull myself onto the land.

"Thank god," I said with a sigh of relief.

I'd felt like I was going to be stuck in that pit without a chance of escape. Who knew how wide the thing could be? The distance I traveled from the middle had to be at least thirty feet. It was still pitch black in the room I was in. I tentatively stood up and extended my arms to feel in case something was in front of me. I moved my arms in the vacant space as I walked forward at a slow speed. I reached a solid wall made of some sort of metal. I felt my way along the wall until I reached the impression of a door. My eyes finally started to adjust to the darkness, and I saw a faint outline of a keypad on the impression.

"Of course." I sighed dejectedly at the sight.

Nothing is ever simple and easy. I focused hard, trying to think of any codes or numbers we may have walked past this day. But the trauma and danger of the last twenty-four hours just kept blocking my thoughts as soon as I made any headway. I felt saddened that my self-importance and false bravado pulled me away from the people I said I'd protect. How could I let them down like this after all that had happened? I had to find a way out of here. I didn't want them to worry about me. I slumped against the wall, feeling defeated. I stared at the ground, my eyes starting to get heavy, and I felt myself slipping away from reality.

Nightmare 7

I woke to find myself still in the darkness. The wisp was gone and all that was left was me. I stared out into the black room and shouted, or at least tried to as no noise escaped me. I listened and couldn't hear anything. I tried to get to my feet, but I couldn't move. I was helpless in my heart. I knew I shouldn't, but I felt like giving up. What was the point of fighting so hard if every challenge I overcame led me to pain? As I thought this, I saw a faint figure in the distance, standing looking down at me. The figure looked similar to Alexa's. They appeared to be at the other end of the room.

I tried again to move and successfully get to my feet. I walked over to the figure, but it disappeared as I reached it. Of course it would, why wouldn't it just leave, I thought to myself. I felt like I was getting nowhere. A voice suddenly burst into my head, much deeper than the child's voice of the wisp, "Ryan, where are you? Where did you go? You were always like this... You rush in without care and get hurt." I had no idea where this voice was coming from or whose voice it was, but it touched my heart. I started to cry. I had no control. I felt utterly helpless. I've felt this feeling before, I thought to myself. Why do we feel these feelings? Despair, fear, sorrow, depression, we experience a plethora of emotions in a day, and it seems the two extremes are the ones we feel the most. Nothing is better than pure and true happiness, but nothing is worse than the indescribable feeling of loss you experience from losing a loved one whether it be a person or pet. Whether it be death or simply growing apart from people you once knew, that feeling of loss can break you. If you let it, loss will swallow you whole, but that's what makes us human. The struggles we face are unique but similar.

I thought this to myself while my tears fell down my face. Then I remembered one particularly important thing, "help is often where you least expect it". As I recalled this message, a door opened in front of me, a rectangle of pure light in the pitch darkness. I walked towards it, calmer than before, and stepped into the light. As I did, I landed in the hiding spot we had used to escape Heather's father. The girls were gone, but on the wall behind where we were hidden, a number was scrawled into the concrete. The number was four. Then another door opened against that wall, and I walked through it into the underground button room. With all fifty buttons lit up green. Then it replayed the pillar with two blades coming out of the wall and moving back and forth the length of the room four times.

The wall opened all the way, and another portal was behind it. I stepped into the portal and got transported back to the pitch-black room. Except it was no longer fully pitch black now, it had mini versions of my memories with the numbers floating above them as if telling me to remember them. Then it started to shuffle them, one with the room memory first, then the second with the pillar memory, and the last being the button memory. The room flashed red slightly, then the memories started to shuffle again. This time with the pillar memory first then the room memory, and last the buttons, it too flashed the room red. It shuffled one more time, with the button memory first, then the room, and lastly the pillar memory. It stopped, and then the room turned a blinding green. I remembered the numbers as the world started to return to me. Fifty, four, two, four.

Chapter 20

I awoke next to the door to the room. Just where I had passed out previously. I touched the keypad and it lit up. I entered the code, fifty, four, two, four and hit enter. The keys flashed green and the door made a very old scraping sound as it unlocked, and I slid it open. Inside the door, a faint light shone through. I stepped into the light and even though it was dim it still blinded me as my eyes adjusted. I squinted my eyes to see a small workshop in front of me.

Tables and bookshelves were lining the walls. All filled to the brim with ancient-looking tombs. With a single leather recliner in the center, with an oak side table. A small candelabra illuminated the room with three light bulbs imitating wicks. I walked up to a bookshelf and said, "What do we have here? Why would that slime room lead to a study?"

A small groan came from behind me, and I jumped away, startled.

"D-d-don't come any closer, whatever you are!" I yelled.

"Shut up, you buffoon," it replied in a snarky voice.

"Alexa?" I said, quietly pondering how she got down here.

"What? That's preposterous!!" the voice responded in a shrill tone.

"Who are you?" I asked.

"Who am I? WHO AM I? WHO ARE YOU?! To appear in my study that I had so securely hidden from the world," they said.

I continued to look around and saw no figure or even shadow of a person.

"I'm sure you're confused, and I bet I pegged some of your questions before you asked them. But you needn't bother talking to me. I am recording this audio log on the off chance someone falls into my trap *cough* secret entrance *cough* and manages to get into my study. For you must be remarkable or perhaps just incredibly lucky. I have long since left this world for I could not find a way to cure the ailments that affect me. On these bookshelves you will find an immense amount of research into a variety of topics, chief among them being my study into the very company that built this building for me. They told me it was to assist in my research, but why would they create such elaborate underground tunnels to be my lab? Couldn't they just create a normal lab above ground? My thoughts exactly. The people I had met during the initiation of this project were all very gung-ho about setting everything up. However, they seemed to be afraid of something or someone, so they added a plethora of traps, one of which I used to be the entrance to a hidden study that they did not know about. Secretly, I watched them, studied their mannerisms, and tried to decode their hidden agenda. I saw many oddities and many actions taken with malicious intent, including some done to children. But none of these ever seemed to have any correlation or sound reasoning as to why they would act this way. In the end, I was unable to do so before my expiration date. So, brave soul who has made it here and activated this message. Please use my research to understand why they are doing what they are. Signing off for the last time, Doctor Zirdan." With that the audio recording ended and I was left with even more questions.

I sighed, "Well it doesn't ever get any easier, does it."

I walked over to a bookshelf and pulled out a few books, all seeming to be dated in a specific way. Not in any normal fashion but almost as if whoever was writing them did not write days and instead ordered them sequentially by days spent in this room. The walls were filled with them. I walked over to the last bookshelf, and the last day number was 765. Whoever Doctor Zirdan was had written a journal each day for more than two years.

I decided that taking out a few books might be a clever idea while I try to look for a way out of this trap he so lovingly described as an entrance to his secret world. Reading these books gave me a foreboding sense of melancholy. They seemed to be detailing one man's descent into madness.

However, it appeared he seemed to recognize that he was going insane and would write to himself in the third person to make him feel more at ease. Statements like "hang in there" or "it's almost time" were words of affirmation he seemed to give himself, as if he would have forgotten in the future what he had written and would find these sentiments upon review of his own writings.

He explained in a series of days what it was like for him to go from doing his work to then hiding in this secret surveillance room/research lab. Explaining how everyone seemed to be normal, but then when he watched them in secret guards would talk in military lingo, and would often use Morse code to communicate via walkie-talkie instead of speaking. It was very strange to him.

Then I finally got to a book that gave more insight into what work was being done at this facility. Doctor Zirdan explained that he was working with human test subjects to alter their genetic code. Zirdan was working with disabled veterans as human guinea pigs, and was trying to find a way to replace limbs and even vital organs by rewriting their genetic code. The only problem was that the facility had not been finished, and so a substantial portion of his specified machinery was never installed or even created for him to finish these treatments. The next journal talked about him rewriting this genetic code to regrow the limbs and organs stronger than before in an almost Frankenstein-like amalgamation. However, he had never finished writing these journals, so I had no clue what happened as the last journal explained that he had been hidden away for four days and knew that they were looking for him. He also wrote almost angrily about his assistants, who seemed to become more adept in their performance as the days went on, and was afraid of being replaced by them in the near future. Whatever the reason these plans were scrapped was not clear to me right now, but what was clear was that I needed to get out of here as soon as possible.

I looked around the room, trying to discern how he would leave this room, but found little clues to explain how I should escape. It felt like this room was completely sealed and the other "trapped room" was more of an oubliette than anything. Where escape could be seen but not obtained as you sunk deeper into the goo to eventually die.

But Doctor Zirdan must have had ways out of here, as he was in and out of this study on a daily basis, it seemed from his detailed writings.

I walked over to the bookcase and said, "If I were an evil scientist, where would I put an exit? Obviously behind the bookshelf. DUH!"

I started tearing books off the shelves and looked for some form of lever or button to press. But none were made apparent even as the bookcase stood barren from my rampage.

I paced around the room, worried about the girls freaking out, trying to find me. It was funny, I thought how we could be in just as much danger as someone we cared about, and would think about them before ourselves. I was sure they were freaking out just as much as I was. They were probably at each others' throats, each trying to pin the blame on the other for not pulling me to safety. But no one was to blame for my recklessness but myself.

I sat in the large leather-bound chair and pondered where a hidden exit could be. Since clichés weren't working, maybe a more obvious approach would do the trick. I walked over to the brick wall that appeared behind the bookshelves when I had removed the books that were blocking it, and stared intently at the pattern. I scanned the wall for what felt like an eternity to see if I could pick out any changes. As I was about to give up, I saw a small hole appear that didn't seem to be from the decaying grout. It was about the perfect width of a slender index finger.

I tried to fit my index finger into the hole but to no avail. Then I tried my pinkie and it worked. I felt the smooth texture of a small plastic button. I pressed the button and the bookshelf slid out of the way to reveal an entrance into the hallways below the library.

I crept carefully into the hallways and used the walls to guide me as this hallway had no light in it at all. The small candelabra from the last room barely illuminated the entrance to the hall. I held onto the wall, slowly sliding along it towards the other end that I had assumed would lead to the main passageways. I couldn't see how far I had left to go, so I just kept putting one foot in front of the other.

I slammed into a solid wall with a large thud, not expecting to hit the end of this corridor so fast. I regained my footing and slid my hands up and down the new wall until I found another small button. I pressed this button, and the wall spun around, throwing me face-first into the underground passageways.

I heard a scream come from the other end of the new hall I had found myself on the floor of, and saw a familiar sight running towards me.

"RYAN!?! Are you okay!?" they said.

"I'm fine. More confused than hurt. Are you two okay?" I replied.

"Of course we're okay. We didn't slide down a death pit," Alexa Responded.

"It wasn't a death pit. I'm alive and well. See?" I said, doing a slight spin.

"Leave it to you to make light of almost dying. But I'm so glad you're okay anyway," Heather whispered while hugging me tightly.

Alexa stared at us, looking upset.

Alexa then walked over to us, slid her hand under Heather's and broke the hug apart.

"Enough of that, it's time to go," Alexa said dryly. She was trying so hard to appear as if she didn't care and just wanted to get out of the underground. I still had no clue why she had been acting like this, but I shrugged it off and agreed with her anyways.

"Yeah, it's getting too spooky for me down here anyways. We should get going," I said.

We walked back through the maze-like tunnels and made it back to where we had originally entered the underground. I walked ahead of the girls to check the corner as we went up the stairs. *It appears they all really did leave*, I thought to myself. How could they leave like that, thinking we had disappeared? Or were they just letting us go to have a feeling of security?

"Hey, are you going to let us in on your thoughts, or are we going to have to beat them out of you, dork?" Alexa said while poking my side.

"I'm sorry, I was just wondering why they hadn't left even one person in case we had just been hiding and not run away from the library. It just makes no sense. Could they have let us go on purpose, to lure us into a trap in the future?" I replied.

"I was thinking the exact same thing," Heather said.

"Well, it's official, this is the first time we are all in agreement this whole time. I'm not sure if that's a good sign or a very terrible one," Alexa said.

"How could it be a bad sign? I for one am glad we're all on the same page," I shot back.

"We definitely need to think of a plan before we continue, and no matter how much we hate this place, it seems like they aren't coming back anytime soon, so we should probably stay here at least for the night," Heather said in a hushed tone.

"It is pretty late. Well, relatively speaking, winter makes everything feel later than it really is. It's actually five P.M.," I replied.

"Yeah, we all know how winter days are shorter, Ryan. There's no need to pretend to be so smart," Alexa snarkily said.

"Okay. It's settled, we stay here for the night. But we should really look for a place with more insulation because this is not going to help us stay alive," I said, pointing to the enormous hole in the roof of the building above us.

"Now that you mention it, I am freezing. We should go towards a more finished portion of the library," Heather said.

"So, it's settled, we split up and look around the first floor for somewhere to get comfortable for the night?" I asked them. Both replied with a nod, and we set off on our separate ways.

I wandered towards the front of the library again, seeing the sunset reflect off the yellowing glass and spreading a dazzling light show into the foyer. I walked over to the finished desk where a librarian would have sat, and dragged one finger along the top of it while I walked. I picked up my hand as I reached the end of the desk and saw the filth my finger had picked up with a sense of melancholy. I looked around and saw the empty shelves in the distance and the sun-stained walls and floors. A deep feeling of forlornness entered me. *What have we come to? Being essentially pushed out of our homes for fear of capture. What did we do to deserve this?* I questioned myself.

I thought this while mindlessly walking in the front portion of the library, stopping at a shelf that had some books stacked in it as if whoever had been stacking them had just vanished without warning, leaving a tilted stack of children's books. I flipped through the stack and came across a book that reminded me of home. "If you give a mouse a cookie..." Seeing the cover instantly gave me a hit of nostalgia.

Thinking of being a child again, I mindlessly flipped the pages of the book, hoping that they would open up into some sort of portal and I could return to the days when I had so much less to worry about. I'd certainly never seen myself embroiled in a chase with some sort of government agency. *Don't we all long for the days when times were simpler?* I thought to myself. As I thought this, I sat down next to the shelf to keep looking, but I felt something poking me from in my pocket. That's right, I had my pen and notebook with me. With all of the stuff that had happened up until now, I'd had little time to think about writing again. But I couldn't think of a better time to write with this deep wave of nostalgia washing over me. Why not indulge it a little more and go back to before this had all happened?

The Lion Who Wanted to Reach the Moon Ch. 5

The lion awoke to a strange sight above him. The sun had risen into the sky. His mind felt more clear than before, but he still felt as though something was missing. He turned to see both his companions fine, sleeping on his back.

"Phew." He breathed a sigh of relief.

Immediately he wondered why he was so relieved to have them still by his side. They had seemed like burdens before, or if not burdens more like minor annoyances. But now it seemed as if he could not do without them.

I can be alone and not worry about it, he thought. I was alone before this anyway. As he was thinking this, the sun started to shrink in the sky until the other stars came out, with the moon not far behind.

The lion walked towards the moon with renewed confidence in his journey. As he walked across the clearing, he found that it had a large ravine between him and the next cliff face to climb. How can I make it across that? he pondered.

"Hey, dummy, what are you thinking?" the snake hissed.

"How am I going to reach the other mountain in front of us? It seems too far to jump but I might be able to if I go to that branch over there," he said, nodding towards a branch that reached half the distance between the two mountains.

149

"I don't know. That branch looks pretty sketchy. Seems like a bad idea," the snake replied.

"How do you propose we make it then?" he said.

After hearing this, the owl sprang to life and flew over to his head.

"I could carry the snake across and then look for some branches to make that particular branch stronger. I could tie some more sturdy branches to it and help its integrity," the owl said loudly, interrupting the two.

"Okay, we will do that then," the lion said without giving the snake the chance to protest.

The owl carried the snake over to the other side of the gorge and then started frantically flying around the other mountain, picking up sturdy branches. The owl flew back and started to fix the branch hanging off the lion's mountain, and then flapped her wings to hover next to it as if she were saying she was complete with her task.

The lion walked over to the branch, and then got a running start to bound across the gap. However, as soon as he stepped onto the branch, it made a loud CRACK! sound, and in an instant he vanished, falling to the bottom of the pit as the snake and the owl cried out in fear.

The lion slowed his descent by trying to hook his claws into the rock, but all it did was marginally help. Eventually, he hit the bottom of the pit, landing on a tremendous pile of leaves, cushioning him. The sides of the ravine fell down around him until they sealed him beneath the rubble.

"Do you think he's okay?" the owl said calmly.

"HOW? Just how could he possibly be okay?! He fell all the way down that pit and was now trapped beneath an enormous pile of rubble," the snake replied, seething.

Meanwhile, a couple hundred feet below the explosive argument on the surface, the lion looked around, his eyes adjusting immediately to the darkness. The small beams of light shining through the rubble allowed him to survey his surroundings in perfect clarity. He shook his head to get it straight as he still felt somewhat dizzy from the fall.

Now. How do I get out of here? he pondered. Hmm, seems going straight back up would be too troublesome. Seeing as I have to break through the rocks above *me to even attempt to climb up, he thought aloud.*

Then an idea comes to him as he stretched his paws out to feel that the wall was made of a soft soil. I can dig into the side of the mountain to get out of here. I need to be careful while building this tunnel, but it should be significantly easier than trying to lift all the boulders above me.

So, with his plan in mind, he carefully constructed a tunnel that wound up and around the rock tomb he was previously in.

As he broke through the soil wall above the rock, he climbed out to see the snake and owl waiting for him.

"What took you so long?" the snake said snarkily.

"We were worried when you couldn't hear us, and the rock pile had stopped shifting," the owl tagged on.

"I am fine now. I had to dig around the rocks because going through them would have taken too much time. Speaking of time, what time is it right now?" the lion replied.

"It appears to be midnight," the owl said to him.

"Then we must make haste. We were almost to the moon before I fell. Climb on and I will use the proximity of these walls to scale up the mountain again," the lion replied with a harried expression.

Both of his companions climbed atop his back, and he started bounding off of the walls, jumping all the way back to where they had started, but with his current momentum, he was able to make the gap the second time, and they landed atop the opposite cliffside from where they had started.

As he reached the cliff face, he felt a sense of heaviness take over his body. All of the work from that night seemed to have finally taken its toll on him. The lion's legs started to burn as he lay down on the ledge.

"Hey, bozo, what are you doing? We're burning moonlight," the snake said, annoyed.

"I need a rest, all of the day's work is beating me down. I feel very faint," the lion replied.

"Tonight has been a very busy night indeed. Take your rest, you deserve it," the owl said sweetly.

"Thank you. I think I will," he replied as his eyelids got heavy, and he looked

up to the moon one more time and gave it an apologetic glance as he drifted off to sleep.

Chapter 21

I put the heavy metal pen I had been writing with into the binding of my notebook and then slowly shut it to find a pair of green eyes staring into mine just a few inches away from my face.

"Oh. Hey, Heather, I didn't notice you there," I said, feeling a little embarrassed.

"It's no problem, I enjoy watching you write. It's comforting to see you feeling better. Will you maybe let me read what you've been writing one day?" Heather replied in a hushed tone.

"Did you guys find a place to lay down for the night? Also, how did you get Alexa to let you out of her sight? She seems to be watching you like a hawk more and more as our time together extends," I asked her, utterly confused, how she managed to shake Alexa.

"I have my ways, and yes we did find a place to settle down for the night," Heather said with a wink that made all the hair on my body stand on end.

I felt a blush softly develop and cover my face, feeling embarrassed that a comment like that could give me goosebumps. Heather just seemed to know how to push the right buttons. I just enjoyed being in her company. Honestly, a part of me is sad that she came back, but the selfish side of me was so happy to see her again. I really had missed her since she left all those years ago. Even in these circumstances, she seemed to be able to bring me out of my own head and make me feel okay about our current situation.

She smiled at me, knowing that she'd got the reaction she wanted from me.

"Come on. Let's go to the place we found," she said while gesturing over her shoulder.

"Okay," I replied, and we stood up and walked toward the science fiction portion of the library, or at least where the science fiction portion should have been.

I looked around at the almost fully empty shelves, and then I walked over to Alexa who was very intently focused on a pair of sleeping bags she had brought in her backpack.

"Looks like you're one sleeping bag short. So, who's going to share?" I said slyly.

"Pfft. You'd love that, wouldn't you? As if we'd end up sharing a sleeping bag. Especially after the day we had," Alexa replied angrily.

"Woah. I didn't mean it literally; it was just a joke. I don't need a sleeping bag, it's not even that cold here," I said, backing down.

"I'd share with you, Ryan," Heather said in a sing-song tone.

"Of course you would… Gah! This entire day has just been the worst," Alexa shouted at us.

"It's fine, Heather. I really won't be sharing a sleeping bag with anyone. Plus, someone has to stay up and watch in case those goons come back," I said, trying to calm the hectic situation.

"No. It's not fair. We should stay up in shifts," Alexa replied in a strained tone.

"Okay, it's settled, we take shifts to keep watch. I'll keep watch first," I said to the group, and they both nodded slightly. Each girl got into their sleeping bag and turned away from the other.

I walked towards the entrance to the section and sat down on a beanbag chair meant to encourage people to sit and read if the library had ever fully opened. I stared up at the ceiling, wondering what I'd done to make Alexa so mad. I mean, I understood that she was just as stressed as we all were about losing our parents and being hunted, but still, why was her anger targeted at me?

I didn't feel like I deserved this treatment. All I'd done these past few days was try to make sure everyone was okay and safe. Too bad everything had to turn out the way it did. Would we ever be able to go back to normal after this? Were we fugitives? I asked myself these questions while I felt the beanbag start to crumple more than it already was. I started sinking backward into it, wishing it would just swallow me whole and I could just disappear. But then I thought about the girls and how selfish it was of me to want it to happen, but it didn't stop me from still feeling like it would all be better if I were just gone.

It seemed everyone I cared about ended up getting hurt whether that be by me or someone coming for me for whatever reason. I looked at my leg and frown.

"This is all your fault!" I quietly screamed at my leg.

I shook my head as tears of anger started to well up in my eyes. All of a sudden, I felt a cold wind blow against my cheek. That's strange, I thought to myself. Aren't we far enough away from the doors and broken glass windows to not have any drafts blow through? I looked around to see if there were any openings that would allow the wind to blow this chilling winter air at me. But it appeared that there were no openings that would allow this biting cold into the section we were occupying. *I should go check on the girls. Something doesn't feel right.*

I turned around and walked towards the place where the girls were sleeping and saw them both comfortable in their sleeping bags. Neither one was moving, which I took as a good sign, there was no tossing and turning so they were fine. Hopefully, we all just needed some sleep to recharge and feel better about everything that had been happening recently.

The cold biting wind then lifted up the hem of my shirt, and I turned around to investigate where the wind was coming from. I walked towards the source of the mysterious wind. It appeared to be coming from the fantasy portion of the library.

I slowly progressed through the library while my eyes started to adjust to the darkness yet again today. I crept through each section, leading towards the wind, to not make any sound that could wake the girls who were just sixty feet away from me. The library had a cavernous set of acoustics that made each step feel like an orchestra should be emphasizing my movements.

The loud echo bouncing off the glass panes and empty bookshelves made me overly conscious of the noise I was making while walking. I finally reached where the wind was coming from, and it was a tiny hole in a glass pane that led to the outside. Weird that I was only feeling the breeze now, and not at all during the rest of the day.

I smirked, happy that for once it wasn't some horrible thing happening to us again. Sometimes things aren't as bad as they seem. In my mind, it was Heather's father returning with his crew to finally tie off the loose ends of the string that he had left blowing in the wind. I had this image of them setting up small portable AC units all around the library to freeze us out and force us directly into their trap. But it wasn't that, thankfully it was just a small chip in a glass pane. I walked up to the chipped hole and ripped a piece of paper from my notebook, sticking it through it and letting the wind blow it flat against the glass. Creating a seal that blocked the slight breeze that was coming into the old library.

After closing the hole, I returned to where we had set up camp to watch over the two most important people still in my life. If anything were to happen to them, I didn't know what I'd do. I didn't know why I did this. I always put others above myself. In a way, I felt that it was not as selfless as I wished to believe, but more of a hollow fear of being alone. Loneliness is one of the hardest emotions to deal with. Humans are social creatures and isolation does terrible things to our fragile brains. We want to pretend we are the pinnacle of evolution, yet without the other people around us we would fall to our surroundings. Isolation brings out the worst in us and is the easiest way to weaken us. This must have been why Heather's dad took our families from us.

To isolate us and keep us on the run. He knew that with enough time he could probably manipulate us into turning on one another. But we couldn't let that happen. We needed to stand strong in the face of this adversity. I was afraid of what was to come but proud of what we had managed to survive thus far. Of course, we had no clue what they would do if they caught us. But I believed that we had what it took to escape and figure this out.

I snapped back to reality when I heard the rustling of their sleeping bags.

I watched as Heather and Alexa lay silently breathing. The soft breaths escaping their lips caused their hair to billow from the wind being created. I saw Alexa in a new light with the soft moonlight peering through the window illuminating them both in perfect serenity.

The angry and sad expressions she had had for most of the day were gone, and a soft smile played at the corners of her mouth. She looked so happy I wondered what she could be dreaming about. I looked over to Heather to see her reaching her hand out toward me in her sleep. As if begging me to grab onto her. I hadn't known that she was capable of sleepwalking. Well, sleep actions, to be more exact. A soft expression of fear flashed over her face as her brows furrowed in horror. The dichotomy of this scene was ominous, to say the least. The panic and the fear in her expression was palpable. I couldn't stand by and watch this anymore. I reached out to grab her hand.

I lightly touched her hand and rubbed the top of it. Her expression began to soften the fear and began to wash away as she slowly opened her eyes and stared into mine. The deep emerald greens of her irises were like tropical swimming pools that I wished I could just dive into to escape this reality. She smiled, staring into my eyes, and squeezed my hand, and I squeezed back.

We didn't need to say anything; we both knew how much the other meant to us. We sat there in silence for what seemed like an eternity. She sat up and then climbed out of her sleeping bag to sit next to me. We stayed silent and just sat there holding the other's hand, softly squeezing.

Then Heather reached both arms around me and hugged me. For the first time, I saw Heather cry, tears welling up in her beautiful green eyes, causing them to glisten in the moonlight. She then buried her face into my shoulder and let all her emotions out that she had been holding in for the past day or days. I put my arms around her and hugged her as she softly sobbed into my shoulder. I rubbed her back lightly, trying to comfort her.

"Shhh… It'll be okay," I whispered.

"H-h-how do you know that?" she was barely able to get out of her lips between sobs.

"Because I'll do everything I can to make it okay," I replied.

"But I feel so hopeless," she said back.

"I don't believe that at all. We can do anything we put our minds to. Look at how far we've come," I whispered into her ear.

"How can we do anything?" she said dejectedly.

"Do you believe in me?" I asked her.

"Of course I do," she said, sure of her answer as she wiped her face on me again.

"Then there is hope," I told her with false bravado.

"Thanks, Ryan. I'm glad I'm here with you. I couldn't keep going if you were gone," Heather said to me with a smile, knowing that I had just said what I thought would make her feel better.

None the less, it seemed that my assurance helped her feel better about our current situation, if only for a little while. That was all I could really hope for anyway. There was no way I would have been able to actually convince her that it was all going to be okay because I could barely convince myself that we were going to be totally fine. How could I expect her to believe something even I was unsure of?

She seemed to understand that I was thinking about our situation, and she put her hand on my head and softly tousled my hair. She smiled and looked into my eyes as she then started to pat my back in a circular motion.

"Heavy hangs the head that wears the crown," she said, almost so quietly I couldn't hear it.

"What crown could I possibly be wearing?" I asked.

"A broken one. But a crown in spite of everything that has happened," I said confidently.

"You haven't answered my question," I replied.

"You'll see. In time. What I mean, Ryan," she said softly, moving her hand back into mine.

She stared into my eyes with a sense of determination and a fire that I hadn't seen in a while. I was glad she'd started to feel herself again. But I was still not sure what she could have meant by what she had said. But right now, that was the least of our worries. We still had to figure out our next

158

steps.

Meanwhile, Alexa was still oblivious to what was going on, sleeping in her sleeping bag. She was still smiling, with a funny look on her face. I smiled as it brought back a wave of memories from the start of this whole thing. Where just a few days ago Alexa was asleep in my front seat, curled up, waiting to get to our next destination. God, how I longed to go back to just a few days ago where the most we had to care about was keeping up a fake facade of being married.

I thought this as Heather squeezed my hand and nodded towards the window with a slight smile. I looked out the window to see that I had spent the whole night awake. Time sure did seem to fly by. My mini mystery of the breeze and the small conversation with Heather seemed to take up the entire night. I didn't know how we would solve our current predicament, but I had a good feeling about the future. For the first time in the last day or so, I had a positive outlook on our next steps.

I smiled back at Heather and squeezed her hand tighter as the sun rose on this new day. The bright orange, yellow, and pink hue illuminated the gray clouds. Today was a new day and one that we would have to use to the fullest. I softly nudged Alexa awake and put some of the stuff we had taken out the last night into her backpack again.

Chapter 22

While I was moving things into Alexa's backpack, she slowly climbed out of her sleeping bag and fixed her messy clothes and hair. Her shirt was all crumpled, so she straightened it and tied her silky blonde hair up into a tight bun.

Heather helped roll up Alexa's sleeping bag. We all stood there not wanting to leave the somewhat safe space we had created for ourselves, for the dangers of confronting our hunters. Silently we all looked at one another and then nodded as we started to walk out to my car.

I unlocked the doors and we all got into the car. Alexa sat up front and Heather got into the back after a small scuffle that Alexa clearly won. I stared at the dash and stuck my keys into the ignition and the engine roared to life.

"Where are we off to now?" I asked.

"I know it's one of the most dangerous places for us to go to, but I think we should head to my dad's office and look for clues there," Heather replied solemnly.

"ARE YOU CRAZY?!?! Do you not remember what happened the last time we went there? That's one of the main reasons we even ended up here. Running from those psychopaths," Alexa yelled, clearly upset by the thought.

"I think we should go there too. I know we got captured last time but we had thought they were the good guys the last time we went. We weren't cautious. Now that we know what to expect we can probably sneak in and look for clues," I said optimistically, looking around the car.

"No way. I will not be going back to that death trap," Alexa said matter of factly.

"Do you have any better options? All the places we could look for clues will be dangerous, and I don't see you throwing out any suggestions," I replied, starting to get angry.

"Fine. But just know I really don't want to do this," Alexa responded with an uneasy anxious look on her face.

"It's settled then, to my dad's office we go. Ryan don't pull into the parking lot of the office, of course. We need to hide your car somewhere nearby and walk to the office, so we don't draw too much unwanted attention," Heather said to us.

"Aye aye, Captain," I replied in a joking way.

I reversed out of the parking lot and started to drive away from the library. Passing through all of the trees felt ominous, as if we were leaving cover into an open battlefield. We reached the stop sign at the end of the small road leading away from the library. For a brief moment we sat there, I looked left and right checking for cars but more so checking for the specific cars that Heather's father and his goons drove. Seeing no sign of them staking out the library, I turned right to ride the outskirts of town.

Going through the main street seemed like a suicide mission. There was no way we would ever be able to get close to the office by driving on the surface streets of the town. By now our hunters were probably hidden down every side street and ally they could find, just waiting to see us and call it in to surround us and not let us escape for a third time.

Part of me wanted to just floor it and leave the town behind us and just disappear. But another part of me couldn't let go of the thought of what happened to my and Alexa's parents. So, we slowly drove around the outside of town while every few seconds I checked behind us to make sure no one was following us. I knew I probably looked like a paranoid mess to them while I sat there neurotically looking behind me over and over again. But that was because I was. I was freaking out. I was terrified of what could happen if they caught us again.

"So, what exactly are we looking for?" Alexa said, obviously trying to break the tension in the car.

"Umm... Good question. I doubt they'd have a file that's labeled 'illegal stuff we're doing,'" I replied.

"Well, I don't know what we are looking for, but I do know where my dad would hide it. He has a safe in his office that he thinks no one knows the code to. I might know it, but I haven't ever tried to break into it. So, I can try the code, and if we get into it, I'm sure whatever we find will be helpful," Heather interjected somewhat confidently.

"Well, I guess that is our best shot, but we have to be careful. Not just normal careful, but like we need this to go perfectly," I said.

"Yeah. Yeah... We get it, Ryan, this is serious. Do you think we don't know that? We get that you're trying to protect us, but come on... We're in this together. You're not alone. So, stop pretending that we're some fragile dolls that will break at the slightest abrasion," Alexa replied snarkily.

"I'm sorry. That isn't how I meant it. I'm just scared," I responded dejectedly.

"Hey, don't worry about it. We are all scared. But Alexa is right, we got your back," Heather said sweetly.

I noded to both of them, and they each gave me a weary smile. They both looked like they'd been run ragged from this. Hell... I probably did too. But I couldn't bring myself to look in the mirror to see how bad I looked. So, I kept driving down the frozen road until we hit the halfway point of the town. We were on the southern side of the town just ten minutes walking distance behind the construction company's office.

With the snow, it probably made it more like twenty minutes due to it being basically waist-high. But walking through the snow would be the most inconspicuous way to get into the vicinity of the building. I looked around us before pulling over off the road and behind a small snow-covered hill. I turned off the car and leaned around, looking at all of my blind spots one more time just to make sure we really weren't being followed. Thankfully, we weren't.

"Phew. We're halfway there," I sighed, relieved that something had gone right for once.

"Now, for the hard part," Heather replied.

"Hate to admit it but she's right. It won't get any easier from here on out," Alexa agreed, nodding slightly.

We all stepped out of the car and started to walk in the direction of the office. The hill I had parked behind was a surprisingly good hiding place. The trees obscured it from higher up on the hills behind it, and the small hill in front of it blocked the view of the street. If we got caught, it definitely wouldn't be because of where we parked the car. I got smacked softly in the small of my back by Alexa jolting me forward into the real world again.

"Glad you're so proud of yourself. But you can get lost in thought after we settle all of this," she said with a sly smile on your face.

"Sooorrrryyyy if I thought my hiding spot was perfect," I replied by stretching out the syllables of *sorry* in a joking manner.

We continue our march to what could surely be our demise but with a renewed sense of determination. We slowly slunk along fences and hid in the shadows as we crept toward the office building in the distance. I slowed to a stop, hiding behind a building facing the office. I motioned for the girls to follow my lead. They both got close, and we crouched down to make our presence smaller.

"What is it?" Alexa whispered.

"It might be a trap. Look at how empty the parking lot looks. Not only that but all of the lights are off as well. The last time we walked around that 'abandoned office' we got caught," I said back quietly.

"Don't worry, this time I know they aren't on our side. I can turn off the silent alarms before they alert my dad. Trust me," Heather responded.

Alexa and I shrugged, and we all continued to make our way cautiously to the seemingly empty building. As we made it to the back door, Heather hit some keys on a keypad and the door lock clicked in a mechanical tone. We all silently rushed inside, and I didn't let the door make any noise as it shut. Heather rushed over to a security panel that was counting down. She entered a code and the screen flashed red. She entered another code and the screen flashed red once again. It then flashed the words "Final attempt before silent alarm triggered". I started to sweat as she entered a third code, and the screen flashed green with a message stating "Silent alarm disabled welcome back Mr. S." I wiped the sweat from my brow and Heather turned to us with a smile.

She held her finger up to her mouth in a "Shh" gesture and then beckoned us with her other hand. We walked towards a door leading to a staircase and ascended the stairs silently and quickly. We reached the top floor and Heather lead us to a corner office with the lights off and we hurried inside. Heather closed the door behind us with a very slight click.

"Nice work. Now to find and break into that safe," I said, keeping my voice as low as I could.

I looked around the office as we pulled out our phone lights to not alert anyone that we are in that space. We were in the midgame now. There was no backing out of this. The office was pretty organized as expected of someone as well put together as "Mr. S". There were very minimal decorations. If Heather hadn't led us to this office, you'd think it wasn't even occupied by anyone. The pen holder had three pens in it that all seemed to have never been touched, let alone used. There were no papers anywhere, even the filing cabinet handles had no smudges on the stainless steel. It was as if this room had been sterilized each night. I wouldn't put it past him to do such a thing, knowing how shady this place was.

I opened desk drawers, and they were all borderline empty with at most one having a ream of paper for the printer that was in the left corner of the room. Was this really a person's office, I thought to myself. As I thought this, Heather walked up to my side and touched my arm. She pointed to basically the only decoration in the office, which was a strange Victorian-style painting of a family hung on the wall. I understood what she was saying even in the silence. That this was probably where the safe was. Just as soon as I walked over to the painting to take it down, I heard footsteps outside the door. They were faint at first, but they were getting louder. Each step echoed off the walls of the small corridors between the cubicles. The thunderous footsteps finally reached the door and we all ducked behind the desk in the middle of the room. Thankfully, the desk had a full privacy panel to cover the person's feet. I peered through a crack between the panel and the desk legs and saw the door handle turn.

The door then was flung open and slammed against the wall with a loud CRACK! Then a large figure stepped into the doorway. He laughed as if he knew we were there and was toying with us. Then from behind the figure a voice could be heard yelling, "What are you doing in the boss's office!?"

"Oh, come on, haven't you ever been curious how the big guy operates and runs this company?" he replied.

"Of course I have, but that doesn't mean I would break into his office just to figure him out. You know what he will do to you if he finds out you went in there," the other guy replied with anxiety creeping into his voice.

"Who's gonna tell on me? You? You're a coward. Even if you tried, I'd say it was all your idea. We're in this together now," he said confidently.

Heather and Alexa were trembling in my arms. I slowly rubbed their shoulders to try to calm them so that they didn't accidentally touch the desk and make it start to shake, alerting them to us. If even they were afraid of what he was capable of then that went double for us.

"I don't like this, man..." said the timid guy.

"Pshhh, he's not coming back anytime soon. He's hunting for those dumb kids. Remember? We have free reign to do whatever we want here," said the cocky one.

"But what if someone else catches us in here? Also, what's so interesting about his office is that it looks like it's basically empty, there's nothing even fun in it, or so it appears," the timid one replied.

"Hey, you're right, what's with that old man? Why doesn't he have anything cool in here? I guess there really is no point in being here at all. I guess I'll just go have a seat in his chair and then we can be on our way," the cocky one said, disappointed.

"He's going to find out that it was you that sat in his chair. There's no way you'll be able to get away with it," the timid one said with fear creeping into his voice.

"Well even if that may be true, I want to feel what it's like to be king of this place. If only once," the cocky one said as he walked over to the corner of the desk.

Alexa and Heather started shaking more and I tensed up, mentally preparing myself to get into a fight with them for us to be able to escape. There was no way that I was going to just let us get captured again. I silently turned around with the two girls hidden deeper behind me against the privacy panel. I saw his large figure start to appear around the corner of the desk and suddenly...

Chapter 23

A loud jarring noise rang out. The cocky guy jumped in fear as soon as he heard it. Then another noise came from what sounded like their walkie-talkies.

"Come here. NOW!" the voice yelled over the walkie-talkies. The voice didn't use a name or a call sign and didn't even give a signature.

"We better get going, man," the timid guy said meekly.

"Pfft. Man, I was so close to getting to sit at the head of the office too. But you're right, I don't want to upset the boss," the cocky one replied.

I sighed a small sigh of relief as I heard the door slam shut behind them. That was a close one, we had almost been caught again. I wondered where they were going. Wherever it was, they seemed to know just by the voice telling them to "Come here".

The girls were still shaking in fear behind me, and I felt each one cling to the back of my arm as soon as the footsteps started to echo away on the other side of the door. They were definitely leaving this floor at least, so we should be in the clear. I felt a faint wet sensation on my left arm, and I looked back to see Heather crying into my shoulder. This must have been pretty hard on her considering her father was the one behind all of this.

I slid out from under the desk to make sure the coast was truly clear. I crept around the corner of the desk and saw the door shut. I motioned for them to stay as I slowly made my way toward the door. I slightly cracked the door open to see the room before this office with all of its lights off.

Thankfully, it seemed like everyone was out of the building for now. I went back to the desk after softly shutting the door and nodded at both of them. I held my hand horizontally, held it up high and slowly lowered it to signify to them that we should keep the volume down. Because we didn't really know if the office was truly deserted or not.

"The coast is clear for now, guys," I whispered.

"That was a close one for sure," Alexa replied in a hushed voice.

"H-h-hearing h-h-his v-v-voice... It's breaking me to think about it. It feels all so surreal..." Heather said quietly.

"I know. I'm sorry for this all happening, Heather. This is really hard on all of us," I said softly as I walked over and gave her a tight hug. She responded by squeezing me the hardest I had ever been squeezed. Then Alexa came up from behind us and hugged us too in a surprising turn of events. I think she'd finally started to sympathize with Heather.

"It'll get better, guys. We always have each other and if I had to go through this again, I would always choose you both to be on my side," Alexa said in a melancholy tone.

"Alright, let's open that safe and get out of here before anyone comes back," I said, walking over to the painting. As I took the painting off the wall, it hit me that the family in this painting was Heather's. I stared into the little girl's sad emerald eyes and saw the same pain Heather had always seemed to carry with her. I looked to her left and right to see her stoic dad and her fiercely beautiful mother. The resemblance was uncanny.

I set the painting on the floor softly and stood in awe of the enormous safe sitting before me, recessed in the wall.

"Okay, time to bust this baby open," I said in a positive tone. Heather walked silently up beside me and started to turn the combination knob. She turned it a total of five times and then clicked the button next to it and the door made a loud clang sound as the mechanical lock disengaged.

"Wow..." I said, flabbergasted that she had just done that.

"That was nothing," she said nonchalantly.

"Show off," Alexa said, scoffing.

We moved the door of the safe open to see the insides. Everything in the safe was in perfect order. I wouldn't be surprised if the entire safe was alphabetized.

"What are we looking for again?" I said, questioning why we were here for the first time.

"Anything. I guess?" Alexa replied.

"No. We need to find the year the construction started on the library. That should be our jumping-off point," Heather said with an authority I had never heard her muster up before.

"I guess that's the best place to start," I said as I started flipping through the documents and looking at the dates. Looking back eleven years ago. Then I found it. 2007. I opened the ledger for that year and all it had on it was the employee numbers that were assigned to the job as well as the leader of the project. That leader's name was just Mr. S. Okay, that was ominous. But obviously, it would be "Mr. S", who else would it be. I started to skim the information and found nothing useful. I flipped to the next page and something caught my eye.

It seemed to be some sort of cipher. Because otherwise, it would have been just gobbledygook on the top of what would be a particularly important ledger. I handed it to Heather, and she looked at it and instantly deciphered it.

"It says 'U.S. Military'," she said.

"Wait, like the U.S. Military?" I replied, confused.

"What other U.S. Military would it be, moron?" Alexa said, smacking me on the back of my head.

"Oww. You're right, that's pretty straightforward," I said, rubbing the back of my head.

"Okay, well now we know who created that library. But the reason why and the cause of the abrupt end to the project still looms," Alexa said.

"Well, if we keep digging here, I'm sure it will be documented," Heather replied solemnly. It definitely seemed like she wanted to get out of here.

"Heather, I understand how you feel. But we can't leave just yet," I said, with a soft smile. She nodded at me with a scared look in her eyes.

I kept pulling more documents pertaining to the mysterious project. At least, that was what I assumed they were as they all had the same filing code name, "Typhon". Whatever that meant. As I was pulling files, I noticed that a large portion of them had a ton of redactions. This really did seem to be a top secret project. I never thought I'd see redacted documents in real life. I only ever thought I'd see them in movies. But here I was poring over hundreds of them. It was so surreal. I felt like a spy in a thriller. But the stakes of our investigation were way higher than any dumb movie plot.

"Ryan!" Alexa yelled at me quietly while shaking my arms.

"What?" I replied, shocked by her sudden outburst.

"Hide... NOW!" she said, whispering this time. I listened and realized that someone was coming. I softly put the painting back up and jumped behind the desk with them. Just before the door swung open with a whoosh!

"Ugh... Where did those brats run off with my daughter?!" the voice shouted as he slammed the door.

"How? Just how could she do this to me? She should know by now that blood is thicker than water. Those pathetic friends of hers. I took her away from this place so she wouldn't become weak and complacent. But it appears I must have done so too late. What am I going to do with her? This insolence cannot go unpunished," he said, slamming his heavy hands against his temples.

I felt Heather and Alexa's soft breaths on my back, both so rapid you'd think they were hyperventilating. I heard him sit down on the couch as it let out the air from beneath him. I was still clutching an enormous amount of paper against my chest. I just kept holding it tightly, focusing as hard as I could on not wrinkling it.

The soft parchment against my hands made them start to sweat. Just as I started to focus on it, he let out another enormous sigh and then clasped his hands together, drumming on his palms with his fingers. Deep in thought, he sat there for a while. Then as if on cue he noticed the painting slightly askew.

"When did this get tilted? Who was messing around in my office?!" he said, fixing the painting.

"Thomas!!!!!" he shouted.

"Y-y-yes s-s-sir?" the now not-so-confident guy said.

"What were you doing playing around in my office? This is the last time you do this, foolishness boy. Next time it's your head. You thought what I was going to do with those kids was harsh. You don't want to know what I'll do with you," he said, his voice booming and echoing throughout the halls.

"S-s-sir, I swear, it wasn't me. I would never touch your th-th-things," he replied meekly. I almost felt bad for this guy for a second. I mean, he really didn't do anything. But right now, I was glad it was him and not us.

"ENOUGH! NO MORE EXCUSES! GET OVER HERE!" he said, shuffling towards the man in the doorway.

"N-n-no, please, sir, I'm sorry!" he said, crying audibly. The footsteps of Mr. S got louder as he got closer to the guy, and then they stopped and in their stead were the horribly gruesome sounds of a beating. His punches ricocheting off the guy's face made enormous slapping and crunching sounds as he mercilessly beat this man. Surely this man would never be able to talk again. I wanted to throw up, knowing that we were the cause of this horrifying attack. I blamed myself for the punishment being doled out. It was sickening. I wished for it to end.

"Find me something to clean my hands with, Jacob," he said as the room fell silent. Jacob must have been the nervous one as he quickly scurried away, running to grab something to clean his boss's hands, which I could only assume were covered in Thomas's blood. What a horrifying thing to experience.

I think hearing it was worse than if I were just watching the beating. My imagination ran wild, filling my head with terrifying thoughts of the scene just a few feet away from me. I felt the girls shuddering against my back and I looked down to see my knuckles white with how tight I was gripping the paper. I must have subconsciously started to squeeze tighter while the beating was happening.

Jacob returned without saying a word and handed Mr. S his towel or whatever to clean his hands.

"Good boy, Jacob. Now take Thomas to the ER. Say it was a really hard fall down three flights of stairs," he said as we listened to Jacob drag what was basically a corpse at this point away. The horrifying gurgling noise that Thomas was making while being pulled away filled me with the fear of God. I could still hear the sound of the body being dragged away on replay in my mind.

Then he walked out of his office, slamming the door shut with an angry grunt, and as he stomped down the hall he shouted, "Now I have to get someone to come in and steam this place because Thomas made such a damn mess!" He said this as if it were a thinly veiled threat to all of his employees.

I sighed softly once the office murmurs started to fall silent as one by one they seemingly left to go look for us. What a terrifying thought. I felt Heather grab onto my arm, and started to cry against it. Her wet tears fell against my shoulder, and I was frozen. For the umpteenth time today, one of these girls has broken down. Honestly, I didn't blame them. I was on the verge of breaking down. But I felt in my heart I needed to be strong for them. Now they needed me more than ever to be there for them. I couldn't just wallow. I sat there thinking this while both held onto my sides. Then I decided we had to get up, so I slid out from under the desk.

"I think it's time to go, guys. We need to grab all of these documents and just run. Enough is enough. That was too close. We almost got caught twice. God knows what they'll do to us when they catch us. We need to just get anything that could be remotely helpful and dash," I said as my voice betrayed my confidence by shaking.

"You're right. Plus, we'll need evidence anyways because no one will believe this," Alexa replied, wiping her tears away.

"Got it all," Heather said, stone-faced now, and then started to slink out the door.

This must be really hard for her, I thought to myself.

"Follow her lead," I said quietly, clutching the papers to my chest. I left the room slightly behind Alexa and shut the door silently. I looked ahead and saw Heather already at the top of the stairs. She rushed down them without making a single noise and Alexa and I weren't far behind. She peeked out the door to the outside and then gave us a hand signal to keep going, so we did. Then she darted outside towards the hill on the outskirts of town where I had hidden the car behind.

Alexa and I pursued her as fast as we could, but Heather was on another level in terms of speed. She had basically vanished from sight before we even reached the main street surrounding town. Alexa and I looked at each other, both understanding we couldn't let Heather be alone right now. When we made it to the top of the snow-covered peak, we nodded at each other and calmly approached the car. I unlocked the doors and we all got in. I turned the car on and set the heater up because the sun was just starting to fall behind the horizon. It was going to be really cold soon. I couldn't believe we had spent a whole day there.

Chapter 24

What felt like just a few hours turned out to be the entire day. I turned off the headlights to my car as quickly as I saw the sun's last rays of light softly slipping away. I did not want anyone to find us hidden behind this snow-covered hill because of some dumb headlights. That would have been the most idiotic way to be captured.

"What do we do now?" I asked in a somber tone.

"We look over the documents and try to decipher them. But more importantly, where are we going to decipher them?" Heather responded in a serious tone. I had no clue where we would go but we needed to find somewhere safe for the time being. Suddenly I thought back to the beginning of this week when Alexa and I had left town for a short time. I thought today would be the safest time to get out of town. We needed to go fast though. Hopefully, they hadn't blocked all the exits to town. Worst case we'd have to do a little off-roading, best case we'd just be home-free.

"We should head to Portland," I suggested confidently.

"Getting out of town would be the safest option," Alexa said, mulling it over.

"That might not work. My dad has probably already blocked off all the exits to the town. But it might be worth a shot. This way we'll know if we're truly trapped or not," Heather replied hesitantly. I could sense the incredulousness in her thoughts. She had no faith that we'd be able to escape. But we had to try. Even if we couldn't escape, it was not like it changed our current situation much, but if we could it would open a whole lot of options up.

"So, it's decided then? We try to get the hell out of dodge and if we can't we find a place to hunker down and read these documents anyway," I said with false bravado. Honestly, I didn't have much faith in our escape either, but even if there was just a non-zero chance we could get out of town, we had to take that shot.

I threw my car out of park and into drive and slowly crept onto the outskirts road, making sure to keep a close watch on my surroundings. Any light from another car and I would have to find a way to either outmaneuver them or straight up gun it and hope we won the footrace.

We slowly made it to one of the only roads leading out of town only to have my worst fears realized. We were trapped. An enormous blockade had been erected on the road leading to Portland. *Nothing was ever going to be easy, was it though?* I thought to myself, feeling slightly hopeless. Then I felt a small hand grab onto my forearm, and I looked down. It was Heather. She gently squeezed my arm and looked at me with a sorrowful look. I understood what her expression meant. I felt the same way.

I turned the car around and then remembered a place where we might be able to hide out. Not many people knew it existed and I was sure it wouldn't have any goons occupying it. I smiled to myself as I started for a secret clubhouse that only I knew about. Similar to the abandoned house me and Alexa used to go to, there was another cabin that was less abandoned and more forgotten. When we were kids there were rumors that the house was haunted and would eat children. But I knew that wasn't true.

As we pulled up to the dirt road that led off into the woods, I turned and gave a slight nod to my compatriots as well as a wink as I took us off the roads and onto the small dirt path.

"Where the hell are we going, Ryan?" Alexa said, irritated.

"A secret place," I replied, smirking.

"You mean the haunted house?" Heather said with a slight smile.

"R-r-ryan, you are not taking us to that creepy haunted house, a-a-are you?" Alexa said with fear drenching her voice.

"I mean, do you have any better places to hide than a haunted house that only kids knew about?" I replied smugly.

"We still have to be cautious. Who knows if they had already come here thinking we would choose it as an ideal safe house," Heather replied with her serious tone returning. Something was definitely not right with her, but I had to ignore it for the time being. I didn't have the luxury of being able to get lost in thought figuring out why Heather had started to become more serious and cold to us.

"Here we are. Home sweet haunted home," I said in a joking manner.

"Stop, Ryan. You know I hate supernatural things, especially since the disappearance of our parents," Alexa said in such a cold tone I could feel it freezing the blood in my veins.

"Sheesh... It was just a joke," I replied, still feeling the menacing aura that Alexa had created.

I parked the car behind the house so it couldn't be seen from the front, and then I covered it in leaves as the girls went inside to start a fire and warm up. When I got into the house the fire was already burning and Alexa and Heather were already poring over the mass amounts of documents we had taken from Mr. S's office.

I sat down with them and took a small pile of papers to look at. As I was reading them, not a whole lot seemed to be out of the ordinary. It seemed like they were pretty normal construction documents besides the whole hidden military base underground part. But why would they even put the military base part in these documents, I thought to myself. Reading these redacted pages made me want to gouge my eyes out. The soft red light produced from the fireplace was giving me a headache. Having to comb through documents with almost more black streaks through them than words wasn't helping either.

"Man, this sucks!" I said, clasping my hands to my forehead and rubbing my temples.

"You just started reading, dummy. How are you already giving up?" Alexa replied snarkily.

"I know, but it still hurts," I snapped back, sounding a little harsher than I had intended.

"Guys... Just focus on the documents, please," Heather said in a somber tone.

Something is absolutely wrong with Heather, I thought to myself. I subconsciously found myself sliding closer to her in this dilapidated house. The wallpaper peeled off to reveal surprisingly not rotted planks that it had been stuck to for years. The floorboards were creaky, and all the furniture seemed to have a slight wobble to it. For a house filled with antiques that hadn't been maintained, it was in really good condition. As I thought this, I realized I was now basically side by side with Heather.

I started to read more documents more diligently as Heather seemed to be keeping one eye on hers and the other watching me. She had this aura I could only describe as bloodlust emanating from her. I wished I could just read her mind.

While thinking about this I noticed something weird on the page I was reading. It seemed to be referring to the purpose of the project and why it had abruptly ended. The problem was both of the reasons were redacted on this document. I tried holding the document at so many different angles to make out the words, but nothing worked. I tossed them up into the air in frustration.

I lay down facing the fire, and as soon as I did the pages landed on my face. Ironically, this way I was actually able to read what the documents had redacted on them. The orange and reddish hues of the flames that shone from the fireplace were refracting through the old paper and showed a perfect image of the words that had been covered up. "The reason we had to shut down construction was because there was too much heat after that kid fell into the site. We didn't let the public know about it and didn't even take 'em to the hospital for the injuries. We just treated 'em in-house. But that was enough to scare the suits into shutting down the whole project." That was what the first line said. At least now we knew why it shut down, but who was the kid that fell into the job site? I didn't remember many other kids hanging around when I was there.

Then suddenly an image flashed in my mind. I saw another kid walking across a beam over a hole in the library. Then all of a sudden, they had been swallowed up by the void. I reached out but couldn't save them. It was too late. They were gone. I wasn't able to make out their faces in this memory. Who were they? Why had I not remembered it until now? Why was I repressing this memory, a memory that was so crucial to our current predicament?

I read the second line, "Project Typhon. A military operation base. I'm not sure what they were going to use this base for but from what the boss has told me it seemed to be some kind of hush-hush genetic sequencing technology. That would explain all of the expensive materials we were using to build the 'bunker' underneath the library. All I know is that it's above my pay grade. Whatever they're going to be doing in there isn't right but who am I to judge? Anyway, this is all going to be redacted anyway so I don't even know why I'm writing all this. P.S. Hi, Janice..." Well, I guessed now I knew what the project was too.

"Guys. This document has what the project was and why it was shut down," I said in a chipper tone.

"What does it say?!" Heather shouted.

"Basically, it was a military base for genetic sequencing and top secret testing. Maybe super soldiers? It doesn't really elaborate. As for the reason it shut down. Some kid apparently fell into the job site and the 'suits,' whoever they are, were too scared to proceed with more eyes focusing on the project." As I finished explaining I looked at the girls, who both had profoundly serious expressions. I wished I knew what they were thinking.

"Well, I guess the mystery is solved as to what the building was and why they ended construction. But that doesn't explain why we're being hunted. We didn't even have this information until just now. So, it's not like we were even threats?" Alexa replied while scratching her head.

"That might be partly my fault," Heather said with panic creeping into her voice.

"I kind of confronted my dad the day before we left about what was going on and both of your parents disappearing. He tried to calm me by saying they had just gone on vacations, but I pushed further and told him I knew what was going on and that I knew he had been tying up loose ends. Of course, I didn't really know that at the time, but it seems pretty legit now. Then he told me to stop, and I said I wouldn't stop until I exposed his lies. I said I couldn't believe he would do this to me. I always knew something wasn't right when we left, but when I came back the feeling got worse. That's why I wanted to help you guys. But I ended up making everything worse. This is all my fault," Heather said in-between sobs. Her sad emerald eyes were leaking perfect crystalline tears. Everything she said made me feel numb. Was what she said true? Could that really be the reason we were in this mess? I couldn't believe it. Her cheeks started to grow more red, and her unkempt hair was falling into her face. I felt so bad for her having to feel like the burden fell solely on her shoulders.

"Y-Y-YOU?! IT, WAS YOU?!?! YOU'RE THE ONE WHO DID THIS TO ME?!" Alexa screamed at her. Alexa's face turned red as tears started to well up in her eyes as she continued to scream her lungs out at Heather.

"ENOUGH! Both of you. Stop," I said matter of factly, trying to put an end to this situation, or at least set it back down from the level it was at.

"AND YOU'RE EVEN WORSE! HOW CAN YOU TAKE HER SIDE IN THIS? SHE RUINED YOUR LIFE TOO, YOU KNOW?" Alexa yelled at me; her face was completely red now. She looked like a tomato with dirty blonde hair as she screamed at me.

"I'm not taking her side. I'm trying to calm everyone down. It's not her fault. Our parents were already taken by that point. She said it was after our parents disappeared. We all need to take a deep breath and try to relax because turning on one another is not going to get us out of this situation. This is no one's fault. We were tied to this the moment our parents vanished, Alexa," I said in a calming tone, trying to soothe both girls.

"She's right. It's my fault. You should just give me up as a distraction and escape. Sacrifice me. I deserve it. If I hadn't said anything to my dad maybe you both wouldn't have been dragged into this. I deserve any punishment he sees fit. I also want you both to be free and not be captured. They won't stop until they get us. But I might be able to negotiate your freedom in exchange for my imprisonment. I had done it once before. Anyways this wouldn't be new," Heather said, wiping away her tears, steeling herself.

"Sure. Let's sacrifice her, Ryan. Life will be better without her anyway," Alexa said coldly as she turned to face away from Heather.

"No. We are not sacrificing Heather. How could you even say that? Have a heart. That is not the girl, I know you're really disappointing me right now, Alexa. Also, what do you mean you have done it once before Heather?" I said, sorrow filling my voice.

"I don't need your approval, Ryan. I'm done with all of this. I'm done being your lapdog. Quit playing both sides. Choose a side, if you don't, I'm leaving. I'll take my chances on my own," Alexa said. Her words stung my heart. She sure got what she wanted. She wanted to hurt us and even I wasn't able to avoid this all-out assault on my emotions. How could she ask me to split us up? We were all friends, weren't we? I couldn't bring myself to sacrifice Heather any more than I could bring myself to sacrifice Alexa.

Chapter 25

I started to remember memories of us in elementary school. I always saw how much fun we had during those times. Sure, it was forever ago, but that didn't mean they didn't matter. We were friends. I couldn't see a world where we split up, especially not with the sacrifice of one of us.

Flashback to when the three of us were 11

Before the fight that ended with Heather leaving, Heather was standing there alone next to the swings after finding out she was about to move away. I walked up to her. "Hey, don't worry about moving. I'll always be here when you come back to town one day. When we're older we'll see each other again. I can just feel it," I told her with a soft punch on the arm.

"What are you two nerds moping about? Heather having to leave town?" Alexa said in a soft tone.

"Ryan was just telling me that he thought we'd all see each other again. I hope it's true. I'll miss you guys. You're the only people who ever really got me. I'll miss you more than anything in this dumb town. You're my best friends," Heather said solemnly with tears welling up in her eyes.

"I'll miss you too, Your Majesty. We'll always remember these days. I hope we all stay friends forever. You both are the most important parts of my life," Alexa said, also starting to tear up. She always called Heather 'Majesty' because she had the biggest house, but she never said it maliciously. It was more playful when she'd

say it.

"I'll miss you too, Heather. You can think of us when you feel lonely. Something my parents always told me when they had to work late was to look at the stars. We see the same sky when we look up at night. If you promise to look at the sky every night at nine o'clock, I'll be looking at you so you can pretend I'm right next to you telling you dumb jokes while we watch the stars together," I said as my eyes began to leak.

"I promise," she replied while holding out a pinky for us to swear on.

"Then it's settled, every night at nine we'll watch the stars together," I said, smiling through the tears streaming down my cheeks and puddling between my feet.

I don't know what snapped in Alexa at that time, but the rest is history. This was the fight that fractured us the first time. Little did I know I would be in basically the same position so many years later.

Remembering this memory of us in elementary school was bittersweet. I found myself on the precipice of another enormous life-defining decision. Why couldn't we just all be friends? Were we always destined to split apart? All I ever wanted was for two of my favorite people to get along, and at times they had and others they were on the verge of killing one another. But I thought that was because we were all just so close that we'd butt heads. I guessed that wasn't the reason.

"Well, stupid, what's it going to be? Me or Her? Choose wisely. You can't take this back," Alexa said with a stone-cold face. She was scary when she was serious.

"I can't. If we have to sacrifice someone, just let it be me. I'm not as smart as either of you and I have been basically the weakest link this whole time. You both deserve better. If it has to be someone, let it be me. If we really can't work this out, I'd rather be dead than lose either of you. We've been friends since that first day in kindergarten. If that friendship is truly over, then what other reason do I have to keep carrying on this charade?" I said in an earnest voice.

"Fine. If you can't, I'll make the choice for you. Good luck with your adventures. But I guess this is the end of our trio," Alexa said, rage dripping off of every word she spat at us. Then she picked up her pack and stormed out of the door, leaving us. She really was a savage despot. It was always absolute with her, and you could never really win against her. If she made up her mind, you either listened or got out of her way.

"Wait!" Heather called out in vain. I knew Alexa was too far gone for that. Alexa kept walking off into the dark forest. I didn't know where she would go but I knew she needed a little bit of time alone. She was like a flame that was burning too brightly. If you kept feeding it fuel it would become a wildfire bringing destruction, but if you deprived it of fuel it'd vanish. Sometimes you just had to let it slowly burn back down to a more manageable size. Alexa was very much out of control right now and letting her cool off was our only option. I didn't want to get burned again.

Chasing her would only cause her to run faster and try harder to escape. I knew she would be fine in my heart, but it hurt to see her go like that. Now Heather and I were alone in the cabin. We found what we needed and had the evidence it was being covered up. Our next steps had to be very cautiously calculated.

"We have to go after her," Heather said with determination in her voice.

"No. This is something she has to do. She needs to cool down and take a step back. Don't worry, she won't get caught. She's too slippery for any of those people to get their hands on her," I said very matter of factly.

"Then what do we do next? We can't just stay here; we have to do something with the information we've gotten. I have no clue what we can do or where we can go," Heather said, finally letting panic creep into her voice.

"I also have a plan for us to be able to resolve that. However, it requires some refining. But all I know is that I don't really care about taking down this insane governmental cover-up or whatever it is. I just want to graduate and get out of this town for good," I responded, feeling a sense of melancholy about our predicament.

"Well, I don't particularly want to deal with exposing this either. This would probably have us be hunted for the rest of our lives and I don't want to live every day with the fear I have right now," Heather said in agreement with my statement.

"Then my plan is to use these documents as a bargaining chip for our freedom, including Alexa and my parents. With these, I think we can ensure our mutual escape from the potential torture and slaughter we might have to endure otherwise," I said with actual confidence. I was sure Mr. S wouldn't want these leaking, because if he was willing to do that to his incompetent employee, then who knew what his bosses would do to him if their top secret information started getting leaked all over the globe? Hopefully, it was as easy as threatening to post this online and send it to newspapers with detailed voice logs, I had been recording basically every time we were even remotely near those goons.

"What if they don't make a deal with us?" Heather said, fear still controlling her voice.

"For the first time, I'm sure that we have what it takes to set us free from this horrible reality we have found ourselves in recently," I replied with true bravado.

"Having the idea is the easy part. Now we have to actually structure this plan realistically so that we can achieve it and also muster up the courage to pull it off. Both are easier said than done," I continued, getting more serious.

"Don't worry about the negotiation. You can leave that to me. Even if my dad is mad at me, I'm still his little girl," Heather replied self-assuredly.

"I guess it's settled. We sleep and then find Alexa in the morning," I said with a twinge of sadness entering my voice. Heather could sense the sadness pouring out of me like a waterfall shrouded in darkness, and hugged me softly. I rolled out our sleeping bags and got into mine after throwing a few more logs on the fire to keep it burning through the night.

I lay there as images of the last few days passed through my head. All with a sort of sepia tone obscuring them, making them all seem jumbled together and far away. I awaited the sweet embrace of slumber, accepting whatever might come as my eyelids grew heavier and heavier.

Nightmare 8

I awoke in a void again this time. Nothing around me, no longer was I reliving memories. I was just there. Existing. Floating in an endless abyss. Honestly, it really reflected how I felt right now. My heart felt like it had been swallowed by the darkness. With Alexa gone, everything felt wrong. Even sleeping right now felt wrong. I wasn't curious about what was happening in the nightmare, I just wanted to see my friend again. Thinking this must have woken up a part of my brain because as soon as I thought that I saw Alexa standing in front of me around a hundred feet away. A floor appeared below us that was seemingly made of water. The water rippled around Alexa's ankles as she continued staring away from me.

I tried to start walking but my body wouldn't listen. Then the figure that I thought was Alexa turned. Something was wrong with her appearance, but I couldn't make out what from this distance. My body let me walk forward finally and as I got closer I noticed the thing that was wrong with her. Alexa's eyes were oozing some black slime from them, and it started to stream down her face and fall into the water below her. It was unsettling, to say the least. Then as I continued to get closer she started to vanish slowly, losing opacity as I approached. Then she was completely gone, and I tried to scream out to her to beg her not to go but my voice wouldn't come out.

I fell to my knees in the puddle and looked up at the pitch-black sky wishing for her to come back. I needed her by my side. I felt lost and small without her there. She had always been there, my whole life. Alexa and I had been together. It was surreal to realize that she was truly gone now. It was all my fault, why hadn't I gone after her? Did she even want me to go after her? What would I have said when I caught up with her? Sorry for being so dumb, I should have chosen you? No, that was dumb. I knew she needed to be alone in my mind, but my heart kept telling me she needed someone to be on her side. Which one of them was right? Of course, I didn't have the answers, but I figured I'd ask anyway.

I looked down into the water and saw my reflection. My leg was glowing again, but it didn't hurt this time. This time it just felt warm. I could feel my heartbeat through my leg as I touched it. It seemed to be pulsating the light and throbbing, but I felt no pain. This was unfamiliar to me. I was so used to it being an excruciating punishment that I had been dealt, but now it seemed more like a minor nuisance compared to what had happened to me recently. As I thought these thoughts, my leg continued to heat up until it was hot to the touch. It was so hot it almost left burns on my hands from just touching it.

I tried to shove it into the black water but all it did was cover the leg and not soothe any heat I felt. This was bad. I needed to do something before it burned me up. I stood up and my leg buckled, dropping me back to my knees. I looked back into the water and saw someone else staring back up at me. This time it wasn't my reflection but Heather. It felt as if she were staring through my entire body. Her thousand-yard stare was beginning to freak me out, and I really wanted to leave so I started to crawl in the direction Alexa had been.

But after a short while, I hit a wall impeding my progress and stopping me dead in my tracks. Heather then rose up from out of the water and walked towards me. Something was sinister about her; she had a bad aura. She made it to me in just a few steps and touched my back softly. As soon as her hand made contact with my back, her hand began to glow. I felt the energy drain from my leg as if she were taking it from me.

Then she vanished as well, turning into a hill of dust that had been swallowed by the slightly rippling waves of water. What had just happened? What did that image of Heather mean? As I thought this, I heard a voice call out to me. It was a voice I knew all too well. It was Alexa. She needed me and I couldn't let her down again.

"RYAN! Where are you?! I'm lost and I really need you!" what what she had said. I looked all around and couldn't see her anywhere. Where had she gone? I continued to scan my surroundings, but much to my dismay she was nowhere to be seen.

Then as if on cue my leg reignited and began to burn again, this time with a searing pain that I had experienced many times before. The pain I was all too used to started returning and crippled me. I couldn't move. I was utterly stuck.

"Wait for me, Alexa!" I shouted toward the voice.

"Ryan! I can't wait. I'm stuck. I need you now more than ever. Please!" she shouted back at me.

I tried to fight through the pain, but tendrils of void lashed out and grasped onto me as soon as I got back to my feet. I fought the searing pain and the beast that *was my own mind holding me back as I slowly took each step closer to my friend.*

I couldn't see her, but I heard her voice getting louder and that had to mean I was almost at her. I could find her like she had found me so many times before. We were more than friends; we were family and family meant that no one gets left behind. No matter how mad or upset you are with your family, that bond breaks down all frustrations. These bonds make us fallible, but they also give us what is essential to sentience. Without familial bonds, we wouldn't be any better than wild animals that accept the fact that many of their kin will die. Sure, it is natural that bunnies who have tens or even hundreds of kids each year shouldn't get hung up on the weaker offspring dying, but that lack of connection to something so precious is what sets us apart from beings focused purely on survival. Sure, in their own way, humans are often purely focused on self-preservation, but it's the ability to recognize that ruthlessness and choose to abandon it or embrace it that makes us so special.

As soon as I made it to where I'd heard the voice, suddenly Heather again appeared from the lake beneath me and grabbed my hand, dragging me down.

Chapter 26

I woke up in a cold sweat, lying on my side staring at the barren wooden wall in front of me. I looked at the time on my phone and it said it was only 5 A.M. Now that I thought about it, when was the time we had fallen asleep? The pitch-black windows made me feel lethargic, but I still forced myself to sit up. My eyes adjusted to the dim room from the faint embers of the coals that were hanging on for dear life. I wanted to look for Alexa, but I couldn't just leave Heather alone here either. I was stuck in an impossible impasse, and thought what better way to pass the time than by throwing more logs quietly onto the fire, and starting to write.

I dug through the piles of papers and pulled out my notebook. Looking at the rough leather binding and the worn pages that had been turned too much gave me a sense of melancholy. But I could feel I was close to reaching the end of my story and I couldn't start to get lazy now. Even while we were being hunted, there was something soothing about being able to tunnel vision on doing something other than just staying alive. That was honestly what had kept me so cool the whole time we had been stuck in this hellish adventure.

The Lion Who Wanted to Reach the Moon Ch. 6

The lion was dragged back into the waking realm by a frantic owl. She seemed to be worried about something, but the grogginess was keeping the lion from hearing what she was saying. He looked around and noticed that the moon was still in the sky, so it wasn't the fact that it was turning day.

"Hey! Are you finally listening to me?!" the owl shouted.

"Yes, what are you squawking about back there?" he replied, annoyed.

"The snake is gone! She has slithered off somewhere and hasn't been back in a while. All she said was that she needed to do something," she said, still in a panic.

"Hmm. Now that you mention it, my back does feel lighter. Well, she must have had her reasons to leave. What point is there for us to worry?" he said indifferently.

"Wow, that's pretty cold. I didn't like her much either, but she was still one of us. How can you be so flippant about her leaving?" she said in a frustrated tone. She kept getting more upset as time went on. The thought that he could just be fine with a friend disappearing infuriated her to no end.

"Fine. If it will appease you, we can look for her before we continue heading up," the lion said with a heavy sigh.

"Yes, that should do," she responded, contented with him making the correct decision.

The lion started towards the edge of the cliff and looked down at the side they had come from to see if the snake had tried to go in that direction. Going down a cliff was easier than going up one. But there was no sign of her. He turned around and paced towards the other end of the ledge. He looked down off this ledge and saw more of the same, just a rock wall facing toward the ever-descending moon.

Suddenly, he heard a voice in his head. It sounded like the snake. It was telling him to keep going up. So, he did as he was told and started to ascend the mountain again.

"What are you doing!? You can't just give up on her!" the owl protested furiously.

"I'm not giving up. I have a feeling she is up here," the lion replied.

"That is insane, how could she climb up so high without you?" the owl shouted back concernedly.

"She had made it up fairly high without my help previously. I think she can manage," he replied calmly.

"Okay... I trust you," she said, her voice falling silent.

The lion continued to climb in silence, feeling a somewhat worrying sensation in his stomach. But each time he wanted to hesitate and falter he heard the snake's voice telling him to push forward. He hoped and wished that she really had continued her way up and that he wasn't traveling away from her. He could sense that the owl felt the same way as she continued to shiver with fear at the thought of her being gone.

Finally, the two had made it to a clearing drenched in moonlight. There was a single tree on this snow-covered peak, and as the moon bathed them in its glow, he noticed a glint reflecting from the leaves. He looked up at the tree suspiciously. He could tell something was up in the tree but wasn't sure if it was the snake or something else.

"Hello?" He roared the question towards the object. Yet it did not respond to his calls.

"Snake? Is that you?" the owl said as she flapped her wings to fly upward toward the object.

"Snake. Reply to us. What game are you playing?" the lion growled and started to get angry.

"Ahhhh!" the owl shrieked in fear and agony.

"What happened?" the lion questioned.

"I've been bitten," she called back down.

"Bitten by what exactly?" the lion shouted back.

"The snake. She seems to have gone mad. She wasn't responding, and when I got close, she lunged at me and bit my wing. I need to come back down," she said as she landed on the lion's sturdy haunches.

"What happened to her? Also, are you doing okay?" the lion continued to question hurriedly.

"I think I should be fine. I'm just a bit dizzy. I have no clue what happened to her. But she doesn't seem like the snake we know," she replied, tending to her wounded wing.

As the lion was about to ask another question, he noticed the body of the snake limply falling from the tree. It appeared the snake had been knocked out, or at least was exhausted enough to just pass out. It fell straight through the fluffy soft snow and slammed into the hard rock below with an enormous THUD!

"Oh no! Is she going to be, okay?!" the owl shouted when she heard the thud.

"I'm not sure but I should probably pick her up and fix her injuries before we head further up the mountain," he said, concern entering his voice. He dressed

her wounds, luckily she didn't have any serious injuries, and he also tended to the owl to make sure she was totally okay as well. Then he made a small igloo-like shelter and dragged his companions inside to rest for the day as the sun slowly ascended into the sky, its creeping tendrils wrestling control of the night sky away from the moon. As he watched the sunrise he curled up into a small ball with his companions and fell asleep in his makeshift igloo.

I finished writing the excerpt I had been working on and decided it was time to wake Heather up. I checked the time again and it was nearly 8:00 A.M. I had been writing for almost three hours. I absolutely needed to go looking for Alexa now. With the sun up, Heather's father's goons probably had been up all night searching for us. This meant that potentially they would be getting sloppier. Which would be the best time for us to make our move, and also search for our missing friend. Obviously, we would only find our friend if she wanted to be found, but I just had to hope she would want to be found by now.

I shook Heather awake and she looked up at me dazed and confused. She stared into my eyes, and it seemed like she realized what I was going to say and quickly got out of her sleeping bag and rolled it up. We gathered all of the evidence we would need to prove our claims and stuck it in my backpack. As I threw the backpack strap over my shoulder it jostled and made the faint sound of loose paper tumbling around. I grabbed some protein bars from my backpack for breakfast, and then we both nodded to one another as we stepped out of the door together to find a friend. In silence, we had both agreed we couldn't just leave Akexa alone. She would get herself caught or even worse just flat-out killed for being obstinate.

"Do you know where she could have gone?" Heather said with an inquisitive look on her face.

"I think I know a place she could have gone. Actually, more like a couple of places that we need to check. She will definitely be at one of them, I know that for sure," I replied in a confident tone.

"Are you sure that this isn't just your hubris talking?" she said, questioning my confidence.

"Surely, you are not questioning my knowledge of one of my best friends in the world. Or do you just not trust me?" I asked, feeling my pride being massacred in front of me while being unable to stop it.

"I was just wondering... Sheesh. It seems like every time you come up with ideas we always end up in dangerous positions," she remarked. I mean, she wasn't wrong, it seemed like every plan I had laid always had some kinks I could never just iron out. I had to admit it, no matter how much I hated doing so.

"What an astute observation. My best-laid plans do often go awry," I responded, quoting one of my favorite books.

"Okay, John Steinbeck... Whatever you say, dork. As long as you know that you usually come up with bad plans," she sniped back.

"Hey, I never said I came up with bad plans! I was just stating that sometimes even when you try your hardest and plan your best, something always messes them up. Why'd you assume I thought my plans were bad? Maybe you're the reason my plans have wrenches thrown into them. Ever think of that?" I yelled in an over-the-top fake upset voice.

"Oh, right, I forgot. The Boy Wonder could never make mistakes. It is us, his lowly servants, that ruin his plans. My apologies!" Heather condescendingly said in a tone I hadn't heard from her before. It was more cocky and callous-sounding than I had ever heard from her. I guessed some people are just really good at hiding aspects of themselves. I wondered if Alexa had hidden any parts of her personality from me. I thought this but immediately I knew better, she was too dumb to create manipulative images of herself just to fool others around her.

Heather on the other hand seemed to be fairly adept and spinning false narratives. Maybe she wasn't as reliable as she always seemed to be. That couldn't be true, right? She never appeared untrustworthy to me but Alexa sure couldn't ever bring herself to trust her. Alexa was often a better judge of character than I, but something about Heather was just so disarming to me. I didn't know what it was about her, maybe her silky hair that flowed so effortlessly with the breeze or her beautiful emerald eyes that swallowed my thoughts when I looked into them. She could always break down the fortress I had built around my heart with the snap of her fingers. It was almost as if she had some form of control over me. Even I recognized it, but there was nothing I could do even knowing she had this gravitational pull on me.

We walked towards my car in the blindingly white snow, and as we reached for the door handles I unlocked it. I broke the ice off of her and my doors, and then we got in and started the car. I drove towards a secret hiding place Alexa and I would always go to, but as we sped across the sprawling fields, I didn't see any footprints laid out in the snow. That meant she wasn't there because it hadn't been snowing last night, so any and all prints would be extremely apparent.

Then I drove back onto the main street that surrounded the town. We drove on it for around ten minutes as I made it towards the back of Alexa's house. Maybe she had come home to sleep for the first time in days. I saw many footprints in her backyard, which meant those goons must have already been there, but it didn't mean that Alexa hadn't shown up after they had left. I parked and got out of the car silently and started to creep towards the house. I peered around the corner to see the street her house was facing and didn't see any cars in either direction. This meant we had to have been safe because there weren't any cars parked behind the rows of houses either.

I walked into the empty house and was hit with a wave of nostalgia. I imagined Alexa's mom making food while her dad opened the front door and made the same tired old joke he did every time he came home from work. I remembered him calling out to Alexa and me to get us to come down and tell him about our days as dinner was about to be served.

I pictured Alexa coming down the stairs in one of the dresses she hated to wear but always changed into because her dad loved them so much. I would never tell her this, but she was stunning, and I was glad she always chose to be my best friend. Thinking this, I started to tear up as I ascended the stairs towards her room. I knocked on the door slightly and opened it when I didn't get an answer. I opened the closet and called her name. No answer still. Heather was just slightly behind me like my shadow. She didn't say any words and stayed out of the light. Alexa was nowhere to be found.

"I guess that was another place we can check off the list. I have one more place I think she might go. Other than that, I have no clue where she could have gone," I said in a sober tone.

"Okay, Ryan. I trust you. Let's go find her and finish this quest we're on," Heather said with determination in her voice.

I walked out of the back door and walked to my car with Heather following me. She was tailing just behind me as we reached the car at the same time. We got into it again and she smiled a soft caring smile at me. She was trying to calm me down. It was telling me not to worry and that she was sure we would find Alexa. She could sense I was starting to panic and was just keeping it inside.

I started the car and the engine hummed to life as I threw it into drive, and we sped off towards our final spot to check. *Alexa has to be there,* I thought to myself because I couldn't bear to imagine what would have happened to her if we didn't find her. Because the thought of someone else finding her first was killing me. Heather softly grabbed my arm and squeezed it, and I felt some of the tension from my body fade away.

Chapter 27

We pulled up to the last place I assumed Lex could have gone. My house. Something told me that it made more sense for her to go to my house than her own. But still I wanted to check hers first in case she had really been there. I was certainly worried about what we would find but with Heather by my side I believed that we'd find her safe and sound.

I parked the car in my backyard and we both got out, silently closing our car doors. I didn't even lock it so that no one would hear or see us at all. I approached the back door of my house and opened it slightly. I peeked in making sure that no one was there and then stepped into the familiar structure.

I crept around the first floor, checking every closet and every hiding spot I knew about from the years of playing hide and seek in this rickety old building. I motioned for Heather to stay close to my side so that we wouldn't have the chance of being separated or one of us be caught and taken away. That was my biggest fear, having all the people I cared about pulled from my life. I ascended the stairs and walked the hallway I had walked down so many times. Never would I have thought that I was going to feel this level of uneasiness walking this hall. I checked all the hallways closets and then went into the bedrooms.

I checked the guest bedroom first. Then I checked the master at the end of the hallway. Finally, I came back to my room as the final spot to look. She had to be here. I could feel her presence. At least, my heart wanted to feel her presence here. I opened the door, and my room was empty. Everything was as I'd left it just a few days ago. Sure, things were slightly strewn about, and the bed was still messy, but it was the same as I'd left it. Nothing seemed to be out of place.

I was starting to get desperate, so I knew I had one more thing to try to draw her out of hiding. I was sure she was here. She had to be. I whistled a tune discordantly. Heather looked at me with a quizzical look, and I just held my finger up telling her to be silent. I continued whistling one half of a call sign, and then suddenly we heard another person whistling the other half of the tune. We harmonized, and I smiled as I pointed to my closet door that was ajar. Out stepped Alexa. Her beautiful blonde hair flowing, perfectly framing her face. She looked very picturesque, and she smiled at me. It seemed some of her trust in me had been restored.

I pointed to Alexa's hiding spot and motioned for all of us to step into the secret clubhouse I had hidden in the recess of that closet. I went in first, and then the other two followed me into the cramped crawl space.

"Okay, we should probably still be quiet, but we should be pretty safe hidden in here for now," I said, looking around with a sense of nostalgia, seeing this room the same as it had been when we were just kids.

"What are you both doing here? It's dangerous to go places they would assume we could go," Alexa said in a lecturing tone.

"Not any more dangerous than running off on your own without a plan," Heather sniped back.

"We aren't here to fight. We need to stick together on this for the plan to work. If we're divided, then we're as good as dead," I said with a grim expression.

"You're right. While Lexi was playing hide and seek, we came up with a plan to get out of this," Heather said mockingly. I really wished they would just get along for once. Like, how hard was it really to just agree on something as simple as not wanting to die?

"Really? You two dunces came up with a plan?" Alexa replied incredulously.

"Yes, we're going to threaten to unredact these files and then post them online and send them to a bunch of newspaper slash stations. But we won't on the condition that they release your parents and we just all pretend none of this ever even happened. Of course, they will probably want the destruction of the files in return, but once the agreement is all negotiated and settled, I believe they will think our offer to be generous," Heather responded with a completely different attitude than she normally had. After Alexa had finished mulling over the information, she finally spoke.

"Hmm. It doesn't sound too shabby. But there is one thing missing. The fact that they could welch on the deal at any point after we destroy the evidence. I say we don't compromise on the destruction of the evidence, maybe we just hand over the originals but make copies to keep in our back pocket in case the deal goes sour. This way they assume all evidence is gone, and if they hold up their end of the bargain then good. But if they don't hold up their end, we release it anyway and blow up their organization. Eye for an eye style. Except of course we probably die if they end up reneging the deal."

"You're right, Lex. What would I do without you," I replied, smiling.

"You'd be dead," she responded with malice dripping off of her words.

"Sheesh… I mean, probably, but did you really have to be so blunt about it?" I said, feeling hurt by what she had said.

"Anyways. What took you two so long to come looking for me?" Alexa replied with a suspicious glare at both of us. Then she and Heather locked eyes and had an extremely intense staring contest. Neither seemed like they were going to back down any time soon, so I just sat back waiting for their challenge to expire.

They kept this game going for a while. Without even realizing it, fifteen minutes had passed while they were just focusing on staring daggers into the other. It didn't look like either was getting fatigued either. They seemed to have infinite stamina when it came to this. I had never seen either of them so intense before. It changed my view on both of them slightly.

"Okay, girls. That's enough of that we need to draft up emails to the news stations and papers as well as get physical copies of this document," I said with a serious expression on my face.

"Whatever," they both said in unison. I decided I'd had enough of their boorish and childlike behavior for now and I would go make the copies alone.

"I'm going to go get the copies done alone. You two can start typing up the emails. Or don't, it's on you. I'm tired of having to act like a parent telling you what you should be doing. I just need some alone time to reset and recharge myself," I said, annoyed. They both started to frown and look down, breaking eye contact for the first time in twenty-five minutes. I saw a deep blush from embarrassment creep across their faces before I crawled out of the hidey hole and looked for my printer.

"There you are. You never let me down, do you?" I said as I approached my trusty printer in the corner of my room.

I reached into my backpack and pulled out the two pages I needed to copy and stuck them in the printer. I copied both pages front and back. I needed the back because the lettering from the redaction bled through there, and that was the only way to be able to actually read it. Good thing my printer was somewhat new because it wasn't super loud, but it was still loud enough to make me cringe as it printed out the copies. In the back of my head, I was still afraid they'd show up at the perfect time to hear my printer, and then catch us all. As I was imagining this, my pages finished printing and I quickly gave them a once-over to ensure that you could read the redaction. When I was able to read the redaction I smiled, did a slight fist pump, and snuck quietly back over to my closet and climbed back to my seat.

When I made it inside the secret room, the air felt unusual. It was slightly warmer than when I had left. They'd probably had a yelling fight while the printer was drowning out their voices. It was either that or they had a quick fist fight and cleaned up in the four minutes it took me to copy and check the documents. I didn't believe the latter, and the former seemed way more likely in my head already. I frowned at them, showing I disapproved of their behavior, but there was nothing I could do to change them.

"I guess now it's time we draft up emails. I scanned the documents for all of us from my printer. We should be able to just hit the forward button and create some emails and type up drafts for social media posts to potentially expose these documents if we need to," I said, feeling some exhaustion hitting me. Even though I had slept through the night last night, all of that active dreaming had wiped out all of my energy even now. With that coupled with the fact that I had to find a missing person, I was completely drained.

Suddenly I felt a sharp pain in my leg. It was as if I had just sat and slammed my ankle into a knife. Then I felt the pain go up my leg. The sensation was equivalent to my calf being fileted off my body. The pain was excruciating. I clutched it up towards my chest and lay down on the ground rolling around. The room wasn't very spacious. It was about six feet by seven feet, so I was basically touching one of the girls each time I rolled over. I didn't want to seem dramatic to them but at the same time I couldn't control my actions. The pain completely overtook all of my brain function.

I silently screamed out in pain, begging to be released from this hell. Yet no one came to answer my prayers. I had been left to rot. In my despair, I noticed the horrified look on my companions' faces. They must have been terrified, but I couldn't focus on either of them for the time being. I felt like I was going to die.

As I was panicking because I thought for sure this was the end for me, my vision started getting hazy, slowly everything started to lose focus and I couldn't see details on even the floorboards inches away from my face. Then my vision started to fade completely. It turned pitch black, and I was alone feeling like I was floating.

I started to focus on the sound of my heartbeat, since my vision had failed me. I figured maybe I could calm myself and alleviate the pain I was experiencing. Slowly the pain began to fade away. Another image flashed into the void I was suspended in. It was the same kid that had fallen into that hole in the library. This time I called out to them. They didn't respond but they did slightly turn towards me. But it didn't matter because, as I was starting to see their faces more clearly, I was awake again on the ground.

The pain was gone, and both of the girls were sitting above me looking down with concern. Heather was softly holding my right hand and Alexa was caressing my cheek. It appeared they both also tried to soothe me.

Maybe it was them who pulled me out of that horrible experience just then. I did wish I could have stayed just a few seconds longer to see the kid.

I was certain that I knew who the kid was, but without seeing their face I couldn't tell who it was exactly. It had to have been someone I knew very well for my brain to be trying so hard to hide it from me. It usually only did that when it thought I wouldn't be able to handle what had happened emotionally.

Honestly, that defense mechanism was a blessing and a curse. Of course, it was nice to not remember every single horrible thing that had ever happened to me. On the other hand, it was also hard to not remember these experiences because it often meant people associated with them would also be forgotten.

Our brain is a magical thing like that. Memories are not retellings of a story but a completely different recount each time. The only problem with my brain is that most recollections start out similar, and then with time they fade into insanity. My mind instead would just completely omit people and events that had happened to me.

As I was thinking this, I felt a single drop of water hit my forearm. I looked up to see Heather crying over me. She was too empathetic for her own good sometimes. I wished I wasn't causing them a similar pain to what I was experiencing. But often seeing a loved one experience a pain like I was, pain that you couldn't do anything to help or alleviate, makes us also feel some of their shared pain.

I smiled at both of them and sat up to show that the worst was over and that they needn't worry about me. But it seemed to have the opposite effect as they both clutched one of my arms to their chests tightly.

"I'm okay, guys, really. I don't know what that was. I haven't been feeling the pain for a while recently. It was odd that it happened just now. But it's done and I really am not hurting anymore. Thank you for caring so much," I said, feeling humbled by their genuine caring expressions.

"Let's just get this dumb thing over with and start writing these emails and posts so that you and our lives can go back to normal," Alexa said with a twinge of guilt entering her voice.

We sat there drafting emails to various different news stations and papers, as well as creating copy and paste-able posts for Facebook, Twitter, and Instagram. After thirty minutes had passed, we all looked at each other with a renewed sense of determination and a deeper feeling of hope that this plan would really work and set us free.

Chapter 28

I quietly climbed out of the closet and stretched because my legs were starting to cramp up. All that was left for us was to confront Heather's father. Once we had done that, we would have our answer as to if we could ever truly be free of this purgatory. I really hoped we could just let this all pass by us and return to normal life. I had missed so much school at this point leading up to winter break, I didn't even know if I'd still be able to take the tests, I needed to pass the current classes I had. But that was a bridge I'd have to cross when I got to it. Right now, I needed to hyper-focus on the task at hand. This was a very delicate game we were playing. Ignorance would spell our demise.

We were standing on the precipice of everything we had gone through. This was the end of this chapter of our lives but hopefully not the full end of our lives. I was having a tough time coming to terms with the severity of our situation. I really couldn't believe that he would be able to kill us. Like, how could his conscience reconcile the destruction of these children's lives? Children that he had watched grow from basically birth. You'd have to be truly heartless to be able to go through with that. But rationalizing it wouldn't work because Heather was certain that he was capable of ending our lives without hesitation.

I slid back into the hiding spot to gather the girls because we couldn't sit there forever.

"Heather, you should text your father. Tell him we want to meet alone at four P.M. This will give us time to set up for his arrival. Give him the location of the abandoned mansion. Tell him if he doesn't come alone the deal is off. We just want to talk to him. No games," I said to Heather to initiate the next phase of our plan. It was currently 11:00 A.M. so we had some time before the meeting. This would ensure we had ample time to work while setting a minor trap in the mansion. As well I wanted to set the location up with something to jam radio signals so he wouldn't be able to call for backup without us noticing.

"Okay, it's sent," Heather replied straight-faced.

"Why did you set it for so late?" Alexa said with a confused look on her face.

"I'm going to set up a few radio signal jammers to place around the mansion so he can't try any tricks," I replied with a smirk.

"Since when do you know how to program? Let alone make a radio signal jammer," Alexa replied, scoffing.

"I took a lot of courses over the summer while you were out camping and traveling," I responded in a more serious tone.

"But do you really know how to make a radio signal jammer?" Alexa continued to question me.

"Creating a universal radio signal jammer is actually fairly easy and inexpensive. I always had a bunch of spare CC1101 boards and Arduino Pro Micro boards to manufacture them. So, rigging up a jammer for our purposes would be a sinch," I replied while I pulled out all of the materials to manufacture the jammers.

It took around twenty minutes, but after the clock struck 11:30 A.M. I'd finished creating and programming the jammers. I smiled down at my creations and made a chef's kiss gesture.

"Bada-bing. My masterpieces are complete," I said, patting myself on the back.

"This just looks like a bunch of junk with wires connecting it to more junk. Are you sure this will even work?" Alexa said with a skeptical look on her face.

"Of course, I'm sure it'll work. It has to work. Too bad we don't have any walkie-talkies to test it out right now. One thing I do need to bring is the two old laptops here. I need to make sure they're charged before we head over because I'm certain that the wall outlets in that abandoned mansion do not work. Not just because no one has paid a power bill in God knows how long, but also due to the fact that many of the walls are heavily water damaged, which usually doesn't play well with more than likely exposed wires, because that thing was made like a hundred years ago," I said back, explaining what exactly I was thinking for setting up the jammers. I'd plug each one into a laptop positioned near places we wanted Heather's dad to stay so we could keep him contained.

The hunters were about to become the hunted, at least for a short while. I was sure that he wouldn't expect us to have thought this far ahead. However, we couldn't be sure when he would show up either. So, we all might be meeting sooner than the requested time. We just had to make it there first to have the upper hand. I plugged in both laptops and checked each one. The first one was basically fully charged, but the second one, covered in stickers and art from years ago, was only at forty-four percent. There was no way that would be enough for our jammer to stay on the whole time we were there. Especially not on an older laptop with a considerably worse battery than the first one.

"Okay, how long do we have to wait?" Heather said with an impatient attitude.

"I'd say we have about two hours to kill to let this thing get up to somewhere in the mid-eighties," I replied, a time frame that Heather was seemingly displeased by as she frowned as soon as I mentioned the full wait time.

"Oh well... I guess nothing can be done. Do you have any other plans besides jamming his signal? Like, are we going to lock him in or something? Maybe hold him at gunpoint?" Alexa said, her deviousness starting to take hold of her.

"No. No guns. I guess we could lock him in, but whoever would be doing that would be open to being captured by whoever else may be waiting outside for him," I said after mulling over the ideas she had proposed.

"You're no fun at all," Alexa said with an evil smile.

"That's still my dad you're talking about. Sure, he may be evil and is hunting us, but you can't treat him like he isn't human," Heather said, starting to sound upset.

"She's right, Lex. He's still a person. He's just doing what he thinks is best. No matter how wrong his actions are, they are misguided and probably come from a sense of duty above all else. Also, if we treat him like an animal, how are we any better than he is?" I said, latching onto Heather's point.

"Of course, we're better than they are. They're evil. They made our parents disappear. They want to kill us. I say an eye for an eye. You reap what you sow. I can't be the only person who is ticked off enough to want to destroy them and everything they hold dear like they did to us." Alexa continued to berate us both with her speech about morality. She pretended that she was better than they were when she suggested we do the same things they would do to us. This was sickening. I never in a million years could have believed that Alexa would be saying something like this in front of me. I literally wanted to throw up, I was so nauseated at the thought of her blood lust.

"Lex. This is going too far. I can't in good conscience allow you to hurt these people in irreparable ways like you wish to. You sound exactly like one of them right now," I said with a solemn expression on my face. The expression didn't last long. As soon as I had finished what I was saying, my expression shifted to one of extreme disappointment in my best friend.

"This isn't too far, Ryan. My life is ruined. Nothing will ever go back to how it used to be. I want to make them feel the same way I do right now. Which is incredibly hollow," Alexa responded as her face flooded with a deluge of tears.

I slid next to her and rubbed her back softly. She stopped talking and just sat there as she let her emotions take control of her. I used to rub her back like this all the time whenever she would get hurt, and it always seemed to bring her back to reality.

I started to hum in her ears softly as I continued to massage her back tenderly. I felt the knots and tension in her shoulders start to melt away. Then after all of that her arms fell down to her sides in defeat, allowing me to win the battle in her heart. Thankfully, this still worked because I couldn't bear to see her go down that path.

I finished rubbing her back and then placed my hand on her right shoulder, giving it a tight squeeze. She frowned and looked back up at me with the tears starting to dry from her eyes.

"I just want them to feel how it feels to be helpless. It's not fair!!" Alexa shouted.

"Shhh. I know. I know. It's not fair. But it'll be okay. I'm here. We'll always be together," I whispered into her ear softly.

"Yeah, Alexa. We're always by your side. I mean that. From now until the end of time," Heather said, sliding next to us and wrapping her arms around Alexa.

"See? We both care about you so much. We'll get through this. We don't need to stoop to their level to beat them. We're better than them. We should show them that they can never break us," I said with a smile slowly taking over my face.

I couldn't help but feel happy and a sense of pride for being able to soothe the angry goddess. If she'd gone off the rails again, I'm sure she would have done something she regretted. But with us here we were able to talk her back from the ledge. She didn't take the plunge and just stepped back into our arms, accepting us.

We sat there and looked at the clock, seeing it was just about to strike 1:00 P.M. All dreading the fact that we were about to leave the safety of my house and my hidden closet hideout.

"I guess we should get going. So, we can set our trap, right?" I said with a slight shrug.

"Yeah, we should head out. We really need to make it there before he does. If we let him beat us there, we lose almost all chance of our plan succeeding," Heather responded in a reasonable tone. She had her head in the game, I could tell. She was a woman on a mission, and nothing was going to stop her from achieving her goal.

This side of her I didn't often get to see. She usually was more quiet and reserved. Sometimes she was almost timid. But this was a complete one-eighty. She was confident and completely certain about what she wanted to do and how she was going to achieve it. Heather had a glow about her right now. The fire inside of her illuminated her surroundings, breathing life into all beings that surrounded her.

I felt refreshed and energized just by her presence. She was truly something else. I could tell that Heather's determination and readiness was infecting Alexa as well because she was packing with much more vigor than normal.

She didn't have much to pack. But what she did she was just throwing into her pack, faster than I had ever seen her do before. Both of these women were on another level. I looked at them and was proud of everything we had done as a team and proud that I was even able to know such supportive people.

We finished getting ready and packed, so I led the way down the stairs and out of the house. We walked into my backyard to see my car just as I had left it. Gone were the times I would have weird notes placed on my windshield or slid into the crack of my door. It was funny to think that just a few days ago Heather had been the one following us around and we weren't even on her dad's radar. Now her dad had caught our scent and like a bloodhound who'd smelled a family of foxes he wasn't going to stop until the foxes were dead.

Even the weather was ominous. There was a dark veil of clouds blocking out the sun's rays. As I was thinking about this bad omen, it went from bad to worse as snow started to come down in sheets. Driving was starting to feel dangerous, but we had to make it to the meeting place before he did. If he was even coming.

As we drove over to the meeting place, Heather's father still hadn't replied to our message. But as soon as we made it out to the mansion, I saw Heather's phone light up with a response from him.

"What does it say?" I asked, curious as to what he would respond to us with.

"All he sent was a thumbs-up emoji," Heather said with a puzzled look on her face for a second.

"That's weird. I figured he'd fight us more on this," I replied, even more confused than she was.

"So was I... I figured he would've said no, he would never give into our demands. With a couple of insults about me being insolent splashed on top. But we didn't get either of those in our response. Something isn't right," Heather said with a melancholy expression on her face.

I parked in the back behind the mansion, and we walked in through the back door. I still wanted to keep a low profile in case he was going to show up early. I looked for a few hiding spots to set up the laptops with the jammers, and found one cabinet that lined a wall right next to the foyer which was perfect. I placed the one with more charge in there plugged in and turned on. Then I looked for another spot to place the second less charged laptop to have more coverage.

As I thought this, I saw the stairs in front of me and ascended them quickly, ignoring the creaking and groaning from the boards as I continued to bound up them. I walked through the decrepit hallways seeing the cobweb adorning the ceilings and made it to a large study-like room. It was almost a library, but it had no books covering its barren shelves. This also seemed like a perfect place for a jammer, so I turned on the laptop and plugged in the jammer. Then I dusted off a shelf and placed the laptop on it carefully. Then I left the room hoping that these jammers would actually work.

As I finished setting up the miniature trap for Mr. S, my phone's alarm went off, letting me know it was four o' clock. *It really took me two hours to find secure places to set up my jammers?* I thought to myself as I descended the staircase. Where could he be? Then as if on cue I heard the sound of an SUV driving over the packed snow and skidding to a stop in front of the doors that I was facing.

Well, this was the foyer, so it made sense they would park in front of the building. Then I heard heavy footsteps compacting the snow even more than it was, and as he progressed, he made it to the wooden front steps, and each creak from the old floorboards was excruciating. I looked down at the girls where Alexa was hidden behind the staircase, and Heather standing at the bottom of the staircase facing the door ready to confront her father.

Then the door handle clicked as he grabbed it, and it groaned as he slammed the door open with an enormous **THUD!**

Chapter 29

He dusted the snow off his shoulders, then stopped dead as he saw Heather. She stared daggers at him. It was the first time I had ever seen her be so intense. The sight sent a shiver down my spine. *Nothing good can come of this showdown,* I thought as Heather's dad cleared his throat and took off his hat. He smiled a wide creepy smile with yellowed teeth and blackened gums from what I could only assume was smoking.

He looked more like a mob boss than the head of a construction company. His black suit had very clearly been cleaned and pressed before he had left to meet us. Worn with a luxury black Borsalino hat that appeared to be made of wool felt. It had a sleek silky look that tied his mafioso get-up together. Meanwhile, we looked like we were basically homeless, with greasy unwashed hair and crumpled dirty clothes. The contrast in this scene was striking.

He slowly took off his hat, revealing his slicked-back black hair. He was like the picture-perfect example of evil. His chilling smile and off-putting demeanor made the scene even more ominous.

"My lovely princess. Why are you trying to break my heart?" he said in a gruff tone. He spread his arms wide as if asking for a hug.

"You know why dad. Also, you broke my heart first," she replied with an intonation that was so cold it could have made Hell freeze over.

"Don't be like that, darling. Worried so much over some street trash. I took you away from this disgustingly nauseating town to keep you away from these treacherous people. After your mother died, I couldn't bear to lose you too," he said, trying his hardest to sound sincere.

"Yeah... Taking me away from the only friends I had ever made and basically keeping me locked away from the outside world was all for me," Heather scoffed, but her stance was unyielding.

"My... my... my... It seems you have been brainwashed again by these cretins. Do I need to remind you where your place is? You belong by my side," he repliedm then began hacking as if he had something stuck in his throat.

"Where are they?" I said, finally interjecting, and my facial expression was hard as stone. I wasn't going to let him know that he made me feel uneasy.

"Stay out of this, boy! This is between me and my daughter," he responded harshly, then snapped his fingers in Heather's direction. Something weird happened at that moment. Heather's head twitched, and she looked like she was struggling, with her muscles tensing up. Then she started to walk slowly towards her father. He then looked me straight in the eye and flashed the most sinister look I had ever seen in my life. Heather then reached his side and turned around. The look in her eyes was empty. Her once green irises turned solid gray. She was acting like a zombie.

"What are you doing to her?" I shouted, breaking my poker face.

"Why, nothing, of course. She did this of her own volition," he replied maliciously.

"Yeah, right. She would never have ever done what you told her to. Heather! Wake up! Shake it off, please!" I pleaded with her. To no avail. She just continued to stare forward blankly, not even looking in my direction. It was as if she didn't even hear me at all. I frowned at my plan completely crumbling in front of my very eyes.

"Yes, boy. Now you understand how futile all of this truly is!" he said in a jovial tone. He truly was a sadistic monster. At that moment I just wanted him dead. I could feel my blood start boiling.

"I still have the proof that can topple your empire," I said, regaining my composure, holding up my phone, and gesturing to my backpack.

"Really? Who would listen to a child's story about a military compound for experimental genetic testing in this dreary town that most of Maine doesn't even know exists, let alone the United States? Doesn't it seem a little too far-fetched? Even with your proof, what does a few redacted invoices really prove?" he said, trying to make my hope falter. But I could see in his eyes that he was scared. He pretended like he wasn't afraid of this, but his body couldn't lie.

"If you read them, you'd know they're pretty damning. I'm also sure that you know that if I did leak them, even if no one believed them you'd lose all credibility to the military and be blacklisted from any future insanely lucrative contracts. On these invoices it says you were paid two-hundred-and-fifty million dollars for services procured to construct this top secret base. I'm sure that the government won't be too happy seeing that you allowed their dirty little secret to be leaked to the whole world," I responded, regaining my confidence.

"Well, I still have one more trick up my sleeve," he said with a devious smirk, and reaching into his coat pocket he clicked something and continued.

"Boys. Come in and handle this situation." There was no response.

"Boys...?" he said again, with worry starting to creep into his voice.

"They won't be coming. We're all alone here. You aren't the only one with tricks up their sleeve," I said while my smile grew wider.

"What did you do?" he said incredulously.

"Just a simple jammer. If you'd like to run outside and call for them, I'd gladly send these documents to every big news organization in America while I have to sit here and wait," I responded while watching his eyes dart around for places a jammer could be. I wasn't sure what he thought he could do if he spotted it but nonetheless it was amusing to watch his eyes frantically dart around.

"Gahh, fine! You're right! If that were to get out, that'd be the end of me! What do you want, you little bastard?!" he said, finally breaking down as he continued desperately searching for a jammer in our current room.

"You know what I want. I want Alexa and my parents returned safely and I would like you to release Heather from whatever brainwashing you have done to her," I replied in a monotone voice.

"That may be a little difficult. Heather is my daughter, and I will not allow you to take her from me," he said defiantly.

"I am not taking her from you. She is not your property. She is a living breathing person who deserves to have the ability to think for herself. How do you feel right now, being unable to refuse my demands?" I said, sturdy in my convictions.

"I hate that I have to give in to your demands," he responded, seething with anger. His face began turning red as his eyebrows only continued to furrow.

"Then how do you think Heather feels? She isn't even able to move freely because of you. What kind of father does that to their child?" I asked him honestly.

"I don't care how she feels. I can't have her leave me. I broke when her mother died. I am not about to lose the only thing left in this world that I care about," he responded, speaking sincerely for the first time since this conversation began.

"She won't leave you. You're her father. Have you ever told her that? That she means that much to you? Or have you only tried to keep her locked away so she could never escape your grasp?" I continued, trying to break down his hangup and get him to free my friend from his mental clutches.

"I haven't told her, but she should have known. Everything I have done I have done for her. How could she not notice how much I cared about her? Why would she choose some ragtag friends over her own flesh and blood?" he replied, basically having a mental breakdown.

"Why don't you set her free and ask her yourself?" I asked him, trying to trick him into setting her free. Heather stood there, still staring blankly into space. It was as if we didn't exist; honestly, it was really concerning that he had this ability to control her.

"I'll have your parents delivered to you later at both of your houses. I will be taking my daughter with me for the time being. We have some things to discuss. But you have my word that she will be returned to her normal state and will be able to decide what she wants for her future. But for now, I just want to be able to talk to her in private," he said very matter of factly as he began to turn and walk towards the door. He opened it roughly and snapped again. As soon as he snapped Heather turned around again and began walking towards the door.

"Wait! You can't take her! Also, please have both of our parents taken to my house," I shouted after him. He nodded without turning around. He completely ignored my pleas to have Heather set free. I guessed there was nothing else I could do. He had already walked into what was basically a blizzard outside the mansion.

Snow was coming down so hard it was whipping against the windows and blowing straight into the house through the open doors. I rushed towards the doors to chase them. But as soon as I reached the front steps that were covered in pure white snow, I saw the headlights of the black SUV that was parked in front of me begin to glow as it reversed and turned around, speeding off.

I fell to my knees in the freezing cold snowstorm at the top of those decrepit steps. I just wanted to let the snow swallow me. Watching the car fade into the distance broke me. How could I have planned for this? How could I have known that she had been brainwashed? Was she always brainwashed? Did she come find us as part of brainwashed orders originally? I began to overthink our entire relationship over the past few days. Was this all some convoluted plan to get mine and Alexa's family to stay silent on the construction project that they had been a part of? Why would it just be our families though? All of these questions weighed on my heart as it was pounding out of my chest in the freezing snow that was now piled all the way up to my chest.

I wanted it to just swallow me and freeze here. I didn't want to have to feel this doubt in one of my best friends. I really wanted to trust her. But how much could I genuinely believe her intentions?

"RYAN!" Alexa shouted from behind me as she grabbed my shoulders and shook me as hard as she could. I felt like I was in a clothes washing machine with how hard I had been spun around. She then dragged me backward and I fell into the house as she pulled me in just enough to be able to close the door.

"Are you crazy?!?!" she shouted in my face.

"No... I'm just numb. Was Heather against us this whole time?" I asked in a dejected tone.

"I don't think that she was. Maybe at the beginning? I'm not really sure, but that doesn't really matter right now. We need to figure out our next steps. Do you really think he's going to let her go again after what she did? He barely let go of her the first time." Alexa questioned me, trying to get me to come up with another new plan, but it felt like I had all of my energy sapped out of me.

"I can't think of anything besides the fact that Heather could have been planning to betray us this whole time. Like she could have been plotting against us at every step along the way," I responded, feeling even more broken as I voiced my thoughts.

"She couldn't have been truly trying to betray us, otherwise she would have done so earlier. She wouldn't have let us stay hidden each time we were almost caught if she were going to betray us. I don't think you should lose so much faith in her," she responded in a caring tone. I wasn't used to Alexa being this caring.

"You're right... She would've sold us out way sooner if she were going to..." I responded, feeling a little better about Heather.

"What we need to think about now is setting her free. We need to go back to her house and get him to set her free. Me and her may not get along too well, but I can't stand the way he was treating her. It made me disgusted to see someone treat another person like that, let alone their own daughter," Alexa said with malice dripping off each word.

"How could we possibly make him set her free?" I replied with a sense of hopelessness consuming my thoughts and voice.

"I don't know. That's what we need to think about. Obviously, the evidence we have isn't enough. But we might be able to find out how she was brainwashed and break it on our own?" Alexa said with less confidence than before.

"How would we even do that?" I asked her with a confused look on my face.

"Well, we do have a lot of Heather's stuff here. Maybe she subconsciously knew she was brainwashed and wrote down things that may help us break her free from it? I mean, it's a start, isn't it?" Alexa said with almost no confidence in her words.

"Hmm... I think I know a place to look for that," I said as I walked back into the kitchen and grabbed Heather's backpack. I dug into it and pulled out a soft leather-bound book. It had a reddish-brown hue and the word "Diary" scrawled on the front of it. I opened it up and began to read from the first page.

Chapter 30

I stared down at the pages of Heather's diary feeling like I was besmirching our friendship. I really didn't want to read her deepest inner thoughts without permission. But this felt like the only way for us to be able to find anything at all about what may have been done to her. I started to feel this inner rage coming back at the thought of her being forced to listen to all the commands her father dictated.

I was seeing red, and it was making it hard to read the words in front of me. I couldn't do this. I needed to calm down but a part of me didn't want to calm down. Alexa seemed to notice me struggling with this predicament and then leaned over and started to gently rub my back.

"You need to cool off, don't you?" she said sweetly and in a concerned tone.

"Yes, but I don't know how. I'm just so angry right now," I replied, defeated.

"I know you are, Watson. I am too. But I think I have one way you can calm down. You just need to focus your energy into something else right now," she said with a tender smile on her lips as she reached down into my backpack that was slumped against the table leg. She pulled out my notebook and flipped to the page I had stopped writing on.

She held the book out for me to take but I just stared at it blankly. Alexa really did know me. She had been with me my whole life. I was glad we could still be as we were. I looked back down and saw the book in my hand. I must have zoned out and taken it from her while I was thinking about the past. Well, whatever the case, I guessed you never knew when a story would appear. Right? I flipped to the next empty page and began to write, letting the real world slip away from me.

The Lion Who Wanted to Reach the Moon Ch. 7

The lion woke up, and the igloo had almost completely melted around them. He shook off the loose snow that had fallen onto his back while he was asleep and looked around, but couldn't seem to find his companions anywhere.

"OWL?! SNAKE!?" he roared as loud as he possibly could. His shouts were deafening, there was no way they wouldn't be able to hear him.

"Yes?" the owl called back sweetly. Her attitude seemed to be more chipper than it had been the previous night.

"Do you happen to know where the snake has run off to again?" the lion questioned, somewhat suspicious of them both disappearing this time.

"Why, I had no clue she was even gone. Maybe she had run off again?" she replied. It was obvious to the lion that she had been hiding something.

"Well, then I guess I will have to look for her again. What another waste of a night," the lion responded, still not totally sold on whether the owl was telling him the truth or not.

"We could always leave her and reach the pinnacle of the peak together and return for her on our trip downward," the owl said, trying to offer a solution.

*"I suppose we could. Couldn't we?" the lion answered, totally suspicious of the owl now. Just last night she had been terrified of leaving the snake behind. Now she **wanted** us to abandon her? This was not anything like the loving, caring owl he had become accustomed to.*

"Onward and upward, is what I always say!" she said in an overtly happy voice. She then seemed to try to calm herself as she realized she was also being too suspicious at this point as she hurriedly flapped to land on his back.

"Okay then... Up we go, I guess..." the lion said skeptically. He began his ascent, climbing the mountain again. In the back of his mind, he was focused on looking for the snake, though. He looked off the cliff at every chance he had. He didn't want to make the owl realize he was scoping out for the snake as he still wasn't

totally sure what her part in all of this was.

As he was climbing, the moon began to hit its apex above them, absorbing the entire sky and covering the land below with a milky white glow. It illuminated everything around the mountain, as it seemed it was directly above it. The lion could now see each crevasse in perfect detail.

As he was focused on looking down, he missed one of his jumps and slipped back down to a ledge just slightly below his previous position. The fall seemed perilous, so the owl fluttered slightly above his head while he regained his footing. Then something caught his eye as he was refamiliarizing himself with his surroundings. A glint of light shot clear into his eyes, reflecting off of some surface. The pearlescent light was a perfect thing to track back to the reflective source. He followed the beam with his eyes and saw the origin of the reflection.

Much to his dismay he saw a lifeless-looking body that was all too familiar to him. He began descending towards the body at an alarming pace. His churlish and reckless actions almost caused an avalanche as he bounded down the mountain.

"What are you doing?!" the owl shouted with a concerned inflection in her voice.

"Finding a friend," he called back to her. He felt her shiver as she readjusted her feathers. She seemed nervous and as he reached the body he knew why. When he had landed next to the body in the ravine the first thing, he had seen that there were flesh wounds. The snake's body was torn up. It had claw marks on its head and its lungs were slipping through the enormous gashes left in the reptile's scales.

At that moment, the lion felt nothing but rage and spun around, staring at the owl. He roared one of the most powerful and painful cries he had ever roared. The owl was frozen in place. She just stood on the branch knowing that the writing was on the wall. She tried to force herself to move but her body wouldn't listen to her. It ignored her brain's impulses to escape and try to survive. Inside the lion, a war was being fought. He desperately wanted to believe it was someone or something else that had done this to what had become one of his closest friends.

The owl didn't even try to deny the fact that she was the one behind this treachery. She just sat there perched above the lion. The lion knew that this was the end of their temporary friendship. All things must come to an end at some point. But why does this one have to end so abruptly and on such a sour note, he thought. He snarled at the owl who tried to approach him as he was grieving.

"I will allow you to live. On the condition that I never see you again," he said in a powerful but also sad-sounding tone.

"Please. It wasn't my fault she tried to attack me again," the owl pleaded.

"Likely story... I will discuss this no longer. I am leaving. Do not follow me," the lion said coldly as he turned and began his ascent, more determined this time to not let anyone or anything get in the way of his achieving his original goal. He slung his friend's corpse onto his back as he climbed. He would take her to see the moon. After all, his goal had turned into her goal when they had first crossed paths all those nights ago.

The owl could just watch as he climbed away from her, leaving her behind. He really didn't care what happened to that traitor, all he cared about was reaching the moon. The thing that had returned to being the only constant in his life. Sure, the journey with friends was fun while it lasted but in the end everyone seemed to fall behind him. He pushed forward, leaving his emotions in the past as he continued to look forward.

The lion's shackles had been broken; he had more fire in him than ever now. He wanted to reach the moon and escape this horrible reality. Where friends could turn on friends and even end up sentencing one to death. What a tragic fate, he thought to himself as he jumped higher than he had ever jumped before. He was almost on the precipice of the tallest mountain in the entire world.

His journey was coming to a close with a tremendously sad note. How would it have felt to achieve this together, he thought to himself. What a hollow achievement he would feel, but he knew that the snake would want him to do it this way. He knew she would want him to carry her along and not to abandon her with that traitor. Why had the owl done what she had done? At this point that didn't matter. He could not control her any more than he could revive the snake.

He came to the top of the mountain finally and stared off into the distance as he frowned. He felt empty. He stared up at the moon and began to call to it.

"Please! Take me to you! I want to run on your surface and escape this detestable reality," he roared upwards; the moon just sat there taunting him. The moon was ignoring his calls as it slowly began to descend as the sun was about to rise.

"Please, before you go, give me a sign! I need you now more than ever!" he called to the moon as the sky began to turn a peachy orange color. He laid the snake's

body down on the cold stone. Then the sun's rays softly whipped the sky as the moon faded from view.

The lion began to sob for the first time ever. Had his quest been for nothing? He felt the warmth of the sun's rays that were a stark contrast to the unforgiving coldness that night brought with it. He slowly began to bask in the sun for the first time ever.

As he did, something strange happened. A beam of light hit his fallen friend's body and it began to glow. As it was glowing the wounds on it began to heal miraculously. When it had finished glowing, the body was placed back on the ground softly. The lion lay there in disbelief of what had just occurred.

"Thank you! It was you who I was looking for! You are the life giver, warm and subtle! I can't believe I had missed it for so long. I was a fool all this time..." the lion cried out as the snake reanimated in front of his very eyes.

"Huh? What happened? Where is that terrible bird?" she asked, more confused than anything.

"I left her behind. I'm so glad you are okay. Look around, I have made it to the top of the mountain," he boomed. He then walked over to the snake and nuzzled her with his cheek.

"Good riddance. Something was seriously wrong with her. How did you find my body? All I knew when I was about to die was that I didn't want you to find me like that. Then I felt the sweet suffocating embrace of death. If only for a short while," the snake replied inquisitively.

"The moon had guided me to your body as if it were taunting me with your demise. It wanted me to feel helpless. I'm certain of it. I cannot believe that I was such a fool and chased after a celestial being that only wished me torment," he said dejectedly, with a big frown on his face.

"It's not your fault. You couldn't have known. Thank you for taking me here. This is the most beautiful place I have ever been. I will never forget this day as not just the day I had been revived but the day that I had been saved by one of the most amazing friends I could have ever asked for. Truly and ,honestly thank you for staying by my side," she said, her voice starting to fade towards the end of her declaration.

"I should be the one thanking you. You are the only reason I made it up here.

221

The owl had kept hindering us for these nights. It was as if she was stalling me, trying to stop my progress. You were the one who kept me going. So, I should be the one thanking you. Even now I wouldn't be standing here without you," he replied with a warm smile taking over his face.

"Then let's raise a toast to our friendship and to the sun. The life giver," she said jovially.

"To us and to the sun!" they shouted together.

The lion stared off into the distance, watching the sun wake up the entire world, and admired the caring fire it brought to the world. Gone was the lion who wanted to reach the moon. For he had reached the moon and been spurned by it. From today onward the lion would be a champion of the sun, and as a gift the sun turned his mane into the embodiment of its own image. He now walked around with the flames the sun had given him as a badge of honor, bringing light to the darkness and erasing the shadows of the world with his best friend by his side for the rest of time.

Fin

Chapter 31

I finished writing in my notebook, and the story being finally finished left me with a sense of relief. It also gave me a strong sentimental sense of melancholy. It's funny, I create these stories, only to keep them away from everyone else around me. When it comes to art, does it really matter what you intend for people to see? Or is the only thing that matters what the audience gets out of your art? That is the inherent paradoxical nature of art itself. You can't control how someone interprets your work. Sure, you can try to lead them to a specific conclusion but ultimately it is up to them how each story concludes.

Even art that has definitive endings, be them written or drawn, people will still wonder what comes next. The artist may finish with a work and never think about it again, but that same work could inspire another to make a sequel to it in their own interpretation of the art. That was what was so amazing about humanity, and perception in general. Even though we could be looking at the same thing, both of us could come up with completely different reasons as to why it might have been made. Even items made with one specific purpose in mind can often be repurposed outside of their intended use by one creative individual.

Thinking this, I set down my notebook and looked at Alexa. She was intently studying Heather's diary as if she had completely shut out the world. I looked at her, and her dirty blonde hair framed her tanned face perfectly. Her eyes, like two deep oceans, were churning as they scanned each page at a quick pace.

I could see her scanning every line. She was always a fast reader. It was so interesting to watch her read. She often bit her lip without noticing, leaving slight teeth marks on her bottom lip. She also would tap her leg quickly and quietly as she read. She looked so pretty right now, I didn't think I had ever seen her in this light before.

She was the picture of serenity. Even though our situation was dire she appeared to be completely calm on the outside. The only way you could tell we had been through so much was from her crumpled clothes. Her hair looked perfect even though neither of us had showered in days. Its silky and soft texture along with its slightly messy appearance made it look as if it was intentionally messy. All of this made her look even more picturesque.

I slid my chair around the table we had been sitting at, so I was right next to her, and just sat there watching her focus. I knew she would never notice me sitting there, with the level of attention she had allocated to reading. She used to do this all the time when we were kids. For someone who made fun of me for being a dork, it seemed like all she did was read back then.

She had been so excited for the new updated library that was coming. It never really made sense to me. Even now it still confused me. I guessed Alexa just liked getting lost in the pages of an enthralling story. Suddenly she paused reading and turned her head towards me, noticing me for the first time since I had finished writing. She smirked and then leaned in and gave me a kiss on the cheek.

I smiled back at her as a deep crimson colored my face from the embarrassment of this moment. I knew we were busy trying to find a way to save our friend, but something about Alexa's demeanor made me feel more at ease than I had this entire week. We hadn't said any words up to this point and I felt quite content just being by her side.

"Did you find anything, Sherlock?" I inquired coyly.

"I think I did, Watson," she said, smiling, and flipped back a few pages to show me what she had found.

Entry 230

Something hasn't been right recently. I feel like I have been losing some parts of me over the last few months. Things I used to like now feel empty and hollow. Also, I feel like there are lapses in my memory as if entire weeks just get erased from my mind. This has been frightening to say the least. Dad seems to think it's just in my head but the way he says it is always so suspicious. I think he's doing something to me. I'm not sure what that something is just yet, but he has been acting rather strange.

Entry 231

I found a secret lab under the house. Dad seems to have experiments going on down there. It had so many beakers and chemicals I didn't know what to make of it. I confronted him and he said that we didn't even have a basement. How could he have a lab? This isn't lining up at all. Am I going insane? I feel like I'm going insane. I saw it with my eyes, but I can't seem to trust them as much as I used to now.

Entry 236...?

I am missing significant portions of my memories from the last week. I don't even remember writing any of the last logs. But they must be true. Whatever is happening to me is getting worse. This is scaring me. All I can think of is the times back in Maine. I miss Ryan. I think about him all the time. I feel so alone here. I'm so scared. Please someone save me.

Entry 240...?

I don't remember the last month. I feel hollow inside and out. I don't want to be here anymore. I don't even remember why I was worried anymore. It feels like my mind is being tampered with. I saw dad earlier. He was going downstairs. I followed him and he snapped at me. He was so angry and then... I don't really remember what happened. I remembered him raising his hand. Then the next thing I knew I was talking to him in my room. When I remember the conversation in the room he said, "We'll figure this out." What did that even mean? Why do I remember those words as the first thing after the missing portions of the day?

Alexa closed the diary after I had finished reading the last entry she showed me. *Yikes*, I thought to myself. I couldn't even imagine what it would feel like to have my brain literally tampered with. He took playing with her emotions to an entirely new level. It was the scariest thing based on fact I had ever read in my entire life.

How could you do this to someone? Especially someone you loved. No matter how afraid you were of losing them, nothing could justify this. This act was more than heinous. It was downright monstrous. It was so hard for me to even fathom the thought process behind such an action. But this had started to feel more common than not for this week. It seemed every day I found something more disturbing than the last.

"Oh my god…" I said, my voice trailing off.

"I know, right. It's horrible. I had no clue she had been going through all of this. Why hadn't she told us about this happening to her? This is legitimately scary. All of the other stuff that happened is child's play compared to what we just read," Alexa said with a terrified expression on her face.

"We have to go find her," I said with renewed determination from resetting my brain with writing.

"Where do we even begin?" Alexa asked with a thoughtful expression on her face.

"I'm not totally sure. We should probably check her house first to see if they had gone there. Who knows, maybe he built another creepy basement into that house similar to the one she wrote about in her diary," I said with a shrug and a solemn frown on my lips.

"Sounds like a place to start. What do we say to try to snap her out of it? There did seem like there was a phrase that released her from whatever brainwashing had happened," she asked as she began to pack up all of our things.

"I'm not totally sure what we should say, but we don't have any time to waste. The only upside right now that we have is that it's basically a blizzard outside and no planes can take off," I said with a twinge of positivity making

226

its way into my voice.

"That is true, but we have to be careful now that we are on the offensive here. We can still die from a car crash in this inclement weather. We're no use to anyone dead. I guess besides Mr. S," she replied with a serious tone while staring into my eyes, making sure I understood her.

"I get it. I get it. No fast and furious. As if I would try that with zero vision. What do you take me for?" I scoffed at her, brushing off her gaze that could probably turn many to stone. But for me that stare was just a familiar sight for sore eyes. She hadn't given me that look in a long while.

"That's right, mister. Now let's go get our friend back," she said, shouldering both her and Heather's backpacks. Then she walked down the hall towards the backyard where I had parked my car and I followed suit. It was extremely refreshing to have her take the lead again. She had been taking a backseat for most of the last few days. This combined with our renewed invigoration made me think things would actually turn out okay.

I opened the heavy oak door that seemed to be barely hanging on, with the sharp winds constantly battering it. It flung open as soon as enough wind could hit it to keep it open. I gestured to Alexa as if to say, *Ladies first.*

"Since when did you become courteous?" she said with a devilish smirk.

"Pfft. I am the most chivalrous saint you could ever meet," I responded as I walked over to the snow-covered car. The soft powder obstructed even the color of the car. If you hadn't known, you would assume this to be just a really oddly shaped hill. I brushed off the fluffy stuff and then opened the passenger door as I walked around the car to get to the driver's side. Alexa climbed in as fast as possible and shut the door tight.

I opened my door and sat down next to her. I stuck my key into the ignition and turned it. The car roared to life, and the first thing I did was put on the heater and the windshield wipers. Luckily, we hadn't been inside long enough for ice to develop, and the windshield wipers just cut through the snow, throwing it to the sides of the vehicle.

"Here we are. On the home stretch," I said, nodding at Alexa as she silently nodded back.

I began driving down the dirt road towards the main street. The trees in the woods seemed more ominous than before with the snow whipping around their trunks. It was as if they were trying to attack us with gusts of wind. You could feel the wind slamming the panels of the car with such force it was a miracle we hadn't been flipped yet.

We slowly made it off the bumpy road and to the main street surrounding the town and turned onto it. I drove down the street carefully as it was slowly being turned white from the sheets of snow trying to cover it.

I drove past Heather's street and sure enough I saw the same black SUV sitting in her driveway idling. I decided not to come from the front, so I turned into the neighborhood right behind hers and pulled up to approximately where her house was. I then motioned for Alexa to switch seats with me because we'd need to get out of here fast after I got Heather.

"I am not staying in the car. Who do you think you are? We all need to be there to get her out," Alexa yelled at me, her face beginning to turn red.

"You need to keep the car running so we can get out of here. I promise I won't do anything reckless. If I can't get her out right now, I'll come back, and we can wait until she's alone for any period of time to sneak in and grab her," I said as Alexa's expression softened and she seemed to accept this answer.

"Okay... But you had better be careful. I swear to God, if I lose you too, I don't know what I'll do," she said in a sad tone as she leaned over to put her head on my shoulder. I patted her head and then got out of the car as she slid over the center console and sat in the driver seat. When she was settled in, she gave me a thumbs-up and I returned the gesture as I walked over to the fence of Heather's behind neighbor. I climbed into the backyard and then walked over to the fence separating this backyard and Heather's. I peeked over the fence and stared intensely at the house. No lights could be seen from the sliding back door. As I was thinking about climbing over, I strained my ears and heard two voices from inside the house. Then the sliding glass door opened, and I could hear them clearly.

"Why do we have to leave again, Dad?" the girl's voice said, and obviously it had to be Heather. But she had a more childlike tone than normal which was giving me doubts.

"Because, sweetheart. I have business elsewhere. We couldn't stay here forever," the man's voice said. I knew this gruff tone. This was definitely Heather's father.

"Awww. But why not?" Heather said. Again, the voice sounded too childish to be Heather's. I didn't want to risk peeking over the fence, but then I noticed a hole in the fence lower so I crouched and squinted so I could see the two. They were certainly Heather and her father. But this only confused me more, with the way they were talking. It was as if he was talking to an eleven-year-old kid, not an almost full-grown adult. Even Heather's voice sounded like that of a child.

"Come on, pumpkin. Let's go, the car is waiting. We fly out as soon as this storm quells," he said to her.

"Okay, Daddy. Let me go grab my diary first!" she shouted as she ran back inside.

"I'll be waiting in the driveway, honey, meet me out there in two minutes!" he yelled after her.

Now was my chance. I had to go save her. As soon as he was out of earshot I jumped into their backyard and rushed over to the sliding glass door.

"Daddy! My diary isn't where I left it. Have you seen it?!" I heard her shout from up the stairs. What was I going to say to her when I confronted her? I had to snap her out of this. I ascended the stairs slowly to not make any noise. Then as I reached the top of the stairs, I heard a door from down the hall slam open.

Chapter 32

"Daddy! Why aren't you answering!!" she shouted as she appeared in the doorway. Then she turned and looked at me with confusion. It was like she didn't even recognize me. She just stared blankly with a slight amount of fear. I could see it in her eyes clearly.

"It's okay. It's Ryan. Do you remember me?" I said, stalling for time to think of how to snap her out of this.

"No, you're not. Ryan is the same age as me. You're an old man," she said matter of factly.

"How old do you think you are?" I asked her calmly, trying not to make her panic. Still thinking of ways to break her from whatever spell he might have put on her.

"I'm eleven. So is Ryan. He's the coolest. But I'm sad because Daddy said I have to leave him behind. So, who are you again, mister?" she said in a singsong voice.

"Heather. I know something is messed up in your mind right now. But could you please come with me? I have something important to tell you," I asked her sincerely.

"No way, mister. Don't you know about stranger danger? I shouldn't even be talking to you. DADDY!" She began to shout, throwing a tantrum.

"Heather, please just come with me, and we'll figure this out, I promise," I said, trying to convince her to quiet down. Suddenly something strange happened. She just fell to her knees and stopped responding to me. I walked over to her and shook her, trying to wake her up. Then I heard the door slam open from downstairs, along with a booming voice.

"DARLING! Do not keep me waiting any longer! We must go now!" he shouted up the stairs. But when no response came, I could hear him start to panic. He ascended the stairs with thunderous footsteps. I wasn't going to hide anymore. I know I told Alexa I'd be safe, but this was our last chance to save Heather. If I left now, we'd never see her again. It was all but guaranteed.

"YOU! What did you do!" he shouted as he saw me.

"I could ask you the same thing," I replied calmly.

"I'll kill you, kid. This is the last time you get on my nerves!" he screamed as he rushed towards me. I narrowly dodged a punch aimed at my face.

He kept throwing punch after punch, blinded by rage. I was starting to feel fatigued. Each blow I avoided was by the skin of my teeth, and if my movements got any sloppier, he'd certainly connect with one of them. I could tell he was running out of steam as well. His breath became haggard, and his swings became more wild in nature.

This made them harder to dodge as he was just throwing his weight around while attacking. Then one of his fists connected with my ribcage and knocked the air from my lungs. I staggered back as he closed in on me. I was going to end up like the guy I had heard beat half to death in the office. I was certain of it. But I don't think he'd hold himself back. This appeared to be my end. I felt the rain of blows landing, knocking me to my back. Then he climbed on top of me and continued to slam his heavy fists into my chest. I felt my lungs were about to collapse and everything was on fire as I strained to breathe. I looked at Heather still lying on the ground, and said I was sorry in my head because I certainly couldn't get the words out in my current position.

He then moved on to my head, slamming blow after blow into my face and temples wildly. My vision began to go dark as I accepted that this was where I would die. It wasn't much of a life, but I'd had a good time while it lasted. As I was making my peace with death, I heard a shrill voice scream out.

"Daddy! How could you?! Y-y-y-you m-m-monster! Get off of him! I love him!" Heather shouted towards her father.

"Stay out of this!" he yelled back as he raised his arm up to snap. I reached up to grab his hand and stop him from snapping his fingers, but it was too late, he had snapped.

This time, however, something different happened. It seemed like the shock of seeing me on the brink of death in front of her gave her the willpower to block out whatever was brainwashing her, and she just stood there instead of going limp.

"Not anymore… Dad, this is the end. I don't ever want to see you again!" she screamed as she ran out of the door.

"Wait! Heather! Don't do this to me! This is for your own good!" he shouted after her as he knelt on my chest to stand up, and ran after her. I was in no shape to stand up, but with my adrenaline pumping I stood up too and followed them both outside.

"Stay away from me!" she screamed as she ran into the backyard.

"There's nowhere to go, honey. Why don't you come back to me, and I can help you forget this even happened," he said in a deep voice you could almost call a growl.

"Heather! Jump the fence and run to the front yard of that house. Alexa is there waiting for you. Both of you should get out of here while you can!" I shouted at her, and each word caused me excruciating pain.

"Boy! Stay out of this! I'll finish you off later!" he yelled at me as he turned his attention back to Heather.

"Both of you stop! QUIT DECIDING WHAT I SHOULD DO WITH MY LIFE! I am not leaving Ryan and I am not letting you kill him, Dad!" she screamed at the top of her lungs.

"Why don't we all calm down," Mr. S said in a gruff voice.

"No, Dad. We are done being calm. You set both of their parents free and let me go. If you let this all go, I will still talk with you and come to visit you. But if you don't, I will kill myself and leave you here all alone. If you kill Ryan, I won't ever forgive you or myself for putting him in this position. So, what's it going to be, Dad?" she said while tears streamed down her face. She was sincere and he could tell she meant it.

"Please! If you died, I'd have nothing to live for, Heather. You mean the world to me. All I ever wanted was to give you the world. I'm sorry for all of this," he yelled as he dropped to his knees, begging Heather.

"Then, Dad, you must let me and them all go. I will continue to be your daughter but if you don't then I won't be anyone's daughter anymore," she said through the tears.

"Okay... Okay... I concede. You all can be free. Just promise me one thing. Take care of her?" he said, looking in my direction.

Heather ran over to me and hugged me tightly, and at that time the adrenaline started to fade so I felt my whole body explode as she squeezed me. I fell to my knees and as I did the entire world went black.

Nightmare 9...?

I woke up floating in the same lake that Heather had dragged me into during the last nightmare. I looked around and wasn't sure if I was really alive or if I were dead at this point. Everything in this place felt so off and weird that I wouldn't even know how it could be out of the ordinary.

I felt a grab at my arm, and I looked around to see nothing in the dark water. Nothing seemed to be there, but I kept feeling as if I were being pulled in that direction. I floated toward the thing that was pulling me until I reached a shining door underneath the water. I dove towards the door and grabbed onto the handle. I turned the doorknob and fell into the light that came from the other side.

I stared up at the sky above me as I landed on my back, half expecting this to be some sort of afterlife because I was still unsure if I had died or not. I stood up and I looked around. I was now in a snow-covered field. I had to shield my eyes or risk becoming snow blinded. I walked through the snow towards the only tree in the clearing. As I approached it, I saw its branches move. I watched its branches move and realized what I had been looking at. This tree seemed to be some sort of clock.

However, its branches were turning counterclockwise which seemed weird. But who was I to say what was weird and what wasn't at this point? Its branches began to spin faster and faster until they were like the blades of a helicopter. Then in an instant they stopped at four o'clock. I wasn't sure if it was morning or afternoon, but judging by the sky, I'd say it was afternoon. After it stopped it let out a loud ringing sound. As it did, a pair of elevator doors opened in front of me enveloping the tree behind it. It appeared like I had no choice, so I stepped inside.

I rode the elevator as it went upwards into the sky. It started to speed up and abruptly stopped. As it stopped it opened the doors, and I looked out to see Heather standing in the cold snow looking down on my body that had collapsed behind Heather's house. Oh man, I thought. Was I really dead? I couldn't be, right? I started to freak out. I wanted to get out of the elevator right then, but as soon as I tried to step out into the scene the doors shut with lightning speed.

Okay, that was weird. I couldn't be dead, right? I was still here thinking away in my mind, wasn't I? I started to pace around the elevator, trying to steady my mind. Then the elevator began to ascend again, going up more. It continued for a while this time, and then again it abruptly stopped, knocking me down to my knees.

The doors opened again, and I saw the library under construction. It was full of life. I could hear what I could only assume to be the foreman yelling orders to the rest of the people working on the site. I scanned the room looking for something out of the ordinary and I saw my parents. I jumped and waved at them. Man, how long had it been since I had last seen them? I thought to myself. I waved at them, not expecting anything in return, then I saw my dad look up from what he was doing with an expression of pure unadulterated horror. He stared in my direction and pointed and screamed at the others around him. I couldn't turn to look at what was happening behind the elevator, but whatever it was, the entire construction site started rushing in the direction the elevator was.

I tried to stop my dad as he walked straight towards me. As he got to the elevator, he passed right through it as if it wasn't even there. As if it were just some apparition. I felt so ethereal right now as if everything around me was fake. I tried to step out of the elevator again to go see what all the commotion was, but again the doors slammed shut, almost on my leg this time.

Okay... No more trying to get out. That was too close of a call, I thought to myself as I began to pace around again. The elevator shuddered and stayed still this time. It wasn't moving at all, instead this time it just sat there. I started to bang on the doors. I didn't know what I was thinking was going to happen from banging on the doors. Maybe I'd be able to pry them open? I tried to pull them apart with all my might but, nope, it didn't work.

The elevator then responded to my desperation as it began to ascend again. I had a bad feeling about it this time. Something was just making me feel uneasy, riding this terrible ride. I had no control over what was going to happen to me. Hell, I didn't even know if I was dead or alive right now. What I would give to just go back to that yard with Heather. I didn't want to be here.

I continued to pace around feeling utterly and totally lost. I started to lose motivation to walk and just sat. Now on the floor of the elevator, slumping down, sad. I was broken. I could admit that, but I didn't think I was this broken. I wished I could have just had a normal life. As I was thinking this, I hadn't even noticed that I'd stopped moving again and that the doors were now open, showing my house.

It was weirdly hovering outside my house though not inside anywhere in particular. While thinking that, the elevator then flew into the front door. I gritted my teeth and braced for impact, but I didn't feel anything. I just phased through the wall with the elevator. I looked around and saw my younger parents sitting at the table with happy expressions on their faces. I waved at them again and they just looked up at me and smiled. Then the elevator began to fly towards the stairs and straight to my room.

It entered my room, but it was strange. I had never remembered it being decorated this way. It had posters on the wall I'd never seen before and also was configured completely differently. As I heard the door open behind the elevator, I looked down to see why it was decorated the way it was, and then the doors shut again on me abruptly.

"What gives? I didn't even try to get out this time?!" I shouted at the inanimate object.

Then all of a sudden it began descending. It was going far faster than it had before. I had never felt it go this fast thus far. After an arbitrary amount of time, it stopped on a dime and opened up again. It opened up facing the backyard I had collapsed in again, except this time the elevator tilted forward as if it were trying to throw me out. I wanted to stay for a bit longer to see what was happening when randomly my leg started to glow. Ugh, really? This again? I thought to myself. I thought this was over with finally? Why is it still happening? I was desperately stretching my arms and legs as far as they could go to hold onto the ever-shrinking doors. Then my knee buckled from the pain of the glowing light, and I tumbled out of the elevator and sort of phased through my own body as I fell. When I landed with a large hard smack into the ground the light of the area all faded away.

Chapter 33

I woke up staring at the gray clouds above me. Snowflakes danced their primordial dance as they fell in slow motion around me. My body was on fire. Every sinew and fiber of my being was ignited in searing pain. A cold hand reached out and touched my cheek. I surveyed my surroundings. I was being held by Heather with her almost frostbitten hands as the snow started to cover our waists. I tried to speak but no words came out. Our eyes met and Heather just leaned forward and kissed my lips tenderly.

"I really do love you, Ryan. Please be okay. I need you to be okay," she whispered in my ear as her hair draped around my face obscuring my vision.

I heard a shout come from the direction in front of us and knew immediately it was Alexa coming to look for me. How long had I been out for? I heard the hard footsteps slamming on the frozen ground mixed with the sloshing of someone running through almost knee-high snow. Alexa came upon us and knelt down next to Heather.

"What happened to him?! This is all your fault!" she shouted, her voice cracking from fear.

"He saved me. He set me free from brainwashing. Of course, he sacrificed himself for that, and I wished he hadn't but we both know he would sacrifice himself for either of us. It is my fault. I wished he had just let me go. I just want him to be okay. Thank you both for coming to me. You can't fathom how grateful I am for both of you being my friends," Heather replied, taking responsibility for everything.

"It's no one's fault but Heather's dad. I should be o-o-okay…" I said, fighting the pain and coughing up some blood, staining the pure white snow.

"You don't look like you'll be okay. Y-y-you IDIOT. HOW COULD YOU DO THIS?" Alexa shouted through her tears. It was so cold, her tears began to freeze as they fell from her eyes, turning into almost diamond-like crystals. It was a beautifully harrowing sight to behold.

"Shhhhh… I'm sorry, Ryan," Heather said, softly caressing my face. As she said that I heard sirens from behind us. Then the flashing blue and red lights came. I heard the voices of two paramedics calling out to each other asking who was injured. Alexa brought them over to the backyard and they both audibly gasped.

"Oh my god. What happened to him? He looks like he got hit by a train," they both questioned.

"He fell out the second-story window," Heather said as if she had planned out what to say, and pointed up to a window I hadn't noticed was open.

"Fell out of that window? Onto what, his face? He didn't try to change positions and just fell out headfirst?" they asked, suspicious at the prospect of someone jumping face first out of a second story window.

"It all happened so fast. I'm not sure. Maybe he did try to change his position but couldn't move in time. At any rate, can you please get the stretchers, we need to get him to a hospital ASAP?" Heather continued calmly as she started to softly pet my hair.

"Right. We can get the full story later. Rebecca, grab the stretcher, please? We need to get him into the ambulance now," one yelled at the other, and then Rebecca came back with the stretcher. They all lifted me up onto the stretcher and wheeled me over to the ambulance.

"Is one of you riding with him?" one of them asked.

"I am. She'll meet us at the hospital," Heather said plainly before Alexa could react. She then climbed into the back of the ambulance with us, and they shut the doors on Alexa as they began to drive off. It was a strange feeling, being tied down to the stretcher, of course, they didn't want you hurting yourself further, but even so I still felt uncomfortable with my arms and legs restrained.

Heather must have noticed, as she grabbed my hand and gave it a soft squeeze. That uncomfortable feeling faded away for the time being. I looked at her with gratitude on my face. She seemed to know exactly what to do. My vision began to blur again. I think my residual adrenaline was fading at this point. I wanted to stay awake, but no matter what I tried, the sound of the road and the murmur of the people's voices started to fall away one by one. Until my eyes could only see colors and my ears couldn't hear sounds anymore. Then I felt the sweet embrace of sleep absolve me of all of my pain.

Nightmare 10...?

I woke up in my room on the day before this all started. Before Alexa and I went to the Old Port. Before any of it happened. I looked at the clock and the alarm was about to go off to wake me up for school. I hit the snooze and went downstairs. When I made it downstairs, I saw a familiar sight. My parents were in their normal spots, making breakfast. My dad was sitting at the head of the table reading a newspaper, and my mom was in the kitchen making eggs, bacon, and hashbrowns. I remembered it was her day to cook. They were funny like that, they always took turns if they didn't do it together.

My dad drank his black coffee as my mom brought the breakfast spread over. I smiled, but when they tried to talk to me, I couldn't hear them. All I heard was murmuring. When I smelled the delicious food, I became ravenous. It was the first real food I had seen in days, and I was salivating just waiting to devour it all. I picked up my fork and put some hash browns into my mouth, but as soon as I did the room began to morph.

The room morphed so much that it completely changed. I was back in my room again, but it was like four years in the past. I could tell it was four years in the past because I still had a poster up from a video game I was obsessed with when I was in middle school. I thought that poster was so cool until I got a couple years older and saw it for what it was. Just a relic of my past personality, the memory of that game gave me such nostalgia I couldn't help but smile at the poster.

I walked to the mirror and even my image of myself was that of a middle schooler.

I was thirteen again, at least in the mirror. This was getting weird. What was I trying to show myself? My subconscious mind had to have a reason for showing me this, right? I began to feel more cautious as I walked down this weird trip to memory lane.

I really wanted to just wake up and see my parents again free, and go back to normal teen life. I never thought I'd see the day when I wanted to go back to hoping I would pass my classes using calculators to see what I needed to get on a final to get a certain grade in the overall class. I couldn't believe I was actually feeling nostalgic about taking tests. What was wrong with me? Maybe all of these wild adventures had started to wear on my mind. I definitely felt the fatigue from them. I think they were especially exhausting because we had no choice but to go on them. The fact that they were mandatory seemed to suck all of the fun out of what an adventure should be.

I walked out of my room as I thought this and down the stairs to another breakfast. This time my father was at the stove and was pulling cinnamon rolls out of the oven and setting them on the table next to some sausage links and fresh assorted berries. The aroma was divine. I wanted so badly to just have a taste of these mouthwatering treats.

I sat at the table, and my mom handed me a glass that she had generously filled with orange juice. I smiled and took a swig. This time the nightmare let me take a sip. The sensation was phenomenal. I was on cloud nine. I then dug into the cinnamon rolls and bacon, both of which tasted better than they ever had before. I finished gorging myself and excused myself from the table. I stood up and walked over toward the couch, with my stomach so full I wanted nothing more than to just plop down and pass out while all the food was digested.

Right as I sat down on the leather couch I started to fall deeper into the leather. I continued to fall until I had been completely swallowed by the chair. Everything around me went black. I blinked and then I was back in my room again. This time I looked around and almost everything seemed the same except for my blanket and sheets. I hadn't seen this comforter or bed sheet set since I was eleven. Okay, strange? I've gone back another two years? I thought to myself as I went over to the mirror to confirm again. Sure enough, I looked like I was eleven, but I noticed something strange in my reflection.

When I looked into my reflection, I saw my leg glowing. But when I looked down, it wasn't. What was going on? I walked downstairs this time, no breakfast was being made. Both of my parents looked to be dressed for work and were about to head out. I waved at them, and they smiled and waved back as they hurried out the door.

I followed them outside, but they were already gone. Then I decided, why not? I knew where they were going. I should go check out the library to see it one last time at its busiest. Who knows when I'd get the chance like this to travel back in time even in my own mind? I walked down the road towards the library, and then made it to the unpaved gravel road that led to the job site. I walked along the path, up towards the library. As I did, I noticed my leg started to ache again. Ugh, really? Now of all times? I thought to myself. I just have to deal with the pain and push on.

My leg began to tingle. It started to affect my pace, causing me to slow down. Each step I took was a sheer testament to my willpower. I had to make it up there. I really wanted to see the building when it had a chance of becoming a real library.

I made it over the halfway mark, and instantly my legs glowed brighter. It was like a beacon at this point, each step I took shook the earth. I was afraid, but also intrigued as to what would happen when I made it into the library.

I sped up my pace, wincing in pain with each step I took. I wasn't about to give in to this pain again. This time I will succeed. I will not be bested every single time. I had to win once, right? I was just ten paces from the front doors of the library. Each step I took now shook all of reality as pieces of the sky started to fall around me in the shapes of giant blue puzzle pieces. They landed all around me as I continued. I was afraid of being struck but more afraid of not finishing. I pushed through the excruciating throbbing pain as I made it to the handles.

I reached out and grabbed both handles and opened the doors. As they opened, my leg's white light began to envelope all of my surroundings. It continued to swallow up the scenery around me until I saw the back of that kid's head again. The one I had seen a couple of times now at this point walking over a hole in the construction site. They walked over the beam and then fell into the black hole below them. I jumped for them to try to grab onto their hand, and when I did, I caught them.

I didn't think it would work. But I then dragged the kid back up and got a good look at them. I couldn't believe my eyes. Who I saw was not who I was expecting this to be. It was a younger Heather. There was no mistaking it. Her emerald green eyes stared through my soul. I'd forgotten she had shorter hair when we were younger. I stared into her unflinching eyes and smiled. She smiled back but quickly her smile turned into a frown. Then her expression became grim. I hugged her and everything went black. For the first time I noticed my leg had stopped hurting. Was this the repressed memory that was giving me pain? I guessed it must have been. I let the darkness consume me, finally at peace with what happened.

I woke up in a hospital bed. After having that revelation, I was so relieved to be okay. All of the pain from before had faded. I felt more numb than anything else. I smiled like an idiot at the ceiling. Was it possible? Were we really free? Was I also freed from my leg pain permanently? I sure hoped the answer to all of those were a resounding yes. I figured that had been the case anyway already because I was actually in the hospital right now. Not like a vet or some weird doctor adjacent business to get haphazardly fixed before going on the run again with the girls.

I looked around and didn't see Heather or Alexa. *Hmm, isn't that odd?* I thought to myself. Surely, they'd both have been there waiting for me to wake up. I continued to scan the room, and that was when I noticed their bags sitting on the table at the opposite end of the room. They must have just stepped out to get snacks or a hospital meal. I mean, any food would be good food right now, even terrible hospital food. When you're starving everything looks and tastes delicious even if you would never eat it if you weren't starving.

I continued to look at my new sterile environment with contented eyes. I felt safe and sound for the first time in a long time. I heard a loud commotion just outside my room. Then the door flew open and slammed against the snow-white wall.

Chapter 34

They rushed in like a whirlwind. The two girls that had cared so much about me my whole life. I looked at them somewhat stunlocked in place. Then they both burst into tears. I couldn't tell if they were of joy or sorrow. Maybe a bit of both?

"I'm so glad you're okay. When you didn't come back, I only assumed the worst had happened. Why are you always so reckless?" Alexa sobbed as she rushed to my side.

"When you collapsed like that, I thought you had died. I'm so sorry that everything that has happened up until this point was my fault," Heather said, also fighting to speak between sobs.

"Shush. It's okay. I just did what I thought was right, Lex. I would've done the same for you. As for you, Heather. It's not all your fault. I got us into this mess when I decided to start looking into all the strange stuff with our parents' company," I said back, struggling to speak. It felt like my vocal chords were on fire still. Even though I had an IV drip I still felt the pain. I must've been really messed up.

"It's clearly not okay though! You could've died! What would I do without you!" Alexa shouted at me, hugging my abdomen.

"Ouch... Could you maybe lighten up there, Hercules? You're kinda crushing my bruised ribs," I said in a slightly sarcastic tone. Trying to lighten the mood even just the slightest amount.

"Sorry..." Alexa said dejectedly, with a twinge of despair creeping across her face.

"It's okay, don't worry about it. It was just a joke," I replied, spreading my arms wide, gesturing to both of them for a hug. They both leaned in and gave me a big hug. Maybe a little too big for my injuries but my brain powered through the pain for their sakes. We stayed like that for a short while until I decided I needed to ask what happened when I was out.

"So... This is nice and all but what went on while I was passed out?" I questioned the two of them.

"Well, you had passed out, so I called an ambulance right away and they showed up. Then I rode with you to the hospital while Alexa drove your car there to meet up with us. When you were admitted we tried to come with you. But after they asked us what happened again, they said that since we weren't family we couldn't go in to see you while they were operating. So, we both panicked while we waited for the two hours you were under the knife. But as soon as they put you in this room, we busted our way through the door past the nurse to see you," Heather answered eagerly.

That was when I noticed the nurse awkwardly standing behind them with a new pillow and clipboard. She seemed more amused than annoyed by the situation. It was strange but she reminded me of my mom. I didn't know if it was just her presence or her age, but the similarities were uncanny. She noticed I was looking at her and gave a warm smile and nod as if to confirm that this was what had happened. The girls then noticed she was behind them and stepped aside as she walked forward and slid the new pillow behind my back as she lifted me forward slightly. Now I was sitting in an almost upright position.

"I will bring your dinner in a few minutes. Please don't strain yourself. We wouldn't want you to get any more hurt than you currently are," the nurse said as she slid the tray that was attached to the chair in front of my lap. I nodded again to tell her I understood, and she turned around to leave, humming a song as she did. After she had left, the two girls then began to explain everything that had happened in excruciating detail. As well as the injustice of them both not being permitted to see me.

"So that's pretty much it. Oh... Also, the doctor said after they took you into surgery you flatlined for a short period of time, but they were able to resuscitate you on the operating table as well as seal up the minor internal bleeding. He said you should stay off your feet for a few days too and said they'd prescribe you some Oxycodone for the pain," Heather said, finishing her thought from before. They both must have had a rollercoaster of a time for the last few hours. From hearing I almost died to not even being allowed to see me. I thought it was slightly funny that Heather was able to pester the surgeon enough after the procedure to get him to divulge that information. Honestly, I couldn't blame him. Heather was scarily persistent when she was passionate about something.

"I briefly died? Woah... That explains the last nightmare's ending. Sheesh..." I replied as my heart sank from hearing the harrowing news that I almost took a dirt nap from those injuries.

"Now, you know why I told you not to be rash. I could've lost you forever," Alexa said, fighting back tears as she leaned her forehead into my chin and nuzzled me slightly. The soft caress of her silky blonde hair against my cheek that still smelled faintly of strawberries from her favorite shampoo. I could tell she finally took a shower after the days we had been in a form of purgatory. She was glowing. I was grateful she took care of herself instead of running herself ragged waiting for hours for me to wake up.

"I'm glad we're all okay. I know it got really scary at the end, but it seems like our luck is turning around, right?" I said with the cheesiest smile I could muster. Both of the girls couldn't help but laugh at my absurd optimism in such trying times.

"By the way. What happened with your dad?" I asked Heather straight up.

"He left. He's getting on a plane right now to fly down to Orlando to one of his many properties, and said that he was ready to wait for me to talk about everything when I was finally prepared to know the 'full story'. Whatever that means. I'm sure he was just trying to trick me into being alone with him again to get brainwashed, but who knows," she replied with a slight shrug. She seemed so nonchalant about the whole thing. I assumed she was probably just completely and utterly over this entire mess we had been involved in for the past week.

"Wait... What happened to Alexa's and my parents?" I said with an inquisitive tone. I could feel my face start to contort from the fear of them still being gone.

"Well..." Alexa started to say before being interrupted by the door flying open again.

"My ears are burning. Was someone talking about me in this room?" my dad said jovially.

"Oh my god... I can't believe it. Is it really you guys? Am I hallucinating right now?" I said, tears welling up in my eyes.

"In the flesh and blood. Your mother's here too, kiddo," he said, stepping aside to reveal my mom, her eyes so bloodshot it looked like she had been crying for days. Tears were still streaming down her face as she ran over to the bed.

"My sweet, sweet boy. I can't believe this happened to you. I'm so sorry you all had to be alone through this. It killed me inside knowing you all had to go through this," my mom sobbed, louder than even the girls had.

"Don't worry, Mom. We made it through it," I said softly, patting her head. Then I noticed two more figures towards the back of the room.

"Ryan... Thank you for taking care of Alexa for us and thank you for helping get us free. We all knew you were a tremendous young man. But to say that we were surprised by your ingenuity, cunning, and sheer strength of will would be an understatement," Alexa's dad said, walking up next to my dad.

"I think it was more the other way around. Alexa and Heather took care of me more than I did. I'm just reckless and dumb, which is how I ended up in this bed," I said, because I truly believed that if I hadn't had them with me, I would've given up a long time ago or worse. But now wasn't the time to think about that. We should be rejoicing, with a new lease on life.

"We will be indebted to all three of you. Regardless of how little a part you may think you played. You all succeeded where we failed. We can't thank you all enough," they all said together as if they had rehearsed it.

"So, Ryan. When are you going to get serious about our little girl?" Alexa's mom said sweetly.

"Stop it, Mom! You always find a way to embarrass me, don't you?" Alexa shouted while pushing her parents out the door. But before she could, her dad shouted something back into the room.

"You have our blessing! Do with that what you will!"

She finished pushing them out of the room and slammed the door on them. A little harsh but knowing Alexa they got off easy. If she'd really been that mad at them, she would've dragged them out of that room all the way home to scold them. Her face was a deep crimson as she turned around, and I smirked at her as we both locked eyes for a second.

"Man, they always are the same, huh?" I said, laughing off the situation.

"They don't seem to change ever. No matter what we've gone through," my mom and dad said.

As if on cue, the nurse walked through the door with a plate of terrible hospital food. But I was starving so I could eat anything and think it was a three Michelin star meal. It was a cup of soup, some crackers, a pile of miscellaneous steamed vegetables, a small side of mashed potatoes and gravy, and to top it off a single sad pudding cup. Ah, yes, my favorite foods. Mush with a side of mush, I thought to myself.

"Well, son, I guess we should leave you three here while you eat. It seems you have a bunch to talk about," my dad said with a smile as he started to drag my mom out of the room.

"Wait. I can't leave him, I just got to see him again..." she protested.

"Honey. He will be home in a few days. Let's let him talk with his friends. Don't worry, we'll have plenty of time to visit with him," my dad said, while he turned to me and gave me a wink and a nod as she continued to try to fight him on their way out the door.

"Sooooo... What's next guys?" I said as I stared at the sad-looking food in front of me.

"I don't really know..." Alexa said, her voice trailing off.

"What do you think? You've been pretty quiet for a while now," I asked, looking at Heather.

"Hmm, I was just thinking about what I should do for the rest of this semester and the next school year. I don't really want to go back to my home. There's a lot of traumatizing places there now that I have most of my recollection back," Heather said, looking down, concentrating so hard on thinking about this. I couldn't stop my lips from curling into a smile. She always looked so beautiful when she was concentrating. I hadn't gotten the chance to watch her like this for a while. It was a remarkable sight.

"Well, maybe you could stay at mine or Alexa's house. Of course, if our parents allow, that is. We both have spare bedrooms, so you'd have your own space no matter where you chose," I said in a chipper voice.

"Hey! What do you think you're offering! She can't stay at your house! She'll just have to live with me for the time being," Alexa said very matter of factly. She was very much back to being her normal self again. Gone was the slightly timid version of her that had taken a back seat for the last few days. Back was the queen of the world. If you didn't bow down, you should prepare to be crushed by her iron fist.

"I guess that's that then. Right, guys?" I asked as I started to eat the now cold food in front of me. It wasn't good by any stretch of the imagination, but I devoured it all the same. I was so full by the end I just lay back in the chair crushing the other pillow down.

"Man, if you had told me we would all be in a hospital right now two weeks ago, I would've laughed at you and called you delusional. But here we are. A girl from the past, a boy on the brink of death, and a queen unscathed," Alexa said confidently, mocking us and the mini quest we had just completed.

"Hey, who died and declared you queen?" I replied sarcastically.

"Technically, you did," Heather butted in and we all burst out laughing. I couldn't help it, even though it hurt to laugh. I lost all control and just winced with each exhale.

"Wow. We finally broke Miss Prim And Proper," Alexa said, doing a slow clap.

"Hey, sometimes you can't pass up an opportunity when it presents itself. You know what I mean, Alexa?" Heather replied snarkily.

"Of course, Lex knows what you mean. She practically makes any excuse she can to make fun of me," I said, wiping the tears from the mixed crying of laughing and excruciating pain in my ribs.

"Ouch... I'm hurt... That my subjects could make such comments," Alexa responded, feigning hurt.

"Okay, guys. I should probably get some rest," I said as I felt my eyelids start to get heavy.

"Okay, Ryan. We'll be here in the chairs if you wake up and need us," Heather said sweetly as she leaned in and kissed me on the forehead.

"Yeah..." Alexa said as she too leaned in and kissed my forehead. My vision started to blur as I collapsed against the pillow, falling into a dark void.

Chapter 35

I lay there still wondering if I was awake or asleep. I had no way of knowing. I could just feel the sensation of floating. I hoped as hard as I could to be finally free from those nightmares. I just wanted to be back to normal. All of a sudden, I was transported out of the void.

Nightmare 11...?

"Damn it! What could you possibly want to show me now?" I screamed at the ceiling.

I was standing in a room that was remarkably familiar to me. It was calming to be in such a place. It was my room. Nothing out of the ordinary and no weird time fluxes here. Just basically my favorite place in the world. The one place that seemed to never change, and if it ever did it was because I changed with it.

I sat up on my bed and stared at the clock, knowing all of this was in my head. It felt so real, but also strangely not. I'm not sure how to describe it. Everything in the room seems to have its color faded away. The faint pastel colors of my room and bedding seemed almost ghostlike with this shading. I slid off the end of the bed, and looked down to see the dirty clothes I had on from the last few days.

"Weird. I'd thought it would've at least changed my clothes when it brought me back here," I said aloud, knowing that no one would hear me where I was. I heard a shuffling from my closet. That's unusual, I thought to myself. What could be making such a noise in my closet? I walked up and opened the door, only to come face to face with Heather. She seemed to be focusing so intently on digging for

something that she completely ignored the door being opened.

"Hey! Whatcha doin?" I asked her, tapping on her shoulder.

"Honey, I told you already. I need to find the dress I wore to prom fifteen years ago," she replied. This took me back. Why would my mind skip so far into the future? Also, why did she call me 'honey'?

"Umm... What?" I said with a nervous chuckle.

"Quit playing dumb, darling. We have a reunion today," she replied, turning around for the first time. She definitely looked like she was in her early thirties. This made me curious as to what I would look like fifteen years from now. So, I walked over to my mirror and admired myself in it.

"Hmm, I seem to have way more wrinkles than I ever wanted. At least I'm not balding yet. That's hopefully a good sign?" I said to myself.

"Honey, of course you're balding. Have you forgotten that you use minoxidil on your scalp to help keep hair growth? You've been doing it for years," she said nonchalantly.

"What is happening here? Am I being pranked?!" I yelled, starting to freak out a little bit. I ran out of the room to see what else was different. I ran down the hall towards the stairs, but as soon as I reached them, they extended themselves downward way farther than they had ever gone before.

I decided to just bite the bullet and sprint down the stairs, hoping I could escape. It was like an endless treadmill, as I kept going, the stairs kept coming. I hadn't even made it halfway down. As I was about to admit defeat, I saw a new colored wisp. This one was a deep piercing blue. I stared at it for a second and then followed it. It had me start and stop walking like a thousand times. It felt like I was getting nowhere so I almost gave up. But then it glowed brightly and burst into stardust, revealing that I had made it to the bottom.

I walked through the new doorway that appeared in front of my eyes and was blinded. It was too bright. I covered my eyes for a short while until I heard a sweet voice call for me.

"Ohhhh Ryan... Where have you run off to?" the voice said.

I followed the smooth and supple voice calling to me and reached the room it had originated from. When I saw who was sitting in the chair, my jaw dropped. There was Alexa dressed in an elegant gown, sipping on a glass of wine by the fireplace.

"Sweetheart, won't you join me? I have so missed your company," she whispered loudly towards me.

"Lex? Why are you talking like that?" I asked her sincerely.

"I always talk like this, Ryan. I have since we became espoused," she replied. What the hell? Who uses 'espouse' that way, or at all even? Couldn't she just say we got married? Something was really off.

"Okay... well I think I should probably go get dinner ready," I said as I looked at the clock in the corner of the room showing 5:40 P.M. At least, I assumed it was the afternoon, with how the faint crimson light flooded into the room from the magnificent sunset.

"Can't you stay for just a little bit longer, my love?" she said as she stood up and sauntered towards me. She did look gorgeous in that gown, I had to admit. As I thought this, I felt a strange sensation on my lips. Alexa had come up and kissed me.

She pulled me firmly towards her, keeping her lips planted on mine. I could feel the passion in her movements. After a minute or two she finally released me as she softly panted. Her hot breath grazing my cheek sent an electric current running through my whole body. But I had to break free of this sensation and get out of this. This was just a dream. This wasn't real life. I needed to know why it wanted to show me this.

I turned away from Alexa and walked out into the hallway again. I walked past the infinite stairs this time and towards the end of the hall. When I made it to the end of the hall and reached for a door handle, the entire door faded into the wall. How was I going to get anywhere if each door handle I reached for disappeared? I kept walking down the hall, trying to grab each handle, but each time it was the same, the handle and shape of the door faded away.

Until I reached a doorknob that let me grab it. I held onto it for a short while and tried to turn it left and right, but neither seemed to work. My hand just kept slipping around the knob. I looked down and took off my shirt to use it to get a better grip on the knob. Then, all of a sudden, I did it, the door slid open and inside was someone I never wanted to see again.

"Hello... Ryan..." Mr. S said, his sinister glare piercing through me.

"What do you want now? We haven't done anything or told anyone anything," I *said confidently.*

"Son... I am not here for that," he said calmly.

"Don't call me 'son'. How dare you," I replied, seething with rage.

"Calm down. I have to tell you something," he said, keeping his tone down.

"I have nothing to say to you and I don't want to hear what you have to say," I responded in a cold tone.

"Ouch... So harsh... I'm going to tell you anyways while I have you here," he said with a toothy grin after feigning hurt.

"What could you possibly have to tell me? I mean, come on," I replied, keeping my tone harsh even though in truth I was a tad curious.

"Well. I thought you'd want to know what happened. Seeing as how Heather was the cause of that little incident, I thought you'd want to know what part you had in it," he said as I began to freak out. I thought I knew how it ended?

"I already know what part I had in it. That part being nothing. I just remember it happening to Heather," I said, looking down to avoid meeting his eyes. He had the same emerald eyes as Heather, but his were so much more intimidating.

"Oh, my silly, silly boy. Do you really think you know everything that happened? You lot really are cocky. It astounds me each time we talk like this," he responded with a hearty laugh. It was humiliating having him talk down to me like this.

"Go ahead and tell me then!" I shouted, starting to get infuriated with him playing with me.

"Okay... Calm down... Well, it was a winter day like any other. Work was progressing at a normal pace. But there was something unusual about this day. That unusual thing began with the fact that school had been closed for the day. So, I and a lot of other parents had nowhere to put our young kids. This meant a large number of us opted to just bring them to the job site. Of course, hindsight is twenty-twenty, and what seemed like a good idea at the time was actually the worst idea we had ever had. We had no clue how to take care of that many kids, let alone run a program to keep them all entertained," he said in a somber tone. I think this was the first time I had seen him vulnerable.

"Okay, and what happened to all the other kids?" I inquired.

"Well, there was an incident involving Heather, and so they had all been sent home for safety reasons. They should have never even been there in the first place

though, to be frank," he continued. I looked at him intensely as if begging him to finish the story.

"I think that's enough for today. You have all you need to know," he said, starting to trail off.

"No way! That's not fair! You can't just tell me what I already know and pretend it should give me some revelation. Please just tell me the rest of the story," I begged him.

"I'm sorry, kid, life's not fair. Also, I think you're starting to wake up, so there's no point when I won't be able to explain to you what happened before you wake up," he said as he grabbed his suit jacket and stood up from his desk. He then turned around and put the jacket on, and as he slid both sleeves on, he vanished.

I fell to my knees. So close yet so far. I almost found out the full truth of what happened. If that was even really true. I already knew what happened. I kept trying to replay the memory in my mind, but it just wouldn't play. I decided to give up on remembering for the time being and tried to walk out of the room I had been pulled into, but when I tried to open the door again it flashed. I saw a brief image through the door. It was the library again during construction. I saw Heather running around. I followed her around the room as the door continued to flash brief glances into that memory.

Then the door flashed again, and it showed an image I couldn't quite make out. I tried so hard to understand what it was but, in the end, I had no clue at all what that last image was. Then the door flashed again and faded to pitch black darkness. Suddenly after the void took over the door, it began to leak out and swallow the room I was in. It slowly crawled over to me. I tried to run from it but it was too fast. It was like a tsunami; there was no way to escape it. Finally, I accepted my fate and let it swallow me. The ooze climbed over my body, enveloping it.

I guessed now was the time this nightmare would end. That was strange, it wasn't as violent, and I didn't feel as scared as I usually did. Maybe everything was truly coming to a conclusion. I was back to having normalish dreams. It was a breath of fresh air to think even for a second that life was going back to normal.

I lay there in the void waiting to wake up and see my friends' faces waiting for me. I started to think about them and smiled into the abyss above me. No matter how bleak things got, I always had them. Our friendship was truly something amazing, wasn't it. Our bond had to be unbreakable by now. I couldn't help but laugh, thinking about it. The two girls I knew that had the two most contradictory personalities ended up becoming friends. As I laughed, I felt the call of the waking world bringing me out of my slumber and I embraced the light as I awoke.

Chapter 36

I woke up staring at the ceiling of the pristine hospital room. I wondered what would happen today. Was it all truly over? Could I return to some semblance of normality? I sure hoped I could. I just wanted to finish up junior year and head into my final year of high school. Man, with the week I'd had and the way I looked, all scruffy and dirty, you'd think I was in my mid-twenties. I certainly had had enough hardships for a lifetime. I guess it all went to show you can't judge a book by its cover. I know it's cheesy and cliché, but it really is true. You literally can't judge an entire story just by its cover's appearance or the thickness of the book.

I think that applies to people too. It's pretty unjust to judge someone purely on their appearance. I believe we all understand this at least on a conceptual level, but personal bias always seems to muddle things, doesn't it. Biases are one of humanity's largest blind spots. We allow biases to control a sizable portion of our thought processes even though it often happens subconsciously without us even giving it a second thought.

I know I am bound to these same thought processes. I think that understanding that we are fallible is one of the best ways to ground yourself and open yourself up to different ways of thinking. But it seems that mindset is now few and far between, sadly. Mr. S certainly struck me as one to stick to his guns because he always believed himself to be right. But maybe that's just my bias speaking. As I was thinking this, I felt a soft hand caress my cheek. I turned my head towards this new sensation and came face to face with Heather.

"You're barely awake and already contemplating the universe, huh?" she said softly, with a smirk.

"Was it that obvious?" I said coyly.

"I mean, it's written all over your face. You always make this dumb face and furrow your brow when you're mentally philosophizing," she quipped back.

"Could you show it to me?" I said, grinning from ear to ear.

She mimicked my facial expressions, and I couldn't hold my laughter in and cackled so hard I snorted.

"Oh my god! I do not look like that. Do I? Now I'm concerned!" I said loudly.

"Okay, okay. I might've embellished it a bit. But that's pretty much the face," she said with a soft chuckle.

"What are you two morons laughing about so early in the morning?" Alexa sniped at us with a groggy expression on her face.

"What time is it even?" I asked as I looked at the clock. I strained to focus on reading it, but when I did, I saw that it read 6:30. Which I could only assume was in the morning. Alexa never was a morning person. She always loved her beauty sleep, as I called it. It was kind of an inside joke. One that seemed to hold less significance in light of recent events.

"We're sorry. I just had to show him how dumb his face was when he was deep in thought," Heather said, dropping her voice to a whisper.

"You mean this one?" Alexa replied as she made the exact same face Heather had just made to mimic me.

"That's the one," she replied with a thumbs-up.

"There's no way that's what I really look like. Come on, guys. You have to be messing with me," I said in protest.

"Nope. That's the face. Sorry, Ryan, no jokes here," Alexa responded, cutting me off.

"You both sure are punching down on a poor defenseless injured person," I said, trying to gain some sympathy points.

"Pfft! Come on, Ryan! Even YOU didn't believe that line as you said it!"

Alexa replied, holding back laughter.

"No, I swear. You both are meanies! Don't you think you should be nicer to your knight in shining armor?" I asked in a mocking tone, feigning offense.

"Come on now, Ryan. You're less brave and more reckless. Always have been," Heather chimed in.

"Ouch... My pride... I'm dying... *cough sputter*," I said, pretending to die.

"Whatever shall we do, Alexa? Our knight has died the most shameful death of all," Heather said, playing along.

"I guess we have no choice but to burn his disgraced corpse. Such a shameful death doesn't deserve a burial," Alexa said, continuing the joke.

"Ohhh. I have been revived by my fair ladies' kind words. Please do not burn me," I groaned, holding back more laughter.

"Heather, did you happen to hear something just now?" Alexa said, ignoring me.

"No, I didn't, Alexa. It must have been the wind," Heather replied as she too had to hold back her laughter.

"Okay, I guess we have to order the servants to incinerate the body now," Alexa said, trying to keep a straight face.

"Please! Don't! My benevolent leaders! I am but a humble knight. Don't burn me alive, your highnesses," I pleaded for my fake life. This seemed to break them as they both burst out laughing simultaneously.

As we were all laughing off that little play we had just put on, a nurse stepped in holding a clipboard. She walked over to my bed, and then stood next to me as she slid my blanket down off of my arms to take my pulse.

"Hello, Ryan, I am going to be running some tests in the doctor's stead. She said you should be fine to leave sometime today. She did say that you should be careful of any exercise or harsh physical activity that may cause the stitching to rip for the next four to six weeks. Other than that, she said if all of your vitals were normal you'd be released today. Isn't that wonderful?" she said in a chipper tone.

"Really? That fast? That's crazy!" I replied, astounded.

"I know. Modern medicine really is something, isn't it?" she said, smiling at me.

"Sure is!" I responded.

"Well, Ryan. I only have good news today. Everything seems to be normal. I'll bring these results to Doctor Miriam and get her opinion. But I think you're going to go home today," she said as she began to leave the room. She got out the door, turned, gave me a smirk and closed it behind herself.

"Isn't that awesome, guys? I have to go home today!" I said, smiling the hardest I had all week.

"I know! It's been forever since we were all last in our own homes!" Heather replied, matching my energy.

"I think in a way I'm going to miss getting to be around you guys like we were last week. I mean, the circumstance sucked but getting to spend so much time hanging out and talking honestly like that was really fun. Even if I seemed like I was upset during parts of it, I truly did enjoy the time we spent," Alexa said in a dejected tone.

"Hey, cheer up. I don't think this is the last adventure we'll ever go on. I'm sure there are plenty more just like this one, maybe some even more perilous," I replied with a smile.

"You always know what to say to cheer someone up, huh, Ryan?" Heather said, smirking.

"What can I say? I'm pretty much the best," I replied jokingly, stroking my own ego.

"Yeah, right. Like telling me I'll be in more danger when I'm around you would really cheer me up. You psycho!" she replied, but couldn't stop herself from laughing through the entire statement.

After that, Doctor Miriam came in.

"Ryan. I've looked over all your charts and I think it's okay to let you leave today. I'll have nurse Lily get you checked out and ready to go. Remember not to exercise too hard and limit excess physical activity if possible," she said, smiling as she patted me on the head and then walked out.

The nurse walked in who I presumed to be Lily right after she left and got me all set to go. Alexa handled all of the outpatient paperwork for me and rolled me out of my car. Heather and her helped me into the back seat, and Alexa hopped behind the wheel as Heather sat next to me in the back seat.

"Well, guys. I guess the next time I'll see both of you will be back in school next week," I said with a smile.

"It's been a crazy couple of days. Hasn't it?" Alexa replied.

"It sure has, but it seems like everything's back to normal. Oh, by the way, you both can drive my car around while I'm kind of bedridden for the next few days. Just make sure to pick me up before school on Monday, please," I told them both while I choke back some tears. I didn't know why my eyes were leaking. Maybe it was exhaustion. Maybe it was a lot of things. Heather seemed to notice and just softly rubbed my back as we pulled up to my house.

They helped me out of the back seat and helped walk me and carried my stuff to my front door for me. I was so thankful to have them by my side. I hoped it'd be like this forever. The door swung open, and my parents greeted me with open arms.

"Thank you both for taking such diligent care of our boy. I know he can be a handful," my mom said as she squeezed Heather and Alexa into a big bear hug.

"Okay, honey. You're embarrassing him. Let them go. But truly, thank you both from the bottom of our hearts for keeping him out of too much trouble," my dad replied with a wink and a smile.

"It was no trouble at all, sir. We're happy to do it," they replied as they shared a glance and headed down the driveway. It was a weird thought that they'd be living together for the next year. But I guessed they already were kinda like sisters at this point.

My parents helped me bring all my heavy stuff into my room. As soon as I made it inside, I inhaled deeply and felt instantly safe again. My room was my sanctuary, and it was finally returned to me. I no longer had to stay away and could lie back down in my own bed for the first time in what felt like forever. I lay down on my back and felt something in my jeans pocket. I slid my hand into it and pulled out a note.

The note said, *"Meet me out back behind your house in 4 hours. ~ H"*

The only name that H could stand for had to be Heather. So, I guessed she really had something to talk with me about. Those four hours seemed to fly by so fast as I had started to reread my own writing. Suddenly I looked at the clock and saw it was exactly four hours from when they had dropped me off.

I wandered outside silently so as to not worry my parents, and walked behind my house. To no surprise the person I saw standing there, her shadow silhouetted in the snow, was Heather.

"What's up, Heather? What did you want to talk about?" I questioned her.

"I have something to tell you, Ryan. I just need you to stand there and listen to what I'm about to say," Heather said, somewhat nervously.

"Sure. What is it?" I replied, suspicious of where this was going.

"Ryan... I'm sorry for putting you in this situation, but I love you. I've tried to hint at it and show you this entire time. But I can't live without you. I really wanted you to just understand how I felt and reciprocate, but it seems like you were just too focused on our problems or oblivious to see my true feelings. But I need you to know that I love you. I always have," she said, pouring her heart out to me, crying. She must have been hurting, holding this all inside for all this time. I couldn't imagine. I couldn't believe I'd never noticed it. I can't lie, I did develop feelings for her too, but how would this affect our friendship dynamic? This was all too complicated for my brain and heart to handle all at once.

"Heather, I don't know what to say. I can't deny I have some feelings for you too, but I'm not sure what to make of them." But before I could finish my statement, Heather rushed over to me, embraced me, leaned toward me, and kissed me for the first time on the lips. Her lips were soft, and the sweet scent of her perfume played at my nostrils as I melted into the passion of our kiss and felt my head start to float. Until...

"Excuse me?!" I heard a shout from behind the tree line. I knew that voice. It was Alexa and she did not seem too pleased. She sounded downright pissed.

"How dare you? How dare both of you?! Ryan, is this really how you're going to end our relationship?!" she shouted at us at the top of our lungs. "Or do you not remember us dating for the last two years?" she yelled as tears began to fall down her face.

"What? Since when were we dating?" I replied, actually confused at what I had just heard.

"Really? Ryan... What happened to you? Why have you been forgetting everything? Did you forget all those days we spent together? Why did you hide everything and never tell me what was wrong? You can't fathom how hard it was to watch you regressing and still hide everything that was hurting you. It killed me, and seeing you with her this last week was like salt in the wound," she shouted as she fell to her knees, utterly defeated.

As she finished her statement, I had a flashback.

Flashback to two years ago

"Man, Ryan. How are we going to survive high school? Everything seems so important, and the school grounds are huge. This is nothing like middle school," Alexa said with a concerned look on her face.

"Don't worry about that, Lex. We have each other. We always will. I'll always be your friend and be by your side," I smirked as I softly punched her shoulder.

"You're so cheesy. But that's what I love about you," she replied.

"Pfft... Isn't love a little too strong of a word?" I laughed off her last statement.

"No. I think it suits my feelings perfectly. I love you, Ryan. We've been friends for so long and I can't control my heartbeat when I'm around you. I don't know when it started, but I don't think it'll stop anytime soon. I want to be with you forever. What do you say, Watson?" she said, staring into my eyes. This was the first time she had ever used that Sherlock Holmes joke. It was just as dumb then as it was now. But at the time it made me laugh.

"I love you too, Alexa. I always will. You mean so much to me," I replied sheepishly as she nuzzled her head into my chest. We were just kids then, but it felt so real. She then got on her tiptoes, and we had our first kiss. It was clumsy but it was perfect. She was my best friend. My confidant. My guiding light. She was truly my world.

End

I stood there shocked. I couldn't believe I hadn't remembered that. Now everything that had happened leading up to the last week, including the events of the last week, made so much more sense. I couldn't believe I had suppressed something so important.

"Alexa... I'm sorry..." I was at a loss for words. I could barely get out that sentence, but I knew deep down it wasn't enough.

"Ryan... I love you. I always will. That's what **you** said to me. Was that all a lie? Will you forget it again? How can I do that to myself?" Alexa said, failing to hold back her tears. I understood how she felt, and it killed me to think I did this to her.

"So, Ryan... Who is it going to be? Me or her?" Heather said in a sweet tone, holding onto my arms. I knew Heather had been through a lot but the way she said that just rubbed me the wrong way. Like this was some power trip for her. The illusion was shattered. Her sweet persona seemed to crumble before my very eyes as I recalled the events of the last week. I took out the notebook I had always kept in my pocket and shoved it into her hands.

"Read this. I hope it clears everything up. You did always say you wanted to read it when it was finished," I said to answer her. I was sure Heather had to have known me and Alexa were dating even if I had forgotten. I was sure Alexa would have told her. I shook her off and turned towards Alexa who was now lying in the snow.

"Of course, it wasn't a lie. I will always love you, Alexa. I'm sorry for betraying you and forgetting. That was never my intention. I will try to keep it ingrained in my brain permanently," I said as tears began to run down my face.

"But... Ryan... That's not fair... I loved you first..." Heather said in a broken voice as she fought to hold onto my hand. I shrugged her off again and walked towards Alexa.

"I will always love you too, Ryan," Alexa said as she ran into my arms, and I felt the familiar sense of closeness and compassion that I didn't feel when I embraced Heather. Alexa genuinely cared about me and didn't just want to hurt someone else. I squeezed Alexa with all my might even though my side started to burn. Then I leaned down and kissed her firm lips, the smell of her familiar shampoo and the feeling of her soft face in my hands. As I cupped her cheek and held the back of her head to deepen the kiss, I knew this was what true love felt like. We loved each other without bounds. We each loved one another more than we loved ourselves and I could feel it in the passion in our kiss. I was hers and she was mine.

When we finally pulled away, I felt her soft, ragged breath on my neck, and I smiled. I started to remember the events of the last two years. Everything started to come back. It stabbed me like a knife through the heart that I had forgotten such an important relationship. But I was simply happy she had forgiven me for all of my faults. We were so caught up in our own world, we hadn't noticed Heather leaving. When we untangled our bodies from the embrace, night had fallen, and I invited her in for dinner.

The rest of the week and weekend passed by in a blur. I mainly focused on resting, and the nightmares seemed to all but fade away entirely. I still had a nagging feeling in the back of my mind, but I suppressed it. Alexa and I texted every day. Apparently, Heather was so upset with what happened that day that she had decided to just leave with her dad and was now in Florida. I had one text from Heather, and it was just an image of the last page of the short story, and an apology hoping we could be friends again in the future. The caption she zoomed in on the last page I had written said, "Dedicated to the most important person in my life. My snake, you may seem scary or even potentially venomous, but you are my rock. Love, your lion."

I texted Heather on and off during the rest of junior year, but we mainly lost touch. Alexa and I had spent the rest of junior year going on many adventures. Hey, I decided, maybe I'll even tell them later, but for now that was how the years of our lives began. I was sure there would be many more interesting ones in store, but that's another story for another time. Like I always say, "You never know when a story will appear." To whoever is reading this, I don't know how you found it, but I hope you learn from my mistakes. I mean, who would read some guy's journal they found? I guess I would.

Epilogue Part 1 of 3

I'm sure you wouldn't expect me to be the one telling you this, but some time has passed since the boy visited me in Florida to get the full story. He entrusted me with two journals and after reading this one I have some qualms with him to hammer out. Since he seemed to neglect telling the true tale of what really happened to him and caused all of this to start, I will now append it with the necessary truths. You know me as Mr. S, a harsh evil man willing to do anything to keep my money and daughter.

This is true. I was indeed a ruthless man. However, Ryan left out a lot of crucial information in his telling of events. While most of what happened was true, some information written down may be less than reliable, to say the least. I had known them all since they were children as Heather was my only daughter and Ryan and Alexa were her two best friends. Heather and Alexa often butted heads on things while Ryan always tried to play peacemaker. He was a sweet little boy and cared a bit too much about others' opinions of him than he really should.

Ryan was also curious, so while he may have been the glue holding them together, he was also the weight dragging them down dangerous paths. Ryan seemed to paint Alexa as some sort of furtive underhanded hoodlum. However, in reality it was Ryan who often took them into dangerous situations.

Neither of the girls were too fond of that library, especially during construction, but Ryan always viewed it as a fun place to hang out. He thought it to be one of his many "secret" hiding places. As if we hadn't all known about the many abandoned houses that they would hang around to pretend they were older than they were.

Ryan and Alexa always seemed to be a little closer than he and Heather were. It tormented her so much. She would never show it, but she really did care about what he thought about her. When he came down to visit, they had cordial conversations, but he was totally shut off from her, and from understanding her perspective. Heather on the other hand cared so much that she could only turn inwards and begin to torment herself. She really did love him for better or for worse. They seem to be on better terms now, but I can still tell that they aren't where she wants them to be. For some reason, she holds out hope. She's like her mother in that way. Always the dreamer. I told Ryan what happened, and he gave me this to read. He thought it might help me understand his perspective.

Perspective is a funny thing, isn't it? I see one thing, you see another. I do not claim to know why Ryan seemed to lose large portions of his memory, but I do know why he kept hyper-focusing on his leg. I didn't think it was possible to feel the physical effects of an injury from so long ago. But I guess the mind is funny in that way. We can never truly understand its inner machinations.

In the past, Ryan loved being in places he perceived to be exclusive. This level of exclusivity gave him a sense of accomplishment. He would often cause problems at the job site by hiding in dangerous equipment or jumping out from behind objects to play pranks on the workers. His mom and dad always apologized for the inconvenience he caused, but any time he was punished he seemed to brush it off or completely forget the event was even happening. He would do things he had already done before, and when he was told that he had said or done something prior he would look at you with a dazed look.

Something was not right with him after the accident. He would forget things he had said or did and then repeat them. Heather and Alexa were always patient with him, almost dutifully so. They would let him tell them the same stories over and over again and pretend that they were new just to humor him.

In his writings, he had talked about a dream showing him that Heather was the reason the library was significant. While a portion of that may be true there is something his mind was obfuscating from him. Whether this was malicious in intent or not I cannot say for certain. I do feel bad for the child to an extent. I'm not too sure how I would handle a debilitating memory problem like that.

However, after that incident and the job got put on indefinite hold, I couldn't bear to see Heather feel so alone in that town. I wished I could set her free from her emotions and attachment to this boy. Her mother and I watched as she obsessed with him. It was unhealthy. We had to just take her away from that environment. When we did, she was upset for a while, but then she withdrew. This once delicate and precious flower folded it peddles in and quit. She quit everything she used to enjoy. She changed completely. She was cold and distant where she used to be bright and cheerful. It was honestly depressing. The thought was so hard for her mom to bear. She tore herself up inside about our little girl. Our perfect angel. When she was diagnosed with stage four ovarian cancer, it took all I could muster to stay strong.

When her mother finally passed, Heather was just as cold and distant as ever. It was like she hadn't cared. But I knew that it was breaking her up inside too. I knew she was beating herself up about being so harsh to us over the years. She started to open back up again, and everything seemed to be getting better. But then I got that dreaded call. They needed me to go back to Maine. I couldn't very well just leave my only kin in Florida without any caregivers. So, I was forced to tell her that we were going back. When I told her, I saw a fire in her eyes I thought had died long ago. I knew nothing good would come of it. All at once my world began to break apart. I knew I would lose her as soon as we made it to Maine. We arrived, and she was normal for a while. Until she started to disappear... I knew at that moment she was with them. Ryan wanted to pretend I was going to kill their parents and had kidnapped them.

This is categorically false. Ryan's parents and Alexa's parents were both called to meet with me. I told them about our kids messing around in the old job site and said that I would talk to them and tell them the importance of not talking about what happened there. They agreed, and then I gave them tickets to Niagara Falls. They said they would leave notes for the kids, but it seems in their haste they had forgotten. This led to my elongated chase after my own child and her friends. I did not threaten anyone. I did beat Jacob but that was a long time coming and honestly a huge point of weakness. Same as when I beat Ryan. I couldn't control my rage; it just consumed my vision.

I was not a good man. I can admit that. I should never have brainwashed Heather. But I couldn't bear to see her obsessing about that boy. Especially when I knew all it would bring her was heartache. All of this is to say that I know what I am. I will never claim to be something else. I think I should end my rambling for now. I know this won't be the last time you'll be hearing from me. It may even be sooner than you think. I'll finish telling the full true story in the future. Until then, what does that kid always say? Oh yes, that's right.

"You never know when a story will appear."

Until next time...

www.ingramcontent.com/pod-product-compliance
Lightning Source LLC
Chambersburg PA
CBHW020311200626
46814CB00006BA/2193